It's a novel - It's an album - It's...

THE ARK OF THE
OVEN MITT

By James Gordon

It's a novel.
It's an album.
It's
The Ark Of The Oven Mitt
By
James Gordon
©2021

ISBN: 978-1-990330-05-6

All songs by James Gordon except 'Signal Faded',
by James Gordon and Katherine Wheatley

Songs contained in this book (lyrics) and available for download:

all songs marked with an asterisk were recorded specifically for this project. The rest are from previous James Gordon albums and one Katherine Wheatley Album

Note from the author:
How to read this book!

This musical novel comes with 36 songs. What was I thinking?

You'll see the lyrics spread throughout. You can download the songs for free by going to

Jamesgordonmusic.bandcamp.com

and looking for 'Songs from The Ark Of The Oven Mitt'. Or if your smartphone can read QR codes, hold the phone's camera up to the code below: it will ask you to open 'flowcode.com' – click on that and, voila, as if by magic, the page comes up for downloading the songs! The songs are a big part of the story and the 'feel' of what I'm trying to convey here, so I'd recommend it.

You can listen as you get to the songs, or listen to them all together as an album.

Whatever you like. It's up to you, really. Enjoy!

Acknowledgements

The author would like to express thanks to the Ontario Arts Council for their support in completing the recording portion of this project.

ONTARIO ARTS COUNCIL
CONSEIL DES ARTS DE L'ONTARIO

an Ontario government agency
un organisme du gouvernement de l'Ontario

Special thanks to Laurie Gough for the excellent editing and nurturing. Eric Alper for the PR work. Ian Bell for the cover art. My "beta" readers who helped shape the final product: Liv Cazzola, Jane Lewis, Sue Merritt, Val Morse, Zhyfhs Millicent, Braden Phelan, Tannis Slimmon and Katherine Wheatley with an extra bow to Braden for his management services. To Evan Gordon who produced and mastered the recordings.

17 of the songs in this book were recorded specifically for this project. The musicians on those songs were James Gordon, Jeff Bird, Geordie Gordon, Randall Coryell, Katherine Wheatley, Anne Lindsay and Evan Gordon. The remaining songs were drawn from other James Gordon albums, and the musicians were Tannis Slimmon, Ian Bell, Jude Vadala, Sandra Swannell, Marion Linton, Shelley Coopersmith, Lois Cherry, Alex Sinclair, Tony Quarrington, Louisa Kratka, Molly Kurvink, Peter Van Althen, Dennis Rondeau, Jane Ellenton, Susan

Smith, Brenda Aherne and David Houghton. Apologies if anyone has been missed on this list!

To Lisa Browning for getting this into book form. I seem to
be a bit of a story magnet. Thanks to all those who have spun
yarns for me on my ceaseless travels- you were planting little
book seeds all along. To all the fans who have supported me
and encouraged me over the years. This book's for you!

Published by Pipe Street Publishing
Canada

PART ONE

**Song numbers correspond to track numbers
on the album download**

In the crisp spring morning, when the sun is just peaking over the townhouses and the industrial malls to the east, a long line of cars snails from the road and back, around a small building that is identical to thousands like it dotted across the waking landscape.

Exhaust from the cars rises straight up in the cool air, looking like coal smoke from Dickensian tenement chimneys, mingling together above, creating a dirty haze that filters out that thin sunlight.

The cars are all lined up: pilgrims at a shrine dedicated to the memory of a dead hockey player. Hockey is sacred. Hockey is holy, so there is an air of reverence as the pilgrims pray with their engines idling, waiting to share in the corporate caffeine communion that keeps them coming back each morning at the same time.

Eventually each car makes it to a small window where they receive the communion like patients in a hospital ward receiving their medication. The cars are empty save for single occupants, sleepy supplicants who hand over a tithe, a humble portion of their earnings offered so that they might receive the blessed cup of hot holy water, handed out by young virgins enslaved by the cult of the dead hockey player.

Inside, the car radios squawk with classic rock interrupted by chipper talk that urges the half-listeners to purchase products that come all the way from China, items that were once made right in their own towns by their parents and grandparents before all those factories closed. Many of those factories were now converted to loft condominiums where many of the owners of those cars live.

Along with their caffeine the worshippers receive wrapped lukewarm packages representing the holy trinity of their daily diet: salt, sugar and fat. This gift is received with gratitude for the miracle that the dead hockey player has performed for them: they can do all this without leaving the cars that they have a similar devotion to. These carbon-spewing chariots bear their occupants from the morning mass at the church of the Holy Defenseman to their jobs that are farther away every year, along arteries as clogged as the ones in their own bulging bodies that are filled with doughnuts from that same church.

The cars lurch along past ditches littered with paper cups that no longer contain their precious fluid, accompanied by plastic lids that the worshippers have struggled to open without spilling their steaming stimulant on the seats of their dearly beloved cars. They love those cars more than they love their families, for they spend more time with them.

Conspicuous in the line of cars is an old battered van that may once have been white, containing two weary passengers and a rebel driver: clearly a heathen who has declined to take the morning communion at the Drive-Through Window of Wonders. He is regaling his poor passengers with a righteous sermon that re-enforces his profane belief that those passive dough-eating parishioners are the real sinners while he, with his Ghandi-esque denial of consumerist comforts, is the saint.

This was in the dying days of the Empire of Oil.

Chapter One

Song 1
In The Dying Days Of The Empire Of Oil

Things were pretty good before they got a lot worse
Before the ice cap melted and the pipeline burst
When there was still enough water to quench our thirst
In the dying days, in the dying days
In the dying days of the Empire of Oil

Summers warm and dry, winters mild too
We enjoyed it while it lasted, what else could we do?
We could see what was coming but it didn□t seem true
In the dying days, in the dying days
In the dying days of the Empire of Oil

Nobody saw the coming storm all
Over town things look kind of normal
Tommy's taking Tammy to the formal
In the dying days, in the dying days
In the dying days of the Empire of Oil

In a rented limo they cruise down Main
Past the boarded-up stores, things seem pretty much the same
Tammy hears the thunder, but it never rains
In the dying days, in the dying days
In the dying days of the Empire of Oil

People still went to work everyday
At least the ones who still had jobs anyway
You could look around and think that things were OK
In the dying days, in the dying days
In the dying days of the Empire of Oil

Drummer Tells

Check one check two. Testing. Is this thing on? OK Mr. Bic Penn the reporter man, here goes nothin'.

Hey, remember Miles' song, 'Fast Food On A Slow Road?' Didn't think so. Didn't get much airplay. It kind of pissed off the commuters listening to morning radio. Anyway, he wrote it when it was sinking in for all of us that the highway that had been our lifeline for so long wasn't really going anywhere anymore for us, and it was more like a 'death-line'. I thought of it when you asked me to start this recording stuff for your article about Miles and Myles. It's sure been on Miles' set list a lot lately as the road starts to wear him down even more and he's not sure where we're heading. Well, I'm no writer, buddy, but this old cassette recorder you gave me oughta do the trick: it's vintage like me, and I'll send it along to you when we get to the end of this tour, not that the tour ever really ends with Miles. Deal? Can you even buy tapes anymore? This might take a while.

Song 2
Fast Food On A Slow Road

Fast food on a slow road
Heavy traffic, long wide load
Classic rock squawk on the radio
This highway doesn't go anywhere anymore

Get in line behind the living dead
Full tank and an empty head
Flatbed ahead shredding tire treads
This highway doesn't go anywhere anymore

Pay the toll, sell your soul, wheels roll on
No heart beats through these arteries
It's long long gone

Water bottles, Tim Horton cups
Fill the roadside ditches up
Thrown away, just like us
This highway doesn't go anywhere anymore

Half my life on the 401
Gas pedal's my trigger, this car is my gun
But there's nothing to shoot for, I am done
This highway doesn't go anywhere anymore

Pay the toll, sell your soul, wheels roll on.
No heart beats through these arteries,
It's long long gone

Fast food on a slow road
Heavy traffic, long wide load
Classic rock squawk on the radio
This highway doesn't go anywhere anymore

So you wanna know about Miles, eh? I'm not sure I'm the right guy to ask, but I'm guessing you came to me because Miles and Dougie wouldn't talk to you. right? I didn't join his band till after all that stuff happened with Maddie, you know, and I'm not really the talkative type, but jeez I reckon I got time now and my people are known for telling stories and all I guess, so I'll give 'er a go. What the hey.

You're gonna be disappointed if you're looking for wild tales of the glamorous life on the road. This is the *Canadian* music business after all. Plus I couldn't tell you about what was really going on inside the complicated brain of Miles. I never got inside his head, just inside his van, which was just as cluttered with crap. I can tell you what it was like working with him, if that helps.

Touring with Miles and Dougie, we got into a routine pretty quick after they took me on. I've got a picture somewhere here. I think it actually got used as the first promo shot for 'Miles Gerber and the Shit Disturbers' 'cuz we looked like pretty badass road warriors, eh?

That's them sitting on upturned guitar cases in front of the Avalon Motel in Wainwright if I remember correctly, and there's me standing in the doorway wishing they'd get off their asses so we could head across the street to Frenchy's Diner before they stopped serving breakfast. Some of the newer places have 'all day breakfasts', but who really has the time anymore?

Anyway, it's fairly easy to recall the conversation cuz it went pretty much like this every morning with a slight variation in theme. Miles would always start: "Two kinds of people in this weary world, Boogie."

"Don't call me Boogie," Dougie would say. In case you were wondering, Boogie rhymes with Dougie. "Do we have to play the 'two kinds of people' game every time someone bums you out, Miles?"

Miles doesn't answer since he's preoccupied with scraping something sticky off the bottom of his cowboy boot, no doubt a souvenir from last night's so-called dressing room.

"Well do we?" Dougie repeated, kind of irritated, which was a semi-permanent state for him.

"Don't call me Dewey," growled Miles. This was actually an important part of the game they'd play. The topic of that particular day:

"Two kinds of people, those who smoke and those who don't smoke."

Dougie flicked his cigarette butt at Miles and muttered. "Here we go."

Then Miles would start in. You'd think that the cars in the parking lot were his congregation the way he'd get to preaching.

"Smokers just don't give a shit about their own health, the health of those around them, or about the fact that the whole smoking thing is a huge corporate marketing scam. Generations of tobacco companies convincing us that smoking is cool, even though it's so uncool that it's killing assholes like you Dougie Woogie. Then there's folks like me who *do* give a shit about stuff. You see someone who cares about the environment and about community, and about the future of our children; they are the non-smokers, and the smokers are the ones being fossil fools and committing the crimes and voting for scumbags if they bother to vote at all. Two kinds of people. That's all I'm saying."

"Not that you'd want to generalize at all, Miles," Dougie said with a large exhale.

It was never all he was saying. As for me, I'm one of the only Indians I know who doesn't smoke. I know, I know: I can call myself an Indian but you can't. Does that piss you off? I won't tell you some of the things we call you all. Heh heh. Life was never fair for us so why should it be for you colonials? I'm still learning about all that stuff so I'm not as angry yet.

Despite ribbing Dougie about this for years on the road, sometimes you'd see that Miles was jealous of the 'business' that went with smoking. In a conversation late at night after a gig Dougie could draw attention to himself by saying something like, "Be that as it may gents," then he'd get a real dramatic pause while he inhaled, squinted, then exhaled towards the nearest non-smoker while everyone anticipated the rest of his sentence. And how you always had something to play with in your hands and in your mouth. You could tell that Miles missed having the kind of theatrical potential that smoking gave you, since he was a show person and all, but it seemed worth sticking to the non-smoking just so he'd keep the moral high ground over Dougie. Miles was right about one thing. Dougie *didn't* give a shit, and somehow he made that an endearing quality.

'Shag Rugs. Swag lamps. Colour TV' boasted the sign squeaking in the wind out front of the Avalon, sounding a bit like when Dougie warms up his fiddle. That sign was unchanged since the days that a colour TV was a novelty worth pulling off the highway for. We always liked the faded glory of those places, it seemed to fit with where we were in our so-called careers. When he'd see one of those signs Miles would pretend he was a dad driving the family Buick Roadmaster and he'd say something like:

"Well would you get a load of that, Marge! Colour TV! I bet *Gunsmoke* would look pretty fine on that tonight! Wadda ya say honeybun?"

The routine was always the same when we'd hit the next town, usually mid-afternoon. Search out the old-school motel like the Avalon where you could drive up to the door of your room. These were mostly gone; the motels, not the doors, silly. They were all put out of business by the big chains, but we'd at least try before settling on the Super 8 or the Motel 6. Couldn't the new players in the lodging game think of actual names for their joints? We'd carry in the first load, we'd all stake our space claims as best we could; jockeying for best position for the amps and road cases. Dougie would straight away look in the tank behind the toilet to see if anyone had left booze behind.

Ya that happens. Miles liked to check the backs of the pictures for cryptic notes from travellers. Yup, you'd get those too. Hidden cries for help. In the generic McMotel rooms, the McPaintings, all the same pastel shades as the bedspreads, are bolted to the wall so this secret form of road communication has died out. I'd check to see what movie channels they had. We'd finish the gear-stash, then we'd have the ceremonial coin toss. After Maddie left, and when things started to get rough in the biz, Miles figured we couldn't afford separate rooms, so we'd get a double. Since manly men like us will not share a bed, especially after that unfortunate incident in High Prairie, the winner of the coin toss got a proper bed. The next flip was for who got the mattress of the other bed, placed on the floor, and the loser got the box spring. Miles always tossed the coin and I could never figure out why I always got the box spring, which I started calling 'The Rez'.

After the gig we'd usually keep things pretty up-beat. The adrenaline would still be flowing which is why bad habits and 'show biz' go together like turds and toilets. You'd need something to help wind down and you'd need something to start up in the morning. We'd talk about the crowd, even if there wasn't really a crowd to speak of. Sometimes it was just me and Miles 'cuz Dougie would get lucky and disappear with a waitress or a fan. Miles never did. His broken heart seemed to have shut off the part of him that would allow anyone else in, even though his music always touched other hearts. Sometimes the 'owners of those lonely hearts' would hear Miles sing one of his 'pining' songs and figure it was an open invitation.

Me? I was invisible, eh? I was the drummer.

In the morning at breakfast the conversation wasn't so perky, since Miles would have counted the take from the night before from the door and from merch sales. The math never added up. I'm sure we'll get into that later. Anyway, we'd be eating breakfast at the place with the best breakfast special. When I started you could get bacon and eggs and home fries for 1.99 and you can still find that for about five bucks. Of course this Canadian road warrior tradition is the worst thing you can do to your body before getting in a van and sitting on your ass for six hours.

You'd get to know the best places, and each time through you'd get to know the waitresses and the hash slingers a bit more too. Usually the most trucks out front was the best sign, not for nutritional value of course but for reliability. Those joints depended on keeping those truckers happy. You probably

recall that old song of Miles' where he sings
   'Breakfast at the places where you'd see the most trucks-
   A dollar ninety-nine make mine sunny side up'. That song
was pretty auto-biographical; Miles' take on our routine after
Maddie left- and it included our actual auto: Nelly-Belle.

Song 3: Small Town Prairie Gigs

There'd be a frosting on the wheat fields
Sparkling in the harvest moon's light
We'd be flying up the Yellowhead
The only ones on the road some nights
On our way to play another small-town prairie gig
Songs about the old days, waltzes and jigs
Towns with nothin' but a co-op and a Chinese Cafe´
But the halls would fill somehow with folks who came to hear us play.

After a church-ladies' supper, jellied salads, casseroles and hams
Their husbands would help us haul our gear out of that rusty old van
From the stage you'd look out at the families in the crowd
Such stories in their faces, weathered and proud
Sometimes we'd take their tales back home with us and then
The next time we'd come through we'd be singing about them.

When the show was over, cold cuts and coffee
While they cleared away the chairs.
The local caller would show up
And he'd holler "Come on gather into squares!"
St. Anne's Reel, Big John MacNeill, all the good old tunes
Ukrainian polkas as they'd hop around the room
And we'd play them "Chase Me Charlie"
and they'd dance the butterfly
Some of the ol' boys out the back sharing smokes and a little rye

Estevan and Weyburn, Humboldt, Athabasca, Kindersley
Neepewa and Nipawin, Minnedosa, Dauphin, Unity
Breakfast at the places where you'd see the most trucks
A dollar-ninety-nine, make mine sunny-side up
When the heater was working and the highways were dry
We were happy guys beneath that impossible sky

Here's a picture from way back
With Dougie scraping hard on the fiddle
That's me on the flat-top, and Drummer on the skins in the middle
God, we looked so young, there were stars in our eyes
Took me all these years before I realized
That back then when we figured, someday we'd make it big
We could never ask for better than those small town prairie gigs

Those breakfast joints were of the old-time variety where if you'd ask for coffee they didn't ask you which kind. And they didn't have a *barista*, they just had a two-burner Bunn on the go all day. Jesus, a true trucker would wolf down the 'air horn special' with a six-ounce steak, six eggs, six coffee refills. Six-six-six, that's the devil's breakfast, heh heh, and a load of potatoes that would make Bud the Spud proud. Then they'd climb into those big rigs. Wow. Eighteen Wheels headed straight to the hospital.

The waitresses in these places were the 'lifers', no actresses or students looking for extra pay, nosirree. These gals wore the comfy sneakers and the drab uniform and they didn't take shit from no one. They could be sweet AND sour at the same time, just like the MSG balls you find in every small prairie town at the Chinese Café. They played the role of moms and girlfriends and psychiatrists for the forty minutes it would take to get you in and out of there.

Those gals would always rib me for not ordering bacon. I don't eat ribs either. But that ribbing was sometimes the only female contact you'd get all day so you'd take it with a smile. Ya, try not ordering beef in Alberta and they'd K.D. LANG you to death. My new Indian buddies say anyone who doesn't eat red meat is just a bad hunter. Heh heh.

So part of the game at breakfast was to flirt with the waitress as much as possible. Both teams expected it, but that morning when we were talking at Frenchy's you could tell that things were starting to unravel for Miles.

After we'd started in to the teasing part of the game, which was similar to the way you'd try to relate to the ladies when you were in grade seven, Miles slammed down his mug and actually stood up and addressed the whole diner.

"Excuse me," he announced, "I'd just like to say that there are two kinds of men in this place right now."

"Here we go," Dougie had to say.

"Those entitled assholes who think it's OK to harass poor Wanda here like we've all been doing, and then there's yours truly, Miles Gerber, who would like to hereby apologize to Wanda in particular and to all the hard working women in the service industry who over the years have taken all the sexist crap we dish out just because they're making minimum wage and they need your tip to pay for daycare while they serve you this slop, with an extra apology to Wade over there who *made* this slop. I can't imagine the number of times I've mistreated the Wandas of the world. Thirty years on the road, probably 250 times a year anyway, that must be about.." There's where he stumbled in his speech till Wanda yelled, "That's 7500 times Dickwad, now sit down, shut up, and finish your slop!"

This got more applause than Miles got last night at the Queen's Tavern. Jeez the Queen must be quite the drinker to have so many saloons named after her!

Chapter Two

OK OK, you wanted the Miles story, and I haven't even got us out of the parking lot yet. Jeez.

So we're at the Queen's Tavern. Ya, the dive bars were pretty well where the band ended up, and of course that's where we started too. That's where we all learned our trade really.

The Beatles had Hamburg to get their chops together. We had the Canadian bar circuit. It doesn't exist anymore really, the multi-night stands in one club. Maybe that's a good thing. I don't know. There was a time though, and I'm telling you this so you understand where Miles came from which might help with understanding where he went, that bars all had live entertainment six nights a week. Disco killed that of course when bar managers discovered how much cheaper DJs were. More recently they've also figured out how to take the job away from musicians by having 'open mic' nights where you play for free, three songs each, and the place is filled with hobbiest musicians and their friends who think they might be getting their big break. Guess what? There's no big break because the only gigs available are *more* open mics.

Way back then the bars would hire you for six-nighters and they'd actually pay you a decent fee instead of like now where they give you the door, and only want to charge a five- dollar cover. You'd start kind of easy Monday nights, feeling out the crowd and the town, and if you were good, (and you'd have to be or you wouldn't get invited back), word would get out, this was way before social media of course. By Thursday night you'd have a following and by Saturday night it would be packed. Why do they call it social media anyways? You're all alone wanking away on your device and you're not actually talking to anyone. How social is that?

Anyway, Saturday afternoons you'd do a matinee too, where you'd have to let drunks get onstage with you to jam.

That was usually pretty dodgy but it helped with the public relations. Sundays you'd have off, which usually meant that you'd work your way towards the *next* six-nighter. You only actually had to have about eight places to play cuz by the time you'd finish up the last place the first place would be ready for you again, and the crowds would welcome you back. The bigger cities all had a few of these joints, so in the early days before they hit it big Miles and Myles would be playing at one place, David Wilcox would be just down the street and maybe the Downchild Blues Band or even Ronnie Hawkins at another, and you'd have a competition to see who could bring in the biggest crowd. That made you play better too. Miles and Myles always had the biggest crowds. They were something, all right.

You'd play four forty-minute sets, 9 till 1, sometimes till 3 in Newfoundland, so you had to have a lot of material, maybe 35 songs a night, not like these wimpy-assed bands today who have half an hour tops cuz the only gigs available are ones where they are splitting the door with three other bands and they are maybe lucky to get gas money. Of course we're lucky to get even that these days.

The club would usually give you a place to stay too, either rooms if you were playing in a hotel or they'd actually have a band house that you'd stay in. These were usually totally trashed but they were like your home away from home, since your actual home was usually trashed too. Heh heh. You'd have the days free. Well, the afternoons, since you'd sleep it off till noon, or just before so you could grab those breakfast specials I told you about. You'd hit the all-night diners after closing time too if the town was big enough, which it never is for the band these days.

So you had all afternoon because you didn't have to drive. So what did guys like Miles do with that time? Well you'd get to writing songs, that's what. And you'd run them by the band and you'd get to try them out the day you'd write them. It was perfect. Sometimes the songs would be clearly not keepers: they wouldn't pass the crowd test. Other times Miles would see that there was something there and he'd polish the little darlin' up a bit and try 'er again later in the week. You'd learn what would work and what didn't work. You learned how to be an entertainer as well as a musician and that's where Maddie Myles came in. Miles and Myles sure had it all going on back then.

They'd built up a repertoire that could adapt to any situation, a mix of covers and originals. Miles wasn't as stuck up then so if they asked for an Eagles song why that's what he'd do and Maddie would be able to pull off a Linda Ronstadt that would knock your work socks off.

They'd do tear-jerkers, shit-kickers, rib-ticklers, head-scratchers, thought-provokers, wrist-slitters, knee-slappers, toe-tappers, heart-breakers and humdingers all in one set, and if it looked like the crowd was partial to one of those in particular, why, they'd settle in to a run of those for a spell.

You knew things were really happening for the band when the crowds would stop yelling out 'Skynyrd', and start asking for the originals.

Miles Gerber and Maddie Myles weren't a couple when they started, did you know that? They just had such a good musical chemistry, and yes chemicals did play a part in the picture then. After all the constant touring it just seemed natural that they would be together. They hid it for a while because I think that part of the draw was that Maddie was every young man's fantasy. Availability was part of the fantasy, like when they hid John Lennon's wife who sure got the short end of that drumstick. So even after they got married and she was Maddie Gerber, they kept her name Maddie Myles for the biz. Miles and Myles had a nice ring to it.

The bigger clubs had two performing venues. One for the louder bands and a smaller one for the solo acts. You'd get to hang out with the other musicians and I think that's where Miles first started to jam with songwriters and learn from them. You'd stagger the sets a bit so you'd slip in to hear some of each other's shows. It was cool. You'd get novelty acts too. Miles would talk about doing the northern Ontario circuit before my time and always running into a guy named 'Gloves McGuinty'. The gimmick was he was a piano player and he'd put this velvet cloth over the keys and wear velvet gloves and he'd play as smooth as, well, velvet. One place he got so popular they named the bar after him. No, not 'Gloves,' smartass, Bic.

You'd get regular fans at these places, and sometimes as you can imagine they'd get to be more than just fans, and you'd have a whole week together and you could honestly say you'd be back.

This circuit wasn't the be-all-and-end all though. No sir. It *was* a good way to bring up talent through the system. You'd get better and you'd get known and you'd be selling albums off the stage, yes actual vinyl albums, and then you'd find you'd get invited to do festivals or concerts in actual theatres and then there was even TV and radio work that paid. Can you believe it? What I'm talking about here was a career. Of course it was no life if you wanted a family or any kind of stability. But who wanted that then?

Well Maddie did eventually I guess. That was part of the problem.

Miles and Myles. The legend grew, and I guess once everyone *did* know they were a couple, living up to the legend was mighty hard. They were like the Canadian Dolly and Kenny or Ian and Sylvia. Oh, they *were* Canadian. Forgot.

Their voices together. Wow. You've heard those songs, eh? You never really knew who was singing lead or harmony, it was just its own unique thing.

In the late 80s though, in the music business in general, it stopped being about the songs. It was about the image. MTV and MuchMusic changed all that. It was all about the look and the attitude. And of course Maddie Myles had that in spades and many other garden tools as well.

Miles, he was getting better and better at the songwriting and he wanted it to be about *that*.

Me? Well I told you I'm not the original drummer, eh? 'Buck Skins' left when Maddie left and I guess that's a whole 'nother story too. I used to actually go and see them play when I was just a sapling. (Miles is older than me. Hell, older than most of us still out on the road now.) They were amazing. I saw them once in Kingston, where those boys from the Tragically Hip, just starting up, used to come and worship at the shrine of Miles and Myles. I remember that club cuz I played it too with my first band 'Red White and his Blues Crew'. Ever hear Red play? Jesus. Anyway that place had an Irish name like 'McBrides' or 'McGrooms' or something like that. That means you'd have to sing one rollicking Irish number to please the bar manager but after that, whatever sold the booze the best was OK by him, or very occasionally, her.

That big room was equally divided between merchant sailors off the lakes, posh sailors off their yachts, students from Queen's University off their rockers, soldiers from the military college and guards from the Kingston Pen. It was a toxic mixture. Fights would break out. I should have been warned off the 'biz' for good by witnessing that scene.

It wasn't long after that that Miles' agent 'Kirk the Jerk' called me up at the saloon I was playing in, and said that Dougie and Miles had heard me play with old Red's band. Maddie and Buck had just left, and Kirk said they had to finish the tour and could I fill in? How could I say no? He was *The* Miles Gerber, after all, and I was a kid straight out of the foster system with nothing ahead and too much behind. Not as big a behind as Dougie though. Heh heh.

I signed on, without telling them that I was in Kingston cuz I had just got out of the pen myself. That's a story you don't wanna hear. This is about Miles after all. Anyway that was nearly 20 years ago, and without Maddie Myles, who was clearly the big draw in the band, we've been working that same circuit ever since. So much driving that it often feels like that's what we do for a living, and we do a little playing on the side. The whole time I've been with them we've had the same van, Nelly-Belle, which they got after downsizing from the tour bus after things went sour. She hums along pretty good considering she's an old gal. I've got to know that hum so well that sometimes I can almost make out what she's saying.

Twenty years. I probably don't need to tell you where Miles was at during those years cuz he wrote, in my view, a few too many songs about the road and about heartbreak. Write about what you know and he knew it well. Did he know about relationships? I'm not his judge. I'm his drummer.

He did get some airplay with those early ones after he and Maddie split; more on the country stations then the pop charts.

Remember 'Took the Long Way Home'? A good example. You could tell he wrote that imagining he was coming home to Maddie, which really wasn't going to happen, and they never really had a home to go to.

Song 4: Took The Long Way Home

Took the long way home
Past the Discount Auto Parts
The empty lot full of shopping carts
Along a trail of broken hearts

Took the long way home
Train tracks and power lines
Rusted cars filling up with vines
Signs of our long slow decline

I took the long way home,
Watched the days turn into years
Watched the laughter turn to tears
Watched the hopes turn into fears

Took the long way home
Tire dumps and oil drums
Lost track of where I came from
Did you think I would ever come?

I took the long way home
Down desperate boulevards
Where everything was cold and hard
I was close but still so far

I took the long way home,
Watched the days turn into years
Watched the laughter turn to tears
Watched the hopes turn into fears

Took the long way home,
And much to my surprise
You were there with love in your eyes
Welcoming me inside

Took the long way home
I came around that final bend
Saw you there my forever friend
I knew my journey was at an end

Chapter Three

Nelly-Belle Tells

Oops. Looks like Drummer is asleep again. The rhythm of the road and the melody that I hum when the highway is dry and I'm really in the groove can be like a cradle's gentle rocking. I could wake him up with a sharp turn or a squealing brake but he could use some rest with what lies ahead for the band. He's left that cassette recorder on. I'm going to give it a go. Why not, right? As if cars can talk, eh? Hey, music and magic are closely related.

These guys are like my big babies. Dougie seems blissfully oblivious to what's happening outside my tin walls so you'd be missing the nuances if he took over the tale-telling, and he's out like a light too. I always thought the wattage of Dougie's light was a little low anyway. His snoring is a nice bass part for my lead line though. Miles is driving as usual, at least I let him think he's in charge. I am holding these babes in my rocker arms, and I'm holding their stories, and the stories we gather like bugs on my windshield as we head west through this vast country. These days that country seems as dented and worn out as I am, though like me, it just keeps going somehow, tied together with binder twine and sticky tape.

Drummer has his stories and I've got mine. Not sure if those stories will jibe. I've got a built-in 'auto correct' though. Ha ha. I'll tell the story while the band gets their 'ugly rest' as Dougie likes to call it, though he often calls me 'beauty'. Yup. I have lots of tales. I've even got a tale pipe. One thing I am good at is watching everything that goes on.

Heading out of town towards the next gig is my favourite part of being on the road of course. It's pretty boring just sitting in a parking lot. Being on the actual road is my purpose, and when I feel Miles' hands on my wheel and his foot on my clutch I really feel alive. I think Miles does too. We're connected in a pretty intimate way. When he shifts me into top gear and I respond with the kind of hum that signals to him that we are in sync, we become one. In that moment it's almost like, well, I guess I won't go too far down that road, if you know what I mean. Car-human relationships are taboo I'm told. Anyway, once we are in the groove, you can feel Miles sit back in the seat, letting me do most of the work, which is the way I like it. He holds me loosely but with care and we just let ourselves go for the ride. I think we're watching the same things as we look out on Canada and sometimes the U.S. spreading out before us. I'm maybe a little more focused on the other cars and trucks going by and wary of those pesky motorcycles. I can tell what part of the country we are in by the average age and condition of the vehicles. In the Maritimes folks are more inclined to hold on to their pavement pals, their horseless carriages, a little longer. They have a sense of loyalty and trust and we respond by giving our all: really making it a team effort. Last time we drove through Moncton along the back streets (Miles' first choice, which bugs his bandmates I know) I remember fondly seeing the older cars up on the front lawns of the old clapboard houses, their humans fixing them lovingly themselves, maybe a new transmission in the driveway ready for a transplant. Hoo Boy. Honk my horn! Those are happy automobiles. As you get farther west through the urban part of Quebec and into Ontario you don't see that as much. Ever since they rammed computers into the newer cars, because they don't trust us I guess, their owners take them into these big impersonal 'diagnostic centres' where nobody cares. By the way, I don't really think of Miles as my 'owner'. We're partners. I'm as much a part of the band as Dougie and Drummer. The fourth wheel with four wheels!

I'm watching the cars and Miles is watching who is in them. He feels a special kinship with the carnies and gypsies, the soccer moms and salesmen, the truckers and tradesmen, the cops and the snow plow operators, the travelling people sharing the blacktop with him. Heading into the sun after a cleansing overnight rain, when you can hear my tires singing and my motor purring, it's like we're at the Church of the

Highway. Hot rubber on a wet road. Hoo wee. We work together passing the school buses and the old codgers heading back to their farms from Tim Horton's till we're in the clear and we go for it. Most of the coffee places that used to be right in the gas stations are gone now. They always made me feel like I was an equal. Miles and I could both get our morning fix at the same place. Gas. Food. I know, an unlikely combo but it worked.

The edges of the towns are getting blurrier these days. It used to be that you were either in the town or in the country. Now there are patches of open space and then the last gas station, a car lot, a wrecking yard, a new subdivision going in on top of what was a hay field the last time through. Makes you want to throw a rod. You see those new self-storage places popping up all over as people get more transient, more vulnerable in their jobs and their family units, yet still unable to let go of the possessions that gave them some sense of security. I think that's why Miles hangs on to me.

Miles will talk a bit as he drives about the shifts in the populations of the places we drive through. Smaller towns shrinking as opportunities diminish, but the larger ones overwhelmed with bleak sprawl. Townhouse developments made for my fellow cars but not really for people, looking like scars on the face of the land. And then finally stretches of farmland or wilderness when I can feel his heartbeat slow a bit, his grip on my steering wheel soften. The rhythm of the road accompanying the sweet song of the green earth. You could tell that Miles felt a sense of place when he was not actually in a place.

Miles is awkward physically, as if he wishes he were a couple of inches shorter and far from wherever he is, but on the stage he's so at ease. He looks natural there. (I only get to see the outdoor shows of course). That 'ease' is changing though since that environment seems very volatile these days, like being on an open stretch of road and suddenly finding yourself hemmed in by two 18-wheelers. Listening to the band talk as I drive them back to the hotel, I sometimes get the feeling that the stage, usually a place of safety and freedom, can also become a prison with just one song that fails to resonate, one comment from a drunken heckler.

On the highways, especially the two-lane ones that we know so well, we could feel the promise of the next gig ahead and take comfort in the quilted patterns of fields in the summer or the blankets of snow in the winter. When the roads are dry and there's gas in my tank, it's nothing but smiles for miles.

I was smiling too heading to the next motel. I'll tell you a secret. The boys seem to always argue about which one to stop at but I got tired of that and I tend to jam my gears and make Miles stop at the one I think makes the most sense, from an automotive standpoint anyway.

I've noticed that they are drawn to the motels that have those retro metal lawn chairs that you only see at the old joints, out on the porches. Of course only the old joints *have* porches or even doors that open straight on to the parking lot. Sometimes they get fooled because some of the new places have imitation old metal motel chairs outside, but it's a trap. It's just a boring franchise operation, but they are using the chairs ironically to attract more hipster customers. I don't get irony. I'm just a car. What do I know? I know rust, and that sounds related.

Sometimes they don't back me in to the parking spot. They drive straight in and leave my headlights on while they unload. I notice that this is mostly when Miles and Dougie have been drinking a bit and backing up is a risky venture. Anyway that's when I get to see into the room. I think they like those older rooms not just because they're cheaper, but because there are layers of stories buried in those cigarette-butt-stained carpets and beat-up old wood-paneled walls. Those rooms usually look pretty desolate to me. Usually if you end up in one of them it's because you are some kind of misfit. You are running away from something or going to a funeral or looking for a job or doing a crappy job that requires you to be rootless. They are not happy places, so it's odd that they boys always seem happiest there.

Ok maybe that was an 'anecdote' not a story, but hey, I'm a rookie storyteller; I'm helping to hold those road stories and

I feel like I'm a part of them. You see, when stories don't get told, they get forgotten the same way I seize up when I don't get driven. Miles is holding those stories too, like he's holding onto my steering wheel: kind of loose but steady enough to keep us on course. I can feel them thrumming in him. I don't think he knows what to do with those stories yet. There's something that is making him collect them but he doesn't understand what they're for. He doesn't yet see that people are hungry for them, that they need them to keep going the way I need gasoline. He doesn't yet see that it's in their retelling that we find their meaning. Miles is turning them over in his mind as we drive, the way waves turn over and smooth out pebbles on a shoreline. When he turns them over enough they will become songs that folks will want to hear, and when he shares them he'll be making the kind of connection that he needs, so he can feel like there's a reason he's out here on this blacktop. He's got them all tucked away like the Tim Horton's cups that get stuffed into my wheel wells. Tales of the farmers who have no farms, the miners who have no coal to dig, the factory workers who have no factories to work in, the lovers who have no one to love.

Miles has all this inside him, percolating like gas station coffee, but he doesn't seem to be aware of it. Right now he just knows that he has to pee and he just passed a sign that says it's just two clicks to the rest stop. Drummer is stirring in the back seat.

Sometimes long periods go by where no one speaks inside me. All you can hear are my wheels whining on the blacktop, the purr of my motor (more like a wheeze if you want to be honest about it) and sometimes Drummer or Dougie snoring in the back seat.

Dougie isn't much for conversation, but he has a habit of reading aloud signs that we pass, or the names on the transport trucks, and he'll make a wry remark about it. He finds it amusing that trucking companies don't admit to being just that; these days they often say 'Logistical Solutions' or 'Intermodal Facilitators', so he says the most pompous names out loud accompanied by a sound he'd make like a balloon deflating, or with a "Jesus, it's just a truck for Chrisakes."

Since we're always on the lookout for motels that aren't chains, he likes to read out the names of the family-run ones too.

"The Bambi. That one is probably a bit dear. Ha ha!"

In Minot, North Dakota, the "Ho Hum. True honesty in advertising, lads."

"The El Rancho. No kidding."

Or in the north, "The Cedars- Free Ice-fishing With Every Room. Jeez that place looks like a real cold hole, but you wouldn't think they'd advertise it like that!"

When they load in to a motel he likes to read the signs in the rooms too. I can hear him from my parking spot while the boys lug gear.

"Do not use hairdryer and air conditioner at the same time. Jeez, we won't have much of a party tonight boys!"

"Please do not cut up your deer in the bathtub. Ok, I guess the bed's going to get a bit messy, fellers."

His favourite though is wildlife identification. His father, Dougie Senior, a decent fiddle player in his own right, was also a taxidermist and a trapper, so he taught his kid to watch for the signs. He sees things in the woods as we drive past that no one else can see. Well, I'm watching the road of course, and maybe no one else is looking, but it's uncanny what he can spot.

Until it starts to annoy 'Miles the Easily Irritated'., A long quiet drive is often punctuated with Dougie's smoked whiskey rasp announcing, 'Porcupine!' 'Deer!' 'Moose!'

The only time anyone responds is when he says 'hawk', and everyone else in unison says 'turkey vulture', since that's what they usually are. They say this in a condescending tone, though I'm not sure why a turkey vulture would be less worthy of being identified than a hawk.

We rumble along like this for miles. The boys were at a low point in a tour filled with lows. Rock bottom for the band. Well, more like country-rock bottom. I didn't see it of course. I was out in the lot, but they were still sulking about an incident back in Yorkton. They had set up and were launching into the first set when Miles noticed that the big-screen TV was on behind them, with a football game that was drawing more attention than the boys. He asked the bar manager to turn it off. The dude said no, it was good for business. The band pressed on for a bit till Miles got tired of hearing cheering happen in all the wrong places so he stopped mid-song and said,

"Either that game goes or we go!"

"See you later," said the manager, to cheers from the crowd.

So it was pretty somber the next day. All quiet except for Dougie, who was having a string of road kill spotting successes as we headed along the trail. The way he could spot them so easily, it made you wonder why the furry creatures couldn't have spotted the murderous vehicles coming at them with that kind of sightline too.

"Rabbit"

"Prairie Gopher"

"Prairie Chicken"

"Another Prairie Gopher!"

"Dog"

"Coyote"

"Human"

He said 'human' with the same bored intonation. I heard it first and slammed on my own brakes before Miles could even put his foot on the pedal.

Everyone piled out faster than at that first pee stop after the Rogers Pass.

I could see the boys in my rearview mirror, standing around what looked like a body in the fetal position on the gravel. A coyote was on a little rise behind us, just watching.

After what seemed like a really long time, Dougie said

"It's a girl."

"Jesus Christ, Dougie," yelled Miles. "This isn't a birthing, this looks like a crime scene. We can see it's a girl!"

"On account of she's naked as a jaybird," said Drummer

"Why do they call Jaybirds naked," asked Dougie. "Don't they have feathers or something?"

"Shut up," said Miles.

"Is she dead?" asked Drummer, his body slack with confusion.

"Looks like it."

"She looks like she's maybe black!"

"Maybe that's a tan from being out here a while. It's more like mocha, I'd say."

"More like Tupelo Honey."

"Get back in the Van, Morrison!"

"Look, she's wearing a tattoo!" I could see them all peering down to get a closer look.

"At least she's wearing something."

"What's it say?"

"Read it, numbnuts."

"SHUT THE FUCK UP!"

Everyone did shut the fuck up, because it was the girl who shouted that out.

Drummer covered her up with his jeans jacket as she struggled to get up. She coughed and looked around- looking disgusted as she scanned the gravel, the piercing prairie sun, the cars whizzing by and the three dopey dudes looking down at her. She tried to speak again but had a big unladylike puke instead.

"Sorry about the jacket, dude," she said in a scratchy deep voice that didn't seem like it belonged with her tiny and girly chassis.

"Are you OK?" asked Drummer.

"I guess if I was OK I wouldn't be lying naked beside the highway with three dorks leering at me, but if you mean am I alive, I guess it's yes, unless this is hell, which looks possible at this moment." More coughing and barfing.

Miles scooped her up, said "Outa my way, boys," and carried her into my warmth, which wasn't that warm really cuz they had left all my doors open. Before Drummer climbed in with Dougie he wiped off his jacket on my front passenger side tire. Imagine! Then the girl seemed to pass out again since it was quiet for a while.

"What do we do now?" said Drummer.

No one had an answer.

"Drive," said Dougie, who was in the back seat now with the girl propped up in the front passenger seat. Miles revved me up. I'd been idling all this time. Don't know why they call it idling—it's hard work for me—and off we went.

Hey Miles! Miles! Helloooo, it's called 5th gear! It comes after 4th gear, and if you don't want to rip my transmission right out, it would be pretty handy right about now. Miles wasn't paying attention to the road. I guess that was all up to me. Oh, we passed a pretty sweet looking red ragtop Camaro. Montana plates. I loves me a fine cowboy ride. Ok, I guess I wasn't paying attention either.

I got a better look at the girl in my mirror.

She was small and wiry, with a young athletic body but a face that looked like it was 10 years older than the rest of her, which I determined to be about my age, 20. She had about the same amount of hair as me too, which is to say none. Shaved head. One large silver hoop earring and two large piercing blue eyes. I know people. That suggested to me that she was a real mish mash of backgrounds. Do they call that mixed-race? Like when they throw a Chevy engine on a Dodge frame? Her nose was covered in blood and gravel, though I'm imagining that this was a temporary feature. The blood and gravel, not the nose.

The boys stayed silent and intent on the road. Miles really had me pushed to my limit.

"Hospital," said Dougie, just like when he was spotting road kill.

"Where?" said Miles.

"No, I mean we should take her to a hospital."

"Do you know where we are, buddy? There's no hospital within three hours of here I bet."

From the silence it was clear that Dougie did *not* know where they were, but that was nothing unusual.

"We gotta take her to the next cop shop."

"No way," said Drummer, who didn't like going near those places.

"No *Fucking* Way!" That was from the Girl. Oh my. "And it says M.G"

"What does?" said Dougie.

"My tattoo, idiot," she said, sitting up and squinting at my cluttered innards.

"Oh" the boys all mumbled, not sounding like they were feeling that much more informed.

"What's it stand for?" offered Drummer.

"Merch Girl."

"You're a Merch Girl?" said Miles. "We used to have a Merch Girl."

"Did you throw her out of your tour bus, cause that's what looks like happened to me."

"Woah," said everyone, including me.

"Yes, Merch Girl is my hustle, and my name is Merch Girl too, or MG mostly."

"Those are my initials, oddly enough," said Miles.

The girl, louder this time, said "Wait a minute, are you Fucking Miles Gerber?"

"I am not fucking Miles Gerber! I *am* Miles Gerber. I prefer Miles Fucking Gerber, or in this case, MFG. It has more of a ring to it."

"Pardon Moi, Miles Fucking Gerber. Pleased to meet with your acquaintance, and I'm guessing these are The Shit Disturbers, in all their glory."

"Yup," said Drummer.

"Do you have names?" She had a good look at each of the boys, shaking her head and smirking at what probably didn't look like her good fortune at the time.

"Yup." Drummer and Dougie spoke in unison.

There was a long pause. Finally Dougie said, "Dougie Morrison, m'aam.

"Drummer. Just Drummer" said drummer, starting to shake her hand before she withdrew it in horror..

"Fuck me," she said, followed by a low whistle that dislodged some gravel from her throat and another flurry of coughing. "Well, not literally fuck me, of course. Just because I'm naked doesn't mean I'm easy, though that's been misinterpreted before in this biz."

"Do you mind me asking how you ended up back there,

naked and all?"asked Dougie, which was a long sentence for him.

"How did you get here halfway to Bumfuck, Manitoba, with the big has-been in the front seat, asshole?"

"You go first," said Dougie.

"Well, I don't really know just now. There were some 'issues' back on the bus after the last show. And besides, I never tell a story on the first date. Hey! We just passed a Tim Horton's! You've just broken Rule #1 of the road, dudes."

"Don't get Miles started on that one," said Drummer.

"OK so no food," said the girl. "How 'bout some clothes?"

I could hear Drummer rummaging in a road case in the back, and soon he came up with a T-shirt.

"Wow, you have Miles Gerber T-Shirts? I bet they're selling like hotcakes. Speaking of hotcakes, you just passed the Golden Griddle."

"First we've got to get you some help," said Miles.

"Well, this crappy T-shirt is a start. Can you crank up the heat a bit? What else have you got to wear in that merch bag?"

"More T-shirts. CDs. Pictures."

"Not of you gents I hope." A wheezy laugh was followed by more coughing.

"Get the lady your drum rug, Drummer," said Miles, and Drummer obliged after more rummaging.

"Thanks, bud. Jesus, this stinks. Well, I guess I'm about Chanel Minus 5 right now myself."

"Who were you the Merch Girl for?" asked Dougie, who was getting almost chatty. Maybe all this time he just needed a woman's presence, other than mine of course.

"The Prideful Scoffers."

"The Prideful Scoffers?"

"Is there an echo in here? Yes, ever heard of them?"

"Oh ya," said Dougie. "We accidentally got on a double bill with them in Fredericton. Big Mistake. Those were some nasty lads."

"Tell me about it. Not like you sweet thangs though, eh?"

"Heh heh," said Drummer.

"We're playing in Needham tonight. We're nearly there,"

said Miles. "We could drop you at the hotel while we set up, and you could get some clothes, if you don't think you need a doctor."

"Thanks, chief. I'll just pull my wallet out of my jeans here. Oh wait...."

"Oh right, sorry," said Miles. "We'll chip in, right boys? Till you get in touch with your people."

"Do I look like someone who has 'people'?"

"I'm trying to be helpful here."

"That's new for Miles, too," muttered Dougie from the back seat.

"There's the Mansteads up there on the left."

I was driving them down the main street. It looked tired. Dusty. Faded. Just like me I guess. The street was looking even dowdier than last time through. Kind of unloved. Most of the shops were boarded up. There was, of course, a Chinese café and a futon shop where there used to be a waterbed store when we first toured this way. Ever the trendsetters in Needham. The Co-op grocery and gas was still there, though the Ford Dealership where I spent a pleasant night last time was closed too. The gig was, yes, at the Queen's down towards the railway and the grain elevators. Three of them! Must have been a going concern back in the day. I don't like to see the decline, but the one advantage to this dying town was that there was no motel, just the sketchy rooms over the hotel, so we didn't have to waste time shopping around. The Mansteads was still open but a big sign announced 'Closing Sale. All Clothing Half Off.' I waited for one of my passengers to remark on that. Easy joke there, but no one seemed to get it. There was once a chain of small town department stores called Steadman's, and when they went out of business a local family bought this one, switched the letters on the sign, and opened 'Mansteads.'

"Ok," said Miles, grinding my gears a bit as he pulled up in front of the store. "MG, we'll go in. You boys stay here with Nelly-Belle."

"Who?" said the girl.

"The van," said Dougie with a little less affection than I was expecting. "Don't ask."

"OK. But MG The Other, I can't go in there wearing a rug, though entering the Scoffers dressing room like that once got me some pretty good blow."

"Right. OK, Drummer, you come with me. Dougie, you stay with MG here. What size are you?"

"Medium for a shirt. 32-inch waist for the jeans."

"Not you Drummer. The Lady!"

"No ladies here, except for your vehicle apparently, but thanks for the compliment," said MG. "You can save some dough by getting the largest size in 'girls' instead of the smallest size in 'women.' Anything for now I guess. We'll do the full fashion show later, boys, thanks a bloody bunch."

Drummer, looking uncertain about his assignment, got out with Miles and left me alone with Dougie and MG, who seemed to have either passed out or fallen asleep again. I just watched the pickups going by while I waited.

Chapter Four

Drummer Tells

Well, Bic, got a fresh tape on your machine. I want to capture what everyone was saying for you. I hope it makes sense to you. Maybe I'll try impersonating their voices. That would be fun. I'm gonna tell it like I'm a big-time writer like you, OK? Here goes.

I don't know why Miles made me go in to that store to look for women's clothing. We opened the door and it looked just like 1958 in there. It was a little smelly, but I suppose that might have been me. After all, I was wearing a jean jacket that a naked lady had recently puked on.

We were the only ones in there. I was hoping we wouldn't be that easy to spot. The clerk was an older lady with a sharp face but a round body. I guess I have to learn not to say 'older lady' and admit that she was just a bit older than me. She was wearing a blue print dress that Aunt Bea would have been happy in, though I guess back then folks mostly dressed in black and white for the TV. She looked understandably suspicious as we moved towards the women's section, and Miles muttered something about a birthday present for his niece.

"What kind of style does she like?" offered the woman.

For some reason I decided that this was Miles' problem, so I said, "Ya, bro, what does Winnifred like?"

Miles gave me the finger behind his back. "Kind of punkish, I guess." "Maybe kind of Goth," I countered, as I pretended I knew what I was doing heading down an isle.

She tried to look as if 'punkish' and 'Goth" meant something to her, and said "What about colour? What does she like?"

"Last time I saw her, I seem to remember kind of brown."

"We have a whole beige aisle over there," she pointed, and I'll be darned if she wasn't right. It was kind of a beige town.

Then she added, "Western wear is very popular around here."

Miles directed me to start looking, and for some reason he started to chat the lady up a bit, which is not a Miles thing at all. Maybe he sensed her nervousness about two strangers in the women's section and he wanted to distract her while I did the shopping. Jesus. I kind of panicked and picked out pretty much the first things I saw in each section under 'Small', but ran for the checkout counter when I came face to face with the bras. Merch Girl hadn't mentioned that! Miles looked doubtfully at my purchases after glancing out the window, but he paid up and somehow we got out of that store with our pride intact and our funds not too depleted. It was my first time picking out clothes for anyone but me, and I'm not too picky, so I was a tad nervous about MG's response, especially as I was learning about the mouth on that girl.

I threw her the bag once back inside Nelly-Belle. She opened it and said, "Woah, are these MOM jeans? Hello? Holy 1982 Batmen! And is that a '*blouse*'? Lahdy Dah! I thought they were extinct. And no underwear boys. Are you kinda kinky or what?"

I admitted that we didn't want to arouse suspicion, two dudes in the ladies underwear section, and besides we thought we'd get her basically covered and she could go in for the rest.

"Thanks but no thanks. I think I can wait till we see a thrift store."

She asked me and Dougie to turn our backs for a moment and said to Miles "Keep your eyes on the road for once, Bucko!"

After we got the no-peaking ban removed, Dougie had to comment.

"Whoo Doggies, but don't you just look like a small-town prairie girl now, except for the shaved head of course and the nose ring, and your skin tone, and your not-so-corn-fed size, but otherwise you'd fit right in here."

"Thanks Mr. Talkative," said MG, "but I am not planning on fitting in here. Even if these clothes *did* fit, which they don't, but thanks for trying. Drummer, you're a natural at the shopping. Is there something you're not telling us? I've got to get off this weird planet you dudes are on and get back, get back, like Jo Jo to where I once belonged."

"And where was that?" Dougie asked innocently.

"Not here, that's for damn sure," said MG.

Miles said they would be happy to take her down the road a-ways after their gig that night, since Needham offered no bus service, and she could find her way back to 'not here' from there, which didn't really take into account her immediate need for accommodation. We turned the only corner in town along the tracks, and spotting a couple more stores MG shouted

"Stop the van. I have an idea!"

"Whoa Nelly-Belle!" the band said automatically in unison.

"What the fuck?" yelled MG. "Man, I've *really* got to get out of here. Hey boss," she said to Miles. "I've got no dough, no ID, nothing. Thanks for the Miss Chatelaine outfit, really, but if you lend me twenty bucks I've got a plan that will get it paid back quick and leave me with a stake to help me get out of Dodge, or in your case, Nelly-Belle, a Ford.

"Why, miss Merch," said Dougie, "on behalf of the entire Shit Disturber organization, I'd be pleased to spot you a green Queen if it enabled your hasty exit."

He handed her a twenty with a grand gesture.

"Wait right here," she said as she headed into the thrift store, which had the compelling name 'Thrift Store.' That was new since last time. Thrifty times call for thrifty measures. Now that she had some clothes on, she could shop on her own, and we watched her in silence through the dusty windshield, wondering what she might return with. She was back outside quickly wearing her purchases, a worn-out and slightly too large pair of red cowboy boots,

(we had forgotten about her feet when we were back at Mansteads), and a two-dollar straw cowboy hat. She was waving a gold belt too, and a bag with what I guessed were some dainties and some improvements on our efforts. She cracked the belt like a whip, jumped in and said

"Ride 'em cowboys!"

"Mercy," said Dougie."What have you got in mind young lady? Whatever it is, I'd be pleased to go first!"

"With all due respect, Asshat, and by that of course I mean

with very little respect at this moment, I have a plan, and it doesn't involve 'horseplay'. But first, can we get something to eat? I could eat a horse turd about now."

"Been there done that," I offered. "It's OK with Tobasco."

"Listen Drummer. Oh I forgot, listening isn't a specialty with drummers, along with counting, but anyways, I'll handle the sarcastic remarks around here, OK?"

"Well", said Dougie, who for some reason had adopted a fake country gentleman act that we hadn't seen since the last time a 'lady' travelled with the band, but that's not the story at hand. "Out here, Miss M, we call those 'Road Apples'. Why don't I see if I could secure us a table on the picturesque patio of that quaint French Bistro just across from the gas station up there. I'll bet they could whip up some sauteed '*pomme du rue*' for you real nice."

"What?" said MG

"He's kidding. They only have the Chinese Café," said Miles as we pulled up in front of the 'Super Happy Garden: Chinese and Canadian Food'. We always laughed at this because there ain't no Canadian food really. Unless it's poutine and beaver tails. What they mean is other bland food that's not Chinese, which we make pretty bland for you gringos anyway.

As a bit of a joke, Miles had the habit of stealing menus from the Chinese cafés and using them in the *next* restaurant, since there was never really any difference. We three always just ordered the hot turkey sandwich, the BLT or the hamburger steak anyway. I could describe the typical prairie Chinese café to you: they haven't changed since the '40s, and they've learned to make a unique kind of imitation Chinese food that is mostly salt, sugar and fat, just like the cowboys like, but we have a story to get on with here I reckon.

Settling in to a Naugahyde booth, MG barked, "I'll have the Chop Suey and the sweet and sour chicken balls, not that chickens have balls," to the tired looking waitress, who looked surprised, since most people only ordered from the Chinese side of the menu on date night.

We made our usual order, and MG got down to business with her plan.

"You know why they call me Merch Girl, right?"

"Do tell," said Dougie.

"BECAUSE I'M A FUCKING MERCH GIRL, YOU IDIOTS. Not just ANY merch girl. The BEST merch girl in the biz."

This hit a sore spot for Miles. "Well, for starters, there really isn't any BIZ anymore, and no one buys merch anymore either. Sales are, let's say, down a little."

"Just about zero," said Dougie.

"That's because you haven't had ME selling for you. Who sells now?"

"Well, we just leave them out by the door and Drummer here hangs out with them for a bit at the end."

"A real salesman, are ya drummer?"

I shrugged. I am skilled at shrugging but I guess not at selling stuff.

"Tell you what. I'll sell your merch tonight for you if you give me 20% of it. You'll make some money. Guaranteed at least 20% more than you would with the Hillbilly Huckster here. I'll make some money, and I can pay you guys back and get you out of my hair."

I pointed out that she didn't actually have any hair but she gave me the stink-eye, which was stinkier than Miles' one.

"Deal? Are you going to finish those fries, Slim?" she said to Miles as he paid the bill, waving off MG's offer to pay her share from what was left of Dougie's loan.

"Now I guess you'll have to spot me a room too."

We explained that at the Queen's there was just a band room upstairs. We shared it with the old coin toss method of sharing two beds.

"Well it's four ways tonight, and I'm not sleeping with any of you and I'm not sleeping in Nelly Fucking Belle." We pulled up in front of the joint which was looking as dowdy as ever an aging monarch could look.

We started to unload the gear when MG stopped us. "Woah, Dudes. Look at the marquee!" A bit of a fancy word for the whiteboard beside the front door. It said 'Open Mic Tonight With Celebrity Judge. Uh oh. I told you about those, right?

"Jesus, take me now if I'm that celebrity," muttered Miles.

"Leave the gear in the van till I sort this out. Miles, better get Kirk the Jerk on the phone. Drummer, you watch Nelly-Belle." Dougie was barking orders.

Miles and I laughed because he'd never done that before. Leadership, decisiveness and initiative; not his specialties. Who is he trying to impress? Oh right. Just then MG chimed in

"Who the hell is Kirk the Jerk?"

I told her about Kirk our agent. He'd been keeping us on the road non-stop but he clearly never put much effort into it. That's why this tour's routing looked like a pinball game. All over the map. To be honest, I wouldn't have cared either if I was him. After all, what's a 20% commission on next to nothing? The real gigs are disappearing as fast as our spruce forests but you'll hear more about that from Miles I expect, if he ever talks to you, Bic. My advice would be don't get him started.

"Looks like I've finally hit the big-time with you rock stars," sneered MG, which kind of pissed me off, so I asked her to stay with the gear while I went inside with Dougie as Miles searched for a payphone. Yes I said payphone. Though they are disappearing even faster than gigs, Miles still hung on to what he seemed to see as a romantic tradition. You know his song 'Signal Faded', right? Back from the M and M days. Made the Country charts. Maddie sang it as if every male listener was at the end of the line. Heartache songs are really suffering for the lack of payphones if you ask me. Actually, no one ever asks me. We'd been doing it around these parts 'cuz it has Manitoba in it, even though Miles doesn't like songs from that era. They just give him more heartache. But if you listen to that VOICE on that recording, you'll understand why Maddie won so many hearts herself.

Song 5
Signal Faded

Bitter coffee, but one more cup
Will give me the courage, to call you up,
With one more quarter, and one more prayer
That this time you'll listen, this time you'll care

Last time we made a good connection
But the static started, and our lines got crossed
when I thought we'd braved a new direction
The signal faded, the call was lost
The signal faded, the call was lost

Manitoba, roadside cafe
Another western, another day
Radio's playing a '70s song
That's just as tired as the road is long

Last time we made a good connection
But the static started, and our lines got crossed
when I thought we'd braved a new direction
The signal faded, the call was lost
The signal faded, the call was lost

I keep on stoppin' in every town
Me and these payphones keep breaking down
From here to Whitehorse takes a long long time
But not enough to drive you out of my mind

Last time we made a good connection
But the static started, and our lines got crossed
when I thought we'd braved a new direction
The signal faded, the call was lost
The signal faded, the call was lost

At the bar, which looked pretty much like last night's dump, the bored barmaid was reading the newspaper. Wow, newspapers are disappearing faster than payphones. Without raising her head from the paper the barmaid pointed into the gloom towards a back table where a small round man with a pocked face was surrounded by paperwork. He had that same pasty look that bar managers all get. He looked a bit like our just-mentioned Kirk the Jerk: slick like a snake.

Dougie, still demonstrating this uncharacteristic spunk, said, "Howdy, Mister, I'm Morrison and this here's Drummer. We're with Myles Gerber. We're his Shit Disturbers."

Buddy looked over his glasses. "I see that, boys. Glad to have you here. Now's a good time to set up before the dinner crowd comes in." The chortle he gave with that indicated that there was never a dinner crowd at the Queen's. "We all sure were big fans of Miles and Myles, did you play with them then too? Golly, that Maddie Myles was something. Something I say!" He pounded the table, spilling his half-full glass of draft. He just left it there, and we just left that thought there.

"There appears to be some sort of double-booking situation going on here," said Dougie, more politely than he's ever been, even though MG wasn't present. "The sign outside says Open Mic."

"You're darned tootin' it does. That'll pack 'em in. Always does. And as you know, boys, no offence, but Miles without Myles does not exactly pack them in these days, capiche?"

Just then we heard yelling from the payphone in the back hall near the rest rooms. By the trash littering the hall it looked like the cleaning staff had taken a permanent rest back in the '70s.

"God damn it, Kirk. I don't need exposure! I could DIE from exposure and I'm not being a fucking judge for a fucking open mic contest. It's humiliating! Is this what it's come to?" Miles was banging his hand against the wall, which was rattling the boxes of empties lining it, while he listened to Kirk. "No way, Kirk! We're just in a little slump till the next album comes out, that's all. We won't get out of this slump if you book us shit gigs like this! I've had it! Maybe you should look for another band to abuse!" He slammed down the phone. That's one good thing about those last remaining payphones. They sure slam good.

We just kinda froze.

"What's the deal?" Dougie said, knowing the answer already.

"I think I just fired our agent". Heading over to the now heavily sweating bar manager, Miles said, "Miles Gerber, and you are?"

"Well I am pleased as punch to meet you, that's who I am!" and he reached out a stubby, greasy hand to Miles.

"Two kinds of bar managers in this world, Dougie," announced Miles without taking the gent's hand.

"Here we go," said Dougie.

"Those who appreciate the value of fine veteran performers like ourselves, who will surely give 'er their all for the good folks of... of..."

"Needham," offered the bar man as he unoffered his hand.

"Needham!" continued Miles. "OR there are those who want to undermine the prospects of us hard-working professionals by bringing in hack locals to play for free. You're saving a few bucks while sacrificing the future of what they laughably still call show business!"

"Now Mr. Gerber," said the dude who now sounded a bit like a snake himself as he hissed out his reply: "This is the future of show business. Keeping it local, keeping it fun, and yes, free! And we're honoured to have someone as prominent as you representing the past here in our fine establishment, someone who can pass the torch so to speak to the next generation of musical homegrown talent. We've got a 100-dollar prize for the winner that YOU PICK, and of course 100 bucks for EACH of the three of youse, plus our luxurious band room upstairs and free drinks on us, plus you can sell your records and what-not. It was all agreed with your perhaps no-longer agent who said you LOVED meeting your adoring public in this kind of format!"

Miles was turning redder than the necks of the regular clientele at Queen's hotels everywhere. I can tell you that amongst other things that 'hundred bucks' remark was a real trigger for him. He often talked about it when we'd do that morning 'settling up' ritual from the previous night's gigs. See, when we all got our starts in this alleged biz, we always thought it was a decent night if we made a hundred bucks. That was the early '80's when you could rent a decent apartment for 200 bucks a month, a hotel room for 20 a night, buy a beater van for 500. Gas was cheap, food was cheaper and Bob was your uncle. Even when Miles was riding high though, with a full crew, management, publicists, the whole shebang, he'd joke that when everybody got paid off he often found he *still* made 100 bucks, and nowadays that magic number still comes up though that doesn't even cover a day's food and gas anymore. Anyway, with that and the situation he was facing, he seemed to be lifting off the ground as he reached boiling point. Just then M.G. fell right in to that burning ring of fire. "Excuse me, boys, is there some sort of trouble? She sashayed towards us looking like, well, more than 100 bucks I'll tell you that right now.

We froze and just stared. She was now wearing a size large yellow 'Miles Gerber and the Shit Disturbers' T-shirt, and that's all, cinched at the waist with her new gold belt, so that it was like a mini-dress, topped and bottomed off with the boots and cowboy hat. Even though she had come into our world naked with no possessions, somehow she had acquired lipstick the same shade as her boots, and she had applied it liberally right here in the middle of Conservative country. She looked, well, she looked ready for business, and something that Needham likely hadn't seen the likes of before.

"Fellers, we have a show to do. Let's get our asses in gear," and she turned on her well-turned out one of the afore-mentioned and headed to where she was setting up the Merch table beside the bar.

MG's entrance seemed to diffuse the crisis and everyone except Miles drifted in to the routine of setting up, even though we still weren't quite sure what we were setting up for.

As it happened, what the gig entailed was for me and Dougie to be the backup band for the open mic acts. Miles was to sit in the audience, judge the acts, and presumably say something nice about them; then he'd do a short closing set with us to finish off the night.

That is if we could lure him down from the so-called luxurious band room upstairs, where he'd retreated to.

MG somehow managed to drag him downstairs eventually. We could have never done that. Took her awhile. Don't know what she said, but it worked.

He took his spot as the joint was filling up, just like the Bar Snake said it would.

The crowd looked different than what we usually get. Families. Oldsters and youngsters. They came in groups with cases for guitars, fiddles and a couple of banjos, god forbid. I bet Nellie-Belle was enjoying watching them arrive.

Chapter Five

Nelly-Belle Tells

Because of all the weird stuff going on when we pulled into town, the guys ended up leaving me right out front. Usually I'm parked by a loading dock in the back. This was a lot more interesting. I'm guessing my boys weren't too happy about the arrangements for the evening, but by 8 o'clock the place was nearly full and I noticed right away that it wasn't the usual suspects, and by that I mean 'L.Ls' as Dougie called them. Lonesome Losers. I was facing the entrance and watching them arrive all convivial like. Well, we've already learned that Needham wasn't really a centre for 'houte couture', but you know what I mean. It was like a party. Since they WERE heading in to an open mic, while they were in there I took a stab at writing my first song! After all I've been listening to Miles muttering lyrics to himself at my wheel for years. I confess that I changed the name of Needham to Russell which is actually a ways east of there, since it had a better rhyme. Wadda ya think? I figure it might sound like the way those folks would be singing in there.

Song 6
Open Mic Night at the Queen's
By Nelly-Belle Ford the 2nd

It's a warm night in Russell
Folks come from all round
There's a little bit of bustle
in this dusty old town
It's usually just dogs barkin'
when the sun goes down
But it's open mic night at the Queen's

Some lean against their trucks
And practice up a bit
There's a whole hundred bucks
If their song is a hit
But they're all just there
for the sheer fun of it
Cuz it's open mic night at the Queen's

Even in a small town you can have big time dreams
Up on the stage, you are making the scene,
You're on the cover of Rolling Stone Magazine
When it's open mic night at the Queens

Families and neighbours it's
Not the regular crowd
Here to cheer their favourites
Who will do the town proud
When the work day is over
and the fields are all plowed
It's open mic night at the Queen's

A little Willie, a little Merl
Some Johnny Cash and golly
Just listen to that young girl
She can sing just like Dolly
A little Hank, a little George Jones

Peggy Sue by Buddy Holly
It's Open Mic night at the Queens

It's a warm night in Russell
Folks come from all round
There's a little bit of bustle
in this dusty old town.

Chapter Six

Drummer Tells

The slimy bar manager all of a sudden became the most genial host you'd ever see. He introduced the band and laid down a few ground rules:

"Two songs each. Call out the key to Dougie over here. Please listen to everyone even if they are not your buddies. Order your drinks in between the acts. I know we all can't wait to hear Miles and the boys after we've all had a turn. HAVE FUN!"

To a granny sitting with her family down front he said, "Hello gorgeous, didn't they ask you for your ID on your way in?"

"And now," pulling a name out of a Stetson, "first up are the Dykstras, Bill and Betty. Come on up and let's get started!"

The cheers they got as they took the stage indicated that they were favourites. They looked to be in their 'golden' years, though I always thought 'the Golden Years" came out of the same publicity team that named 'Greenland'. B and B were weathered in a nice kind of way, from the prairie wind I reckon. After Dougie helped Bill tune his guitar up we launched into 'Jambalaya' with Dougie on the fiddle and Bill thumping his flat-top with pretty good rhythm for an old white guy. Their harmonies were perfect; honed around kitchen tables and on truck rides for years, you could tell. They had everyone singing along and, well, me and Dougie were already having ourselves some fun only minutes after we were thinking this night was heading to the top of our 'gig-from-hell' list, which I have to say was pretty long. Next up Bill and Betty channeled their best Tammy Wynette and George Jones for 'We're Gonna Hold On' and I'll be darned if I didn't get kinda choked up back there behind the kit. They totally nailed it, and suddenly that corny old song became relevant. You could tell Bill and Betty were holding on to their marriage through thick and thin, to their way of life that was threatened more and more, to that little town, that was right with them for that wailing chorus. You could feel the tenacious caragana trees holding on to that prairie soil so it didn't blow away like in the Depression. The audience was holding on to every note. Things were off to a roaring start.

Next up was a young woman who drew a couple of wolf whistles from the back, which is where wolf whistles are born. Penny had that prairie look down real good. Pretty well every female in the joint had bleach-blonde hair, maybe the co-op store had a special on, but she was pretty convincing in hers. She didn't dress like a cowgirl; she didn't need to. That country charm just kind of oozed out of her the way she was oozing out of her jeans, which didn't come from Mansteads that's fer sure. I looked over and, uh oh, Dougie was in love. After a brief huddle, Dougie borrowed Bill's guitar and stepped out to join her, and since she was Patsy Inclined, she belted "I Fall To Pieces" and sure enough, we all did. Then she said in a shy voice, "I'm gonna' switch it up a bit here," and she *totally* nailed The Pretenders' "Brass In Pocket". The place went as wild as a bunch of polite prairie folk can get.

And so it went. Some of them weren't very good, though if I do say so, me and Dougie raised the bar quite a bit for them. It didn't matter though. They were all real. Sincere. Heart-warming, and we all felt like we were a part of something special.

Miles had started out the night even crabbier than usual, which is saying a lot. After a couple of twin teenaged boys got up and murdered two Everly Brothers songs, I looked up and, blow me dry and call me dusty, Miles was smiling!

I hadn't actually seen him smile since the late 1990s so it was putting me off beat a little. I know I know, a little more off-beat than usual, Dougie would say. Miles is smiles without the 'S,' but that didn't mean he'd made it a regular part of his repertoire of facial expressions. It was part of his image too, I guess. The brooding songwriter. And speaking of one letter off, Drummer was dummer with an extra 'r' and Miles wouldn't let me forget that very often.

That smile grew wider as the night grew longer. Bar-manager-guy pops back on the stage after a half-decent "Orange Blossom Special" from a kid who looked to be 10 max, with me and Dougie keeping that train on the tracks.

"Thanks fellers, looks like you got yourselves a new band member. Wadda ya think, Miles?"

Miles headed down to the stage to applause left over from the young fiddler. He raised his hands in the air in acknowledgement, cleared his throat into the mic, and said, "Well, folks," and he paused. Dead air. The pause mosied past awkward, through embarrassing, and was headed straight for career ending ala Loretta Lyn when a giantess at the bar called out,

"We love you Miles!"

"I love you guys too," said Miles, "and you know what, I guess I didn't think that I would, so I'm a little at a loss for words, which can be fatal for a songwriter." There was a bit of nervous laughter and he kept going.

"See, it's been a bit rough out on the road lately, and I was getting ready to whine about that to you, I guess. But hell, all I can say right now is that there's two kinds of people in this crazy world." Dougie face palmed and I gave Miles a rimshot in the hope that it might keep him from continuing.

"Two kinds, Ladies and Gentlemen. There are righteous old self-absorbed burned out has-been bastards like me, and there are genuine, honest, hard-working real deal folks like you. I'm humbled and honoured to be in your company tonight. And I'm thinking that I'd be even more honoured if instead of playing you a concert set, all you pickers and singers gather up here and we'll jam for a bit."

The audience seemed to be mulling over their options when there was a loud whistle from the back of the hall. Wouldn't ya know it but MG bounds on to the stage and grabs the mic from Miles.

"Howdy everybody, I'm new in town here, and I was pleased to have met these boys earlier today. I'm such a huge fan that I was thrilled when after telling them I had lost my previous job rather suddenly that they said for tonight I could be their merchandise sales representative! Now I know Mr. Gerber here hinted at it, but making a living in the music business is pretty near impossible these days, considering that money is tight for all of us so we can't pay much for tickets, and it's too darned tempting to get all that great music on Spotify or free downloads or on YouTube and what-not. Why wouldn't you take something for free if it was offered to you, ammaright?" The crowd nodded. "You know that old prairie joke about what a farmer would do if he won the lottery? Keep farming till the money ran out?" Some people chuckled at that one, I noticed. "Well music is the same now, except that no one is asking you to give away your grain for free, though it must seem like that with the prices this year."

"Yes, Ma'am!" called out a lady from the back.

"What I'm trying to say is that, since they promised me a little slice of the sales tonight, and I'm unemployed, I'm hoping you'll consider supporting Miles and the boys here. Even if you don't have a CD player in your truck, if you've got one of those fancy new bluetooth thingies instead, here's your chance to help these song farmers keep on farming for a bit longer, by supporting them, by showing your appreciation for all they've done over the years to brighten your long winter nights. If they can't afford to tour, they can't keep doing this, can they?" Lots of 'no m'aam's' there! "So wadda' ya say? You can get an autographed CD or one of these fine 100 % cotton t-shirts which I just happen to be modeling right now." MG gave a little wiggle which revived those same wolf whistlers from earlier on. "And, you know you can't download a T-shirt yet, so here's your only chance!"

Bar Snake, OK let's call him Jake for argument's sake and an extra two points for the rhyme, called out, "Thanks young lady, but perhaps first we should get Miles here to announce tonight's winner!"

MG grabbed the cowboy hat that held the contestant's names. From the back of the stage I saw her palm something into it, real smooth, and she said, "But mister, look there's one more name in that hat!"

Jake looked in and said, "Golly, Missy, you're right. It says here Muriel Gilmour! Is she still here?"

MG looked all bashful and awe-schucksy and exclaimed, "Why, that would be me! I'm just arrived from down in Estevan. And you can call me MG for short".

Everyone cheered, and Jake said "Well, I'll be! But maybe just the one song cuz we're running late now, honey!"

She whispers to Dougie. He shakes his head no, but she gives him that stink eye and she says, "This here's a song by none other than Miles Gerber right there. Some of you know it I'm sure from the Miles and Myles greatest hits album, which y'all have right? But in case you don't it's available at the back of the room." She must have thought that in Estevan, the deep south of Saskatchewan, folks would say 'y'all', so that's how I knew she was NOT from there. She also had no idea that she was breaking a cardinal Miles rule. Yes, he sold that greatest hits album to keep some bills paid, but except for rare pre-approved exceptions Miles and Myles material was off limits. Oops.

She launched into "Lonesome Cowgirl's Lament", a smart choice of course since it mentions Saskatchewan in it. It had been a duet sung by Miles and Maddie that was a cross-over hit back in the day.

Song 7
Lonesome Cowgirl's Lament

There was no blind on the window
She looked outside and watched the wind blowin'
The snowy tracks that led to that ten-dollar dive's door
That same driving wind
Had swept her there again
Although she swore she'd pay no mind to its cries anymore

She used to think she'd find
Out on the road somewhere a sign
That would tell her what this restless windblown wanderin' meant
Maybe she'll find out listening to that cold Saskatchewan wind
Whinin' like some lonesome cowgirl's lament

Oh the whispering wheels
And the wind at her heels
Would often fool her into thinkin' she was gettin' somewhere
But if she stopped to look behind her
She usually would find
There wasn't really any difference between here and there

Somehow every year about this time she starts to spend
All her days in wanderin' where the hell the last one went
Maybe she'll find out listening to that cold Saskatchewan wind
Whinin' like some lonesome cowgirl's lament

Many times she's still reminded of those tear-filled eyes
That she left back in Ontario in '85
She knows that she could never make him realize
That like the wind she must keep movin' just to stay alive

She's headed west out to Lethbridge
She suspects some kind of death wish
Keeps her always on the highway in the wintertime
She simply can't keep still
And all across the Cypress Hills
She lets the whistle of the wind sing her a lullaby

She wonders if she'll ever know
What it is about the blowin'
Wind that keeps her gypsy heart from feeling content.
Maybe she'll find out listening to that cold Saskatchewan wind
Whinin' like some lonesome cowgirl's lament.

As soon as she started in, with a kind of fragile innocent voice that was very different from her rather aggressive speaking manner, she had everyone wrapped around her fingers, which were wrapped around that microphone like it was a lover leaving for war the next morning. It took a lot of guts to sing a sensitive song like that, but MG seemed to have more guts in her than a store-bought wiener. When she got to the refrain about the Saskatchewan wind whining everyone sang along 'cuz they remembered it fondly. Miles actually *was* a part of the fabric of our nation, but don't get his head all swole up by telling him that. She gave it a big finish and it seemed to take a minute for people to want to break the mood by applauding, but when they did, holy smokers.

Without asking Miles, Jake the Snake came out and gave her a bunch of flowers and the hundred bucks with great cheers from the crowd.

She bowed, and said "See y'all over at the merch table," and they formed a lemming-like line unlike anything us Disturbers had ever seen before. Miles hadn't even played yet.

Dougie and I followed her, caught up in the brouhaha with our signing Sharpies in hand. I heard Dougie say, "Jesus, your name is Muriel Gilmour, and you're from Estevan Saskatchewan?" MG, who at that point seemed to answer to 'Jesus' said , "No and no, Bozo.

I just was trying to fit in a bit with you and your bar full of losers".

"Miles gives pretty much that same pitch for product sales every night, but it never worked like that," said Dougie.

"That's because he says it with anger, I'll bet," said MG, "and I said it with a word that you seem to have lost track of: R.E.S.P.E.C.T.; Just a little bit. Just a little bit", and she started to do a little Aretha as she smiled and worked that table. She was some slick.

Meanwhile, on stage, Miles turned off the P.A. and put some chairs in a horseshoe shape, got out his Gibson acoustic and took a seat. Others soon joined and soon the song swap was in full swing. There was some western swing in there, more old school country, and some Joni since she was a local gal.

Miles chipped in a couple of his originals.

Betty said, "Hey Miles, sing your newest song."

He looked even more wistful than usual and said, "I can't remember back that far," before singing a pretty cool one that I don't think I'd ever heard before. He obviously had a stash of MMMs-'Missing Maddie Myles' songs that he'd written and hadn't shared.

Song 8
Without You

I busy myself, when I'm out on the road
With Zen and the art of counting hydro poles
And I'm getting pretty good at not letting it show
That it's harder and harder the longer I go
Without you

You never would guess that I'd be still
Looking out this windowsill
Trying to finger out how in the hell I will
Ever get these endless hours filled
Without you

They call this the Journey's End motel
But that cannot be true
My journey's never over till I'm holding you

You say your favourite Beatle was Paul, mine was always John
It's a wonder that we ever go along
But we did somehow and now as time goes on
It's more a question to me of what wrong
That I'm without you

I drum my fingers on the steering wheel
I wonder if this is how I'm always going to feel
Without you

At the end, after cheers, Miles gave MG a look which said 'that's what I'm dealing with so be careful.' He sang that song for a reason, and also I think MG had, by 'breaking the rule', kind of given him permission to 'go there' with his material. It was kind of a departure for Miles eh? Speaking of which, the departure never quite happened. The jam went long after last call but Snake got out his harmonicas so he didn't care. By the time everyone went home, why, we felt like locals too, which was gratifying for us wanderers. We felt like we had kind of created something cool, though of course it still was, if looked at sideways, a shitty gig in a shitty town. Nothing new there. Whatever happened, Miles had a look on his face I hadn't seen in a while. Satisfaction I guess.

When we finally staggered upstairs, MG was nowhere to be seen.

Chapter Seven

Nelly-Belle Tells

Wow, the boys sure slept in.

MG *did* sleep in my warm embrace, and I welcomed the company despite those things she said about me. I made sure she was safe in the belly of Nelly. She still had the key from when she was setting up the merch and the boys don't load out until the morning after a gig. (I've heard them argue about which is safer, a bar-room or me for overnight thievery but the bar usually won that argument when we weren't in a motel.)

They didn't even check me out when I saw them heading down the street to the Chinese café for a late breakfast. They left me where I was, so I don't know what they said over their eggs, but I bet it was a lot. Two sentences was normally a lot for those boys.

MG was still snoozing when the boys knocked on the door. After all it was only the day before that we picked her up at the side of the highway, so she was pretty worn out I bet. They were probably more concerned about the key than MG at this point though.

"There you are," said Drummer. "We looked all over for you." This was clearly a lie, since I'm assuming I'd be the first place they looked after they scoured the bar, which probably hadn't actually *been* scoured since the '80s judging by the smell.

"We figured you'd taken your share and boogied," said Dougie.

I'm guessing they had settled up the so-called profits the night before. So-called because there seldom were any, but maybe things were a little different this time.

Miles said to her, "You know, you were way out of line last night." Then he gave a pause approximately equivalent to a dramatic Dougie cigarette inhale and said, "I loved it".

Miles didn't use that L word very often, except in his songs. Something special must have happened.

MG was now sitting upright so the boys climbed in. With quite a flair she gave Dougie back his twenty bucks and another 20 went Miles' way for the dinner.

"Where to, fellas?" asked MG.

Dougie said "Well, miss MG, I was under the impression that we were to part company now, on account of you have some resources now, and you have places to get to."

"Are you kidding me?" she said. "We're a team now, isn't that obvious? And there may be no "I" in team, but there's an A and that stands for the Assholes you'll all be if you can't see how we can rock this thing together!" Then she whipped out a wad of cash. "Minus my commission you so kindly let me bully you into, I've got 320 spondoolicks for you, which is more than your total stake from that so-called gig. So who thinks they're dumping me now, huh?"

Miles started me up. Mmmm, I always like the way he does that. I'm a manual transmission gal, you know, so the 'getting up to top gear' is always a pretty personal connection between the two of us. Just as he was shifting into second though, MG yells "HEY STOP." I guess no one noticed that she hadn't had breakfast or cleaned up yet. After a brief discussion they settled on take-out, and the boys were deep in conversation about all the new developments while MG was inside getting her order and taking a bit too long in the washroom, or so I gathered from the gesticulations of a large farm woman who was standing outside the ladies room. I'd love to see inside one of those some day. What's in there that makes it special for ladies anyway?

When we finally headed out of town, the talk was jovial, from what I could hear. MG actually turned my radio on and Miles didn't even make her turn it off, though he did put a stop to her frequent requests to change channels.

At the first pee stop Miles actually asked Drummer to drive so he could work on a song in the back. I've noticed that the boys stop a lot more as they age. One thing hasn't changed though. The side of the road remains an acceptable peeing spot for them. They usually go through this silly routine about topping each other with euphemisms for 'having to pee' and they really went to town on this for MG, who seemed to enjoy it. It always went something like this:

"Is that nature calling boys? Cuz I feel like we should answer."

"I have to see a man about a dog."

"I see a fire to put out over there."

"Hey dogs, time to lift a leg."

"Those flowers seem to need watering gents."

"I have to cool one of the tires." This was the most offensive to me. Jeepers!

And so forth. It was nice to have a woman on board.

The radio went off and I could hear Miles strumming his acoustic in the back: humming a bit. He never shared lyrics till a song was done.

He urged Drummer to step on my gas so that we could get into the next town early enough for him to keep writing. He said he was inspired by a chat with a sheep farmer from the night before. Wait. He actually talked to members of the audience? He put the guitar away though when the others wouldn't stop talking about their plans and current situation.

We were heading East, which was confusing since we had just come from there but Kirk the Jerk never did seem to have much geographical sense to his tour routing. Of course no one told me that he was fired the night before, so that's one thing among many they were chatting about. I didn't catch everything, they were all talking at once, but I gathered that MG was offering to take the Jerk's place.

"What do you have to lose?" she said. "I booked the Prideful Scoffers for two years."

"Was your success at that endeavor the reason for your sudden departure from the tour bus, Miss MG?" Dougie offered, still with that weird way of talking. I DID notice that the lads were all showered and shaved and a little tidier than usual.

"NO THAT WASN'T IT, DIPSTICK," and she added that MG stood for 'Manager Girl' too. Not sure why she took offence to my dipstick, one of my more useful attachments. She then explained that she needed a laptop and a cellphone and something called a rocket stick, and it seemed that as part of her negotiations that the band was to pay for that. I can't believe they didn't argue much about that. Miles said there were still ten gigs left on the tour that Kirk had booked, right through to Toronto.

"Toronto!" said MG "You guys actually play REAL places too? (It was the Horseshoe Tavern as it turned out. Worst parking in the country, but it's not all about me I guess.) They seemed pumped about getting back there.

Spirits were high and there was lots of chatter. I was heading towards my birthplace so I was happy too. In all the excitement my rad boiled over a bit as we re-entered Manitoba, and it was actually MG who lifted up my hood and treated my royally.

The drive wasn't a long one, it turns out. Dougie only spotted one prairie dog and two coyotes. We stopped by about 3 pm at an actual motel in Nixon, called The Pines, despite its lack of trees, and they parked me just the way I like it, with my butt facing the road and where I could see into the room. Oh wait, rooms plural it looked like! MG was getting one, though she was muttering "I'm fixin' to be nix'n Nixon from the next tour," after they told her at the desk that she'd have to wait till Brandon the next day to get her electronic gizmos and personal supplies. That wasn't far either, and the big new stores in Brandon were the reason Nixon didn't have much to offer shopping-wise even though it was bigger than Needham. It was the same everywhere these days.

Miles headed straight to the other room, banishing the boys who decided to check out the legion hall on foot while he kept working on his song. MG bolted the door and I could hear the shower going. Miles had the window open. The song was shaping up pretty good. I heard him make a call from the room phone to the sheep farmer he met the night before, saying, "I've got your song done," as if he'd just repaired the guy's tractor or something, and he told him they were playing at the

Nixon Legion that night and he'd wait till he saw him in the crowd till he played the song if he could make it.

Chapter Eight

The battered old van carrying the three pilgrims has a new occupant now as it lurches into a new town on just five cylinders. If the shrines to the dead hockey player are the church of consumerists, the Big Box Stores are the cathedrals, and the large number of these creeping west towards this struggling town, like an invading army, makes it clear to the van occupants that the downtown they are headed for will be largely empty.

The main street leads towards the railway station, still grand though abandoned. The tracks are torn up so that no one could ever think of bringing back the trains that were once the lifeblood of towns like this. Instead, a gravel trail overgrown with weeds and strewn with trash heads towards nowhere, with only a coyote passing by to interrupt the solitude. Beyond the trail is the river, filthy and forgotten like a hobo in a back alley.

The empty shops still bear the names of what they once were, like tombstones in the boneyard of the street that is now just a skeleton of its former self.

Reid's Hardware. Daynard's Department Store. Sid's Shoes. Ryan's Formal Wear. Bev's Fruit and Veg; all named after proud owners who would spend their days at the cash register greeting customers by name and asking to be remembered to their folks.

The storefronts that are still open are there because they offer what little the big box monsters don't: pawn shops, tattoo parlours. Drop-In centres. Thrift Stores. Junk shops. Food banks.

The passengers are looking somber as they wind up their funereal procession and join a small row of cars in front of an establishment that remains unaffected by the winds of change, the Legion Hall.

Song 9
Another Big Box Store

See that old photograph in the window
Those are my grandparents way back when
They started this store in 1904
And it's stayed in the family since then

If you took them today out to the highway
They would never believe their own eyes
Instead of green fields and trees
They would see there the reason
Their little business must die

Another big box store
Just a couple more
And there you go

It's been quiet down along King Street
They closed the IGA
You can hear them talk
In the coffee shops
Of how you can't stand in progress' way

But if you listen late in the evening
You can hear the pioneers cry with one voice

Another big box store
Just a couple more
And there you go

Drummer Tells

If you are comparing the bottom-feeder rungs on the showbiz ladder, legions are one step above saloons. Reason is this: often the legion hall has been booked out by a local promoter who has a stake in the game. He's rented the hall, hired the crew, done the postering and that stuff you do on computers that apparently makes people come out to the shows, so he's going to make sure that there is a crowd there. Speaking of crowd, I've noticed that as the music business rides into the sunset, we've downsized the definition of 'crowd'. It used to take hundreds of people to make a 'crowd', not 'three' like the saying goes. Nowadays as long as there are more people in the audience than on the stage, we call it a crowd. Heh heh.

So the Nixon Legion Hall was looking like Carnegie Hall compared to the Queen's in Needham. It's all relative I guess. Dougie would always rate a venue based on how sticky the floor was in the men's room.

Miles did something that he hadn't done in years, so we actually thought he was joking when he called a rehearsal. Rehearsing is for wimps he used to say. He had this new song that he wanted to teach us. Kinda different. About a sheep farmer. I know what you are thinking. Just the topic those Nashville song pushers are looking for these days, right? Forget boy-likes-tight-jeans-on-girl-invites-girl-to-tailgate-partysongs. Sheep farmers. That's where it's at. Ya right. I liked it though. He wasn't trying to write a hit song, just tell a story about some guy he had been chatting with the night before. Chatting to someone in the audience was new for Miles too, so with the MG thing and all, we had lots to get used to all of a sudden. I drove Nelly-Belle for a while that day too, which always gives me a chance to zone in on the rhythm of the road a little more. Being a drummer, and after that jam session in Needham, I was stoked to beat those skins at the gig.

MG had the merch booth looking spiffy, and she'd got some bristol board, I guess at the Co-Op, and she had a sign that said 'PWYC' with a little explanation underneath. She said 'Pay

What You Can' was gonna work with these farmers who were a little tight with their money. It was better to get *something* for those albums than to have a lot of stock taking up space in Nelly- Belle, since there was now an extra person on board. I was skeptical. Skeptical is my middle name. Well, I guess you can't have a middle name if you don't have a last name. Her idea seemed to work though as we found out later.

The joint was about half full, which is all you can ask for in these troubled times, and if I do say so, we sounded fresh. We were kicking Nixon's ass with the tunes. Then just as Miles was introducing the last song of the first set, after MG had given another Oscar-worthy pitch for the product, the sheep farmer from Needham walked in and hollered out to us.

"Howdy Fellers. Hope you don't mind! I brought a few friends along." I'll be danged if half the gang from the open mic came in right behind him! There was a bit of jostling for seats and ordering of drinks, so Dougie launched into what I think was the same fiddle tune he did with those kids the night before. I can't tell. All fiddle tunes sound the same to me. Idle-dee-didle-dee.

The audience, which was now a bona fide, card-carrying 'crowd', clapped along till Miles shushed them, turned to me and Dougie and said, "Let's do it boys!" Then to the audience: "Two kinds of people in this world, folks."

"Here we go" said Dougie.

"Posers like us up on the stage here, and genuine salt-of-the-earth honest folks like my new friend Burt down here." Burt whooped and waved his ball cap. "I was pleased that Burt felt safe in telling me his story, and I figure it's a story that some of you can relate to, so I wrote this little ditty today. Doesn't even have a name yet, but this one's for you Burt!"

Song 10
First November Snow, (Burt's Song)

Grand-dad would be ashamed
He'd say I stained the family name
By selling off the ranch and moving to town
We'd sit on his porch when the day was done
He'd spin his yarns as the western sun
Would paint his quarter-section a golden brown

When it costs you more to raise a sheep
Then you can sell it for, there's no sense keep-
ing up that dream he had so long ago
Old man, times have surely changed
You can't make a home out on the range
I'll be gone with the first November snow

Crossbred ewes and Purebred rams
feeder or slaughter market weight lambs
We ran a decent rangeland operation
Suffolks, Hampshires and South Downs
We'd sell 'em at a hundred pounds
But all we're raising now is frustration

The bank will take what the cayoots don't
When all is said and done I won't
Look back , though I know that'd make him cry

They say that over Moose Jaw way
Folks somehow are making it pay
But I won't pull the wool over my eyes
So when things are all settled up
I figure I might have enough
To say goodbye to these big prairie skies

The audience drank that sucker right up, as if they were as thirsty as the prairie dirt was that year. I'd say that the crowd went wild, but this is Canada, where we're too polite to cross over into officially 'wild' territory, but I can tell you that we got our first 'standing O' in a long time after we finished. At the end, when Dougie did his best Elvis with a 'thankyou, thankyouverymuch, and announced that we'd be back after a short break, half the throng rushed the stage to thank Miles for the song, and the other half mobbed MG and her merch booth.

We didn't even go back to the dressing room like usual in the break. For one thing, they didn't actually have a dressing room, and for another thing, everyone wanted to chat and buy us drinks. Did I tell you that I just drink pop though? For about ten years now.

We had that joint really jumping in the last set too, and half-way through Miles stopped and said, "I'm honoured that my little song for Burt here seemed to mean something to you all, and I thank Burt again for the inspiration. Stories like yours, Burt, are like a gift to old songworkers like me." He always called himself a 'songworker' so he'd feel some kinship with welders and lumberjacks I guess, but I always thought that was a little too pretentious. "Anyone here in Nixon got a story they'd like to share?"

This threw us for a loop in our lariats, but sure enough a woman stood up from back near the bar and started to speak. Miles interrupted her and invited her up to the mic. She was hesitant but once there everyone urged her on. Said her name was Marta.

She looked maybe to be of Ukrainian descent but what do I know? All white people look the same. Bleach blonde like the night before, but by her complexion she could'a been blonde originally before life took over. I figured about 50 with a big toothy smile and a few too many church social pies in her.

Marta had that western knack for using words frugally as if each one had a high price tag on it. Not like on the East Coast where they will spin you a yarn that takes three beers to listen to. Beers don't have ears though (isn't that a Hank Williams song?) but you know what I mean. You probably wish I had Marta's gift for 'economical' gab. Heh heh.

The place was dead quiet as she spoke in a soft but determined voice. I wish Miles could command that kind of attention with his ballads. She spoke of losing her husband in a farm accident, and the next year losing the farm too. Losing everything she knew. She said that she had two grown kids, one on the oil patch, sending her money when he could, and the other in Vancouver married to a veterinarian and doing real good, but she seldom saw her. Folks in town have been kind to her, she said, but she felt like there are no jobs and no future there. Nixon feels like it's just going through the motions of being a town.

"You got that right, darlin," shouted a guy who looked like a trucker from somewhere near the back. Why do guys who shout stuff always stand at the back, anyways? "But we all look out for each other," he added. " Ya don't get that in the big city."

Marta nodded. You could tell that she was taking it in that yes, at least people looked out for her.

Miles was sitting right beside her, perched on my drum riser.

"Marta, thanks for sharing. Sharing is what it's all about here."

It was? That was news to me, but it WAS starting to feel like that.

Miles stood up and put his arm around Marta. Wow. First he's 'sharing' and now he's showing affection?

"Do you have a dream?" he said, still holding her.

Marta started to cry a little bit, something that western farm folk frown on, so the room got kind of uncomfortable.

"My dream is to *have* a dream," . She looked up as if that's maybe where dreams come from. "Something to work towards, something to plan for, something to keep me going, somewhere it feels like I need to go. I don't even dream at night. Just that recurring nightmare of finding John hanging upside down from that old Massey Harris with a permanent look of surprise on his face."

Even me, the stoic Cree dude, got a bit blubbery with that.

And I wasn't used to sitting on stage without drumming so I didn't quite know what to do with myself.

Miles said, "Well, Marta, there's somewhere you *could* be tomorrow if you like. Your story moves me, and I'm powerful grateful for that." The crowd all applauded her then and she was looking mostly embarrassed but kinda' proud of herself too. "If you'd grant me permission, I'd like to turn your story into a song by way of showing my appreciation. I think folks would like to hear what you had to say." People started clapping. "I bet I could get 'er done by showtime if the boys here load in the gear and all." Oh, I get it, I thought, Miles just wants us to do all the work. "Can you get yourself to Brandon, Marta? We'd perform it for you if that would be all right with you."

"I'll give her a lift over. I've got a delivery there tomorrow," shouted that same shouty guy. See I told you he was a trucker. A woman that seemed to know Marta said she'd tag along if there was room, and you could tell that Marta felt a little more at ease about that, just jumping into a stranger's truck and all, so she nodded and took her seat. The Applause-O-Meter went sky high with that.

We finished the show, though the rest of it seemed like a bit of an anti-climax. Everyone was talking to Marta and chatting with each other about what had just happened. Miles had given a shout out to MG, with a little story about how we had found this nice young lady who had fallen on hard times and we were helping out a bit, so they could help her by buying some product. MG whooped accordingly, enticing folks over to her table, but seriously, I could tell that the 'have pity on a poor lost waif" routine was one that folks really weren't buying. We changed that up by the time we hit Brandon.

The party kept rolling and I noticed a few other things that were new. Dougie hadn't disappeared with a local gal. He was sort of like an ambulance chaser when it came to hooking up with women. They'd gather backstage looking for Miles, who would politely reject them. As they started away, disappointed and all, Dougie would be there smiling and putting on his routine which actually worked more often than you'd guess, looking at him I mean. He *had* been a handsome dude at one time, folks say. Tall with what they call 'chiseled' features I think, but the chisel was missing its mark lately. He knew he was the consolation prize but consoling was part of his act.

Secondly, Miles invited the promoter and Marta and some other locals back to the motel. Hadn't seen that in a long time. It was a nice night and we gathered outside in front of our rooms on those official metal chairs. I know it sounds funny but Miles often likes to hang out near Nelly-Belle so she's included. Some arrived with guitars and fiddles and flasks. We used to play the 'Fiddle and Flask' pub in Brampton. Often in the smaller towns you'd get what I call the 'fiddle sniffers'- amateur fiddlers who wanted to look at Dougie's fiddle and share fiddley stories. The promoter, who was a lot younger than your typical Disturbers fan these days, asked Miles to play a couple of Miles and Myles favourites. Miles always declined this, but this time he did it rather graciously and instead jammed like the night before on old country and folk songs, with me slapping one of those chairs to beat time.

MG borrowed a guitar and sang Lowell George's "Willin" with that same sweet voice that was still a surprise as it seemed opposite to her brassy style. We were quiet for a bit after that, and I realized why Dougie had hung around. He moved closer to MG and joined in on the fiddle, moving Marta and others to tears.

You could tell that her talent kind of impressed and irritated Miles at the same time. There'd be more talk about that later, I reckoned.

Miles actually started strumming the beginnings of Marta's song on the spot, and like I said he never shares an unfinished song. That was the start of "Dreamin' of a Dream". Real pretty without the tough-guy vibe that most of his post-Maddie stuff had.

As the non-drinker there was an unwritten rule in the band that I was the one to somehow bring the gathering to a close. I had a good excuse that night and no one argued. After all, Miles had a song to write and we had to get to Brandon early for sound check and for MG to get supplies. She stood at the door of our room, and before leaving gave everyone heading out a hug and the address of the Brandon show, though I don't know how she knew that. We got hugs too, another new thing, though Dougie got the finger when it looked like he was going to follow her to her room. Miles actually climbed into Nelly-Belle for a bit with his Gibson to work on the song some more so we could get some shut-eye. In my dreams Coyote came to me in human form and said 'not yet Drummer, but soon'. What a trickster that guy is.

As you can probably guess, breakfast was pretty lively. MG actually banged on our door to wake us up saying there was an awful lot to do that day.

The motel had one of those breakfast deals that came with the room. Those weird scrambled eggs that look like a chicken had never had anything to do with the process. Looked like you had to get up way earlier than we did to get the bacon, and the toaster could toast you an English muffin in under 10 minutes. They had one of those waffle-making machines, but in all my years on the road I've never seen anyone figure out how to use it. As crappy as it was, it was free and there was a little nook to eat it in, so we had kind of a business meeting right there.

MG reported that sales were OK considering the current state of affairs. Most of the audience had come to ask her which album Burt's song was on, which gave her an idea that she said she'd talk about after she got her supplies in Brandon. She figured that with us tech wizards it would be easier to show us than explain. Speaking of wizards, Brandon was starting to sound like the Emerald City for all the wonders she pictured there.

Miles reported that thanks to that keen young promoter the take from the door was pretty good. We made more than Kirk the Jerk's guarantee.

"About this 'story' thing" said Dougie. "Are you going to do this every night, boss?" He was looking even more perplexed than usual. He actually had a kind of permanent perplexion on his face.

"What do ya think? Should I?" asked Miles, as he emptied

the third creamer into his coffee, in case that gave it some taste.

"Of course you should," said MG. "It's not a case of 'should', it feels like you've turned onto a road that you need to follow to see where it leads." MG had a habit of talking like she was quoting lyrics from bad Nashville songs. The difference was she was sincere about it.

We packed up after giving up on the breakfast and piled into Nelly-Belle, but Miles asked me to drive again.

Dougie only took a turn when we were doing a long-distance haul, since we found that it was hard for him to keep his eye on the road and on the wildlife at the same time. I obliged and soon found out why.

"Boys," Miles started, clearly including MG now as 'one of the boys', "I think I have Marta's song done, and I'd like to sing it for you, if you don't mind, since I have something to run by you. He had left his guitar out of its case and he was ready as rain and as keen as a kid with candy in his sights.

He sang it for us then, and it seemed like a momentous occasion for a number of reasons.

You'll probably recognize it from these lyrics, maybe not the "Dreamin'Of A Dream" title because after he started doing it, and he told the story that went with it, folks mostly requested it as "Marta's Song" though she isn't mentioned in it.

Song 11
Dreamin' Of A Dream

If I had a dream to fly on,
I'd let it carry me away
Something I could rely on
To get me through these lonely days

If I had a dream to try on
that fit me like a glove
I'd need no shoulder to cry on
I'd be on my way to love

Dreamin' of a dream
That could deliver me
From this broken cowboy town
Something to hold on to
To drive away those thoughts that want to
Always bring me down

If I had a dream that was mine
To nurture like it was a child
I'd raise it tall and fine
And I'd let it run wild

If I had a dream I could ride
Like it was a noble steed
It would lead me to a sign
That would set me free

Dreamin' of a dream
That could deliver me
From this broken cowboy town
Something to hold on to
To drive away those thoughts that want to
Always bring me down

The prairie dust blows down my street
Gathering around my feet
It's in my eyes so I can't see
Beyond these messed up memories, but

James Gordon

If I had a dream to fly on,
I'd let it carry me away
Something I could rely on
To get me through these lonely days

We all looked at each other when it ended and there was much congratulating and gratitude and more mushy stuff than we'd ever seen inside Nelly-Belle. I actually had to pull her over to the side of the Trans-Canada for a minute to show my proper appreciation.

Miles nodded his thanks humbly.

Then Dougie looked at MG and said, "Glad you like it, 'cause if you didn't we'd-a stripped you nekked and thrown you out on the road."

"Heh heh" I said.

"Fuck off," MG said, but gave him a pinch. Part of him grew an inch.

"So here's the thing", Miles said. "I think what I've done here for Marta is write a song that really should be sung by a woman, and though that brings up some shit for me as you can imagine since every night some clown yells out for Maddie, I'm thinking there's one with us here that could do the job for us."

"Nelly-Belle can't sing worth a damn," said Dougie, already anticipating a good kick which he clearly misinterpreted as juvenile flirting, the kind he was familiar with.

Miles, taking off his cowboy hat and looking down at his boots, said "MG, though we haven't talked about it, when you sang 'Lonesome Cowgirl's Lament' it brought up some issues for me that I don't really want to talk about. That was sung by Maddie and you know it, so you also probably also know the risk you took."

MG played it all innocent and such, but I learned over time that there was a method to her madness. She made things look like she was flying by the seat of her mom jeans, but nope.

"Sorry," said MG. That word wasn't really part of her vocabulary, and words mean more if they haven't been worn out.

I realized then that, though Miles doesn't like to discuss his personal baggage, he'd put something of himself into that song too. Those 'messed up memories' were his as well as Marta's, and in fact he must have been carrying that thought since MG sang the lament, which is why he stuck that 'cowboy' part in the song. He and Maddie had been 'living a dream' to him, and when that dream died he seemed to have put dreaming away. I'm no songologist, but it felt like this was a good example of what Miles always mentioned as a secret to a good song: a combination of the personal and the universal. Marta's story would touch many listeners as he started to perform it, but that was because some of it came from his heart, a heart that had been absent from his songwriting for a while. Well, since songs were how he shared about his heart, and he was all closed up tight, I guess that is why he had pretty well stopped writing. We were witnessing the resurgence of a master craftsmen, who had been silent too long.

"Just play the fucking song again," said MG, "and show me those chicken scratches of yours there, sailor." She wasn't fooling any of us anymore with the tough talk, you could tell she was emotional about it too. With four of us in Nelly-Belle there wasn't enough room to swing a cat or a fiddle. Dougie dug out his mandolin and they started to work on it with me tapping the steering wheel and if I'd had one I would have pulled my harpoon out of my dirty red bandana. MG nailed the vocals really quickly, with Miles singing that close Everly Brothers kind of harmony that made them sound eerily like Miles and Myles, which was not missed by any of us. Miles looked like he was having second thoughts when those ghosts started to roll around in the van, but he screwed up his courage, which is better than screwing up his life like folks say he had. He slapped a capo on the second fret once he figured out MG's best key, and they went for it. Was he saying in that song that he could hold on to that dream he shared with Maddie without the grieving part if he could move on to another dream?

We'll never really know cuz Miles won't tell you, but it's all there if you listen to the songs he was writing at that time.

It wasn't that far into Brandon, even with me at the wheel, but they had that song shining like a national guitar by the time we pulled in to what Dougie liked to call the 'Worst Western' which was paid for by the promoter of the show at

'Deckers'.

"Deck'er, damn near killed 'er," said Dougie, as we passed it on Rosser Street. We had to beg the hotel to let us check in early, and as soon as we got settled, and realized that the club had actually booked *three* rooms for us, we divided up naturally with the "Disturbers" in one room and Miles and MG each with their own.

MG showed us her shopping list and wanted to get right to it, though when we saw that the first thing on the list was 'get a new driver's license' we knew that she needed a chauffeur for the journey. Dougie offered a bit too enthusiastically, though I had an inkling that MG would have felt safer with me. I'm always 'the safe one', and the designated driver. I wish it wasn't so obvious that I was 'safe' but it was true.

We took the instruments out. The shopper and her valet headed off after extracting Miles' credit card from him, which was part of the deal. She said that was the only thing we had that gave an indication that this was the 21st century, before climbing into our late 20th century wheels.

Chapter Nine

Nelly-Belle Tells

Dougie was driving me, which I never liked. He's a bit rough with my gears and rides the clutch and brake pedal like they're flippers on a pinball game or something. Drummer was OK but really my heart belongs to Miles.

"Baby, take me shopping," MG said to Dougie.

"Now you're talkin' darlin," even though Dougie hadn't shopped anywhere other than a truck stop since I became the official transportation to the stars. MG still couldn't believe that none of the boys had any digital devices, especially since they were on the road constantly, so she was struggling with the placemat-sized city map from the front desk at the hotel.

"As much as I loathe the corporate grossness of it, let's dive in whole hog at the aptly named Brandon Shoppers Mall down 18th," she said. She had already been warned by Miles that if she went to Walmart, her employment would be terminated, and we were soon to learn why, as it turned out. Brandon was kind of a rebel western town in that the north-south streets were numbered like most prairie cities, but the East-West streets had real names just like back east. Fancy.

She announced that her first order of business was some real clothes so that she wouldn't look like a hooker cowgirl or a church lady, her only two fashion options at the moment, before going anywhere near the license bureau to get some I.D. She'd heard that without any I.D. a license is a good place to start.

Dougie wanted to chat, and more, I'm guessing, but MG wasn't having any of it.

"Later honey. I've got work to do," she said dismissively. Dougie didn't look as keen about his chauffeur duties after that, since he seemed to have a different kind of interaction in mind. We were at the mall in a jiffy, though I'm not actually sure what a jiffy is. We parked beside mostly pickup trucks, the silent kind who don't like to gossip, so I knew I wouldn't have any fun either. MG insisted that Dougie hunt down some take-out lunch.

"Bring me an egg sal san on brown if you can find it," she yelled as she slammed my door. Ouch. Poor Dougie wasn't even going to get to take her out to lunch! But I was happy to hear that he dutifully agreed to meet her back in 90 minutes since she couldn't text him when she was done. He didn't even have a watch but I have a clock on my dashboard which I think was still on Saskatchewan time which was the same as Manitoba time only half the year. Don't ask. She gave him a peck on the cheek, which probably gave Dougie the wrong idea again, and made a run for the main entrance while Dougie moseyed off. Moseying was one of his specialties and it suited his lanky frame.

I waited patiently, which is one of MY specialties. I don't know what happened in there, but MG returned with an entire shopping cart full of boxes and bags looking pretty proud of herself. Dougie was already sitting on my running board with his lunch and a paper bag for MG.

When he handed her the bag, she looked inside and said, "Seventy-five percent correct, . it's white bread, but thanks, bud. Not bad for a dude. Next stop, the hunt for I.D. at the license place over on 1st street." He was staring at her a bit dumbfounded, so she said "We haven't got all day. Let's go bro!"

I know why he was slow with turning my key. She was already wearing a new outfit—I guess she couldn't wait to lose that other stuff—and she looked good, maybe a little too good, for Dougie and the boys, but good! Better fitting jeans, tight black ones. Still the same boots and belt. A white man's shirt. I mean not specifically for a white man, I mean, well you know. You could see a hint of a red undergarment, the kind the boys had been too shy to purchase before. A suede-ish jacket over that, topped off with what looked like a newsboy's cap from the 1920s.

At the license place, MG hopped out and said, "Wait here. It shouldn't take long."

When we were alone, which wasn't often, Dougie sometimes talked to me. He had quite a one-way conversation going about what her chances were in there, and what his chances with *her* were.

She came out awfully quickly so we knew it hadn't gone well.

Jumping back in she said, "Guess what? Turns out you have to have I.D. to get I.D.- go figure! I'm fucked. Don't give me that look, Dougie. I know I should have known. Now that I've got a phone and a computer I guess I have to track down the Scoffers, but they have probably thrown out my stuff by now. You know what? Screw it! I.D.s are for slaves to the system. I'm done with that. Time to engage with the alternative economy right? Let's Boogie Dougie!"

Just two more stops. At a music store downtown, MG wouldn't say why, but she carried a big bag out of it, and to another thrift store where she *did* let Dougie join her. They came out with some more clothes and an old suitcase. Dougie had a vintage vest on now and you could tell that MG had picked it out for him. Sweet. Then it was back to the Not-That-Bad Western. She got Dougie to help her load all her stuff into her room and asked him to come get her when it was sound check.

I tried to have a nice afternoon nap in the sun but was bothered by something I saw on the drive back. We passed 'Deckers' on the way and I noticed a lot of motorcycles in the parking lot and a really large sign that said 'Karaoke', a smaller one that said 'Wing Night' and a very small one that said 'Miles Gerber and the Disturbers, Tonight Only!' I put that in my tailpipe and smoked it for a while and could come up with nothing but trouble ahead.

Chapter Ten

Drummer Tells

Uh oh. Bikers. That's the first thing we noticed as we drove into Deckers. The next thing was that big Karaoke sign. Jesus. GFH potential fer sure. That's Gig From Hell, by the way.

Let me explain the biker thing. Maybe those dudes were just there for the Buffalo wings advertised on their marquee where our names should have been, but it's more likely that they were part of what we'd taken to calling Steve Earl Syndrome. Steve's a great guy and a great songwriter. We opened for him a couple times. Fought off some real demons he did. He had a wendigo on his tail for a long time, I tell ya. He wrote a couple of songs that were hits, the most famous being 'Copperhead Road,' that fans interpreted as redneck anthems. Apparently rednecks themselves couldn't see that Steve was being a storyteller, that he was using the character of a hillbilly in those songs to bring those tales to life. They thought that *was* Steve, and that he was one of their tribe. Just like people think I'm this backwoods Cree drummer, when really I'm a graduate of the London School of Economics. Not.

Well, Miles was a victim of that syndrome too. He still gets his share of TT (Trailer Trash) out to shows because of the first album he released after he and Maddie broke up. That was the first thing I recorded with him. Do you know it? It was called 'Miles Away'. He was pretty messed up and angry after Maddie left, and boy did that ever show up in his first music without her. He told me he wanted to experiment with new sounds too, to make a clean break from Miles and Myles. He did that all right, musically if not emotionally I guess. Music is still the only way Miles knows how to express his emotions, though I think he's better at expressing *other* people's. That's the sign of a true storyteller maybe.

The first single off that album was "Burning Rubber", about

leaving everything behind on, yes, a Harley. It was a revved-up country rocker. Fun. Just like with poor Steve though, if you didn't really listen to the lyrics, just the 'tone', you'd figure that the narrator of the song *was* Miles, and that he was a bad biker dude just like them. I'm guilty of it too. I tend to listen to the groove and the 'feel'. I don't actually know what the hell Miles is talking about in most of his songs. It's like Springsteen's 'Born in the U.S.A'. It's become a patriotic anthem. Check out those words some time. It's anything but. Miles'chorus, as cheesy as it was, became kind of a biker's anthem:

> Burning bridges, burning a doobie,
> I got a burning desire to get back to Ruby.
> She's the flame that keeps me alive
> As I'm burning rubber down the I-95.

Yikes.

Quite a few of the songs on 'Miles Away' had a basic 'fuck you' stance that brought him a new audience, but not one that he always appreciated.

Hence the bikers at 'Deckers'. Don't get me wrong, we were grateful for their business, but they reminded Dougie of his old 'rollicking Irish' band days, where the crowd only wanted to hear 'The Black Velvet Band' and 'Right Up Your Kilt' and didn't pay attention to anything else. Made it hard to put on a good show. Miles usually would get those tunes out of the way early, so that those who'd come to hear them could choose whether to stay for the more 'mellow singer-songwriter' stuff. That way they wouldn't be hollering for it all night too.

There was a good three hours to go between sound check and starting time, though there was a warm-up act that night- 'The Stoned Wheat Thins'. Thankfully they weren't that good when we heard them at their sound check. They were a bunch of hillbilly crackers. Heh heh. (We always liked to be a lot better than the warm up bands so folks were grateful when we took the stage, and it used to be written into our contract.) Their set went on a little long. Those biker lads were gonna be hammered by the time we got to their song!

MG was busy setting up all kinds of extra techno doo dads and ho hos along with the merch booth. I couldn't tell you what she had going on there. She asked us to wait till the second set for Marta's Song, and requested Burt's song too.

"Don't you boys worry your pretty little pointy heads about it, all will be revealed later," she said. Looking out at the biker boys Miles got nervous about doing those new songs, but after we went back to the green room, which was really the storage room for the empties, and practiced 'Dreamin' of a Dream' again, this time as a real duet, MG said, "Trust me, my brave knights of the endless highway, you will not perish this fine night."

And, as usual, she was right.

I was fussing with the drum kit a bit before show time and I saw her working the crowd, dressed in some new duds she must have got with Dougie but showing off the Disturbers tee shirt as only she could. I know, you city slicker reporters would call that sexist, right? I've spent about 20 years trapped in a van with two other lonely guys, so you can't blame a fella for lookin'can ya? I don't know anymore.

She went around to each table of bikers and chatted them up and down. Don't know what she said, but somehow they ended up being so well behaved in the show that they shoulda been drummed out of their tough-guy gang. Then, as predicted, the crew from Nixon arrived. It almost looked like they had chartered a bus since they all came in together, with Marta ushered in by her new trucker friend. Didn't see their 'chaperone gal' so those two must be getting' along good. They both seemed surprised that so many other Nixonians had followed them. By now I wasn't. MG greeted them as if they were family, and led them to seats down front. There were even some Needhamites too! (Bikers, by nature, had chosen to sit in the back, which they'd all done since grade 3.)

I was at the back too with MG watching the opener. I had to watch, since I had leant them my drum kit so the changeover between sets wouldn't be too complicated. Dougie and Miles never listened to the warm up bands so they didn't have to pretend they were good if they met them afterwards.

MG was the only one who clapped for them between numbers, and her encouragement seemed genuine.

The local radio DJ who had interviewed Miles in the afternoon acted as MC for the night, giving a polite thanks to the 'Wheat Thins', and then giving us an overblown intro, making out as if he was our best 'ol buddy even though I'd never met the dude. We launched straight in to 'Burning Rubber' and kept the energy up with 'Sleazy Rider', one of Dougie's novelty numbers from way back, and the bikers were suddenly pussycats lapping us up like milk in a bowl. They reacted like, well, like Canadian bikers: enthusiastic but still relatively polite, on account of MG's little pep talk I guess. Another new thing: Miles didn't give his usual 'Hi Brandon, we're-the-disturbers-and-we're-searching-for-the-end-of-the-music-business' intro, thank goodness. That never landed well even though he took to doing it every time. He let Dougie handle the opener.

"Good evening, Ladies and...it looks like there might be a gentleman out there somewhere," began Dougie. "We're delighted that you have chosen to waste an evening with us. You'll never get it back." The crowd laughed, which helped us slow things down a bit with some of the newer stuff. The Nixon crowd was already Jonesing for their song, but Miles promised it would come after the intermission. By now MG had kind of explained about her new recording equipment, which is why the merch booth was now near the mixing board. MG was one smart cookie, though I could never figure out how intelligent a cookie was supposed to be.

She whooped a good biker-chick whoop when she heard her name and I could see her playing with all her new tech toys.

Miles then surprised me and Dougie by calling out a song to us that he *never* did because it was a Miles and Myles 'classic'. Hell was freezing over while Miles was clearly thawing out his own frozen heart. 'Kootenay Mountains' mentions Brandon and Winnipeg, so it was a real crowd pleaser in those parts. Right on cue, when it came to the chorus, MG appeared like magic onstage and joined him at his mic, singing perfect

'Maddie Harmonies' and winning any hearts left to win in 'Deckers'. Miles is about a head taller than MG so when he lowered his mic to her level and leaned in, why it was just like old times.

Song 12
Kootenay Mountains

She found herself in
The Kootenay Mountains
In a January Snow
Round about Nelson
She started countin'
All the Miles left to go
Across those prairie fields
Towards the Canadian shield
She got a feeling way down in her bones
She wasn't going home

Southern Alberta,
Through Medicine Hat and
All across Saskatchewan
She thought she heard a
Voice telling her that
She was living her life wrong

Under those magic northern lights
In that big sky at night
For the first time it felt right to be alone
She wasn't going home

She made it through Brandon
Made it through Portage
In the Manitoba dawn
She thought about her man and
Her job and her mortgage
She knew that she could not go on

Down that last stretch of road
Towards Ontario
That rocky road had turned her heart to stone

She never made Winnipeg
Though she pleaded and she begged
When she tried to tell him on the telephone
And as she pointed her car

Towards the morning star
And disappeared into the snow
She knew that she was home

This was pretty poignant for that rowdy crowd, and I doubt that many had paid enough attention to notice that it actually was about suicide. Maybe you didn't either. I never knew till Miles actually explained it to me.

To pick up the pace, as MG headed back to the Merch table to much applause and whistling, Dougie signaled to me and we launched into a western swing fiddle medley that got the Brandonites up and dancing. You should have seen it. Dirt farmers from Nixon and Needham, truckers, bikers, townsfolk, all up. The farmers mostly did 'Canadian Man Dancing', where the rule is you sway your upper body a bit but not enough to spill your drink, and keep your feet planted firmly on the ground. The ladies were letting loose though, and the 'Stoned Wheat Thins' carved out a corner for themselves for some good ol' Woodstock Hippy Dancing. Their fiddle player Melba, the only talented one in the band, jumped up with us and we kept those tunes going till Miles announced an intermission and let MG give her pitch, this time with musical accompaniment.

Chapter Eleven

Nelly-Belle Tells

Just jumping in here to say that intermissions are my favourite part of the show, no offence to the boys. The audience drifts out my way and I can tell by their body language how the band is doing. Sometimes they lean on me, which Miles hates but I secretly like. You know, 'Lean on me, when you're not strong, and I'll be your friend'. It gives me a sense that I'm contributing somehow. Mostly of course I get the smokers, who tend to be a little more cynical and jaded, otherwise they wouldn't cling to that habit so stubbornly. Funny, I've been with Miles long enough to remember when it was the other way around. The more puritan non-smokers would come outside for some air back when smoking was an essential part of the club culture. They were a little more upbeat. Anyway, there was a real excitement in the air that night in Brandon. There was a group huddled right by me who it seems had driven in from Portage La Prairie for the gig. They must have been chatting with MG, since they were cooking up a scheme to have the band stop by their town on the way to Winnipeg the next night. I was up for that. When we all heard Drummer and Dougie start warming up for the last set everyone skedaddled back in quickly so you know they were keen for what was going to happen next.

Chapter Twelve

Drummer Tells

There was a big line-up at the merch table, a new pattern, so it took a while to get going again. MG even asked me to help her, since that kinda used to be *my* job. She gave Melba a little corner of the table to flog her band's home-made CD. She wasn't getting any takers but there was plenty of interest in Melba herself, what with her flowing hair and legs that reached clear to the floor from a pretty high-up starting point. She reminded me of that old Jimmie Rodgers song that had that line 'she got eyes like diamonds, teeth shine just the same. Sweet ruby lips, and hair like a horses' mane.' I guess that would be a good description of Maddie too. Melba was taller, but she actually looked a bit like Maddie, and I'm guessing that was on purpose. Same sort of hair colour too. What's a cinnamon for rust-coloured? Heh heh. Melba had it all going on, so if she could just lose that loser band she'd have a future, though she had apparently made it quite clear already to Dougie that the future did not include him, since he was looking all sulky at the end of the bar. Miles was with him, chatting with some folks, which was a surprise. He usually barricades himself in the back room for the breaks. I caught his eye and he gave me the nod so I shoved Dougie off his stool and we started up our 'second set routine' which was right out of the Country and Western playbook, corny as hell, and about the only concession to 'showbiz tradition' that we indulged in. Of course it only worked if there were more than a dozen people in the audience who gave a shit, but this was one of those nights fer sure.

Dougie and me would start in to 'Continental Drift', kind of Miles' own take on 'On the Road Again'. Because of our frequent middle-aged-guy pit stops, MG took to calling it 'Incontinental Drift'. After a bit Dougie would introduce Miles, in a dramatic mock tribute to professional wrestling intros, but Miles wouldn't come out. Dougie would do it again, in an innuendo-filled bit that would offer varying explanations as to why it was taking him so long, and then we'd urge the crowd to start chanting till Miles appeared and launched into the vocals. It was all done very 'ironically' since we all hated that stuff, but it worked for audiences who were hip enough to 'get it' and also for those hick enough to not get it. Anyway as you might guess, the crowd was as rowdy as modest prairie folk could muster and we were away to the races.

Having successfully seized back the spotlight, (though the lighting at 'Deckers' was pretty sketchy, a relic of the disco era), Miles shushed the crowd and introduced Burt, asking him to come up. Burt made his way towards the front, but sheep farmers haven't made public speaking part of their training, so he sheepishly waved and gave a little bow and gestured for Miles to tell the story.

"Well folks," Miles began, "I've been traveling this land for too many years now. It's all I've ever done. Playing towns like this, though of course none quite so nice as this." Audiences always ate up that corny line like it was pie at the church social. "My job has been to ask good people like you to listen to *my* story that I tell in a few little ditties that I've written down in the hopes you might take away something from them."

This false modesty and overly folksy-ness was making me a bit nauseous but the crowd ate it up like it was bacon on a donut.

"I didn't figure it out till just recently that I need to switch things around. I need to be listening to *your* stories and using what little skill I have to turn those stories into songs, so we can learn more about who we are, what we have lost, and what we want to..."

"DO BURNING RUBBER!" a biker interrupted, who must have arrived late or just wanted to hear it again. Uh oh. This was bordering on a speech, which wasn't what the good people of Brandon had come to hear. He was losing them.

"Well," said Miles, "Burning Rubber" itself is a story, and I'm pleased to hear that it meant something to you, and we did it in the first set. It's about a biker getting the hell out of town when things got tough for him in a relationship. Now Burt here told me a story the other night about his own struggles. I only heard it cuz I stopped being so uppity for once and let folks share their tales with me. Uppity just wasn't getting me anywhere I guess, and I'd have to say I have a new friend for pointing that out to me. I'd like to share the song I whittled down from his story with y'all. OK I'll shut up now if you'll let me share this brand new song with you".

Just then MG bounced onto the stage. Bouncing was her primary mode of propulsion.

"Howdy again, everybody! Just before Miles sings this beaut of a song, and trust me it's just as pretty as Burt here is handsome," Burt blushed. Everyone cheered. She was pretty slick at working a crowd.)

"I have a favour to ask. See those two mics up there? And see my little rig back there at the Merch Booth? I'm trying something new as the chief manager and babysitter of these boys. I'm going to record this song live, and the next one too, and I'm hoping you'll be a part of it by being the best audience you can be; quiet during the song and of course enthusiastic applause and whooping at the end. Then I'm going to load the songs up onto the brand new 'miles2go.ca' website. Look for the link, and you can download it tomorrow if you like it. It only costs one Canadian Toonie per song, which goes to support us in these tough times we're going through. Yes we've got miles to go on this tour, but you can have Miles To Go right now, kind of like take-out food, only more delicious cuz it's a song!"

Wow. She had the tech stuff figured out and the marketing for it all rolled into one.

"Take off your shirt!" yelled another biker.

"That's a different kind of bar you are thinking about, honey," she shot back, "but thanks for reminding me about these fine T-Shirts." She gave a model's 'turn' with that. "Just a few left at the back, and the boys'll sign one for you after the show when we can do a little business with you. Luckily we're not selling gotchies cuz we wouldn't have a pair small enough for YOUR little business, mister!"

A big 'ooooooohhhh' ran around the room after that. She went a bit far but it worked.

"Ladies and Gents, and you too, Asshole," she said to the T-shirt dude in a way that even he thought was all in fun, "heeeeeere's Miles". She bounced back to the booth, pressed a button on her computer and signaled Miles to begin.

Miles waved me and Dougie off and decided to sing the song solo, a real risk, but he started in quiet and he nailed that sucker. Watching bikers bawling is a sight I never thought I'd see, and wouldn't recommend.

The crowd did their part for the recording perfectly, and Burt got up and took a bow with Miles. The resulting picture was spread far and wide within minutes in ways I still don't really understand. Next up was Marta. MG had obviously shown Melba what button to press and so forth, so she bounded back to the stage, bringing Marta with her, who was happy to share her story and introduce the gang to her new trucker friend and thank Miles for what he was about to share. When she counted in the song and Miles leaned down into her mic for the harmonies, there was not a dry eye for the debut of 'Dreamin' of A Dream'. It was so powerful that for the first time it really sunk in for me as to what was happening here. I looked around and I could see how many folks could see themselves in that story, and they felt instantly like they were a part of something important. It was such a 'moment' that folks forgot to applaud at the end until MG prompted them. Then the floodgates were open and Marta took her bow with Miles too, which was of course the start of a tradition. Those were the pictures that accompanied the downloadable songs on the web thingy and the storytellers had their moment of fame out of it. Dougie got an idea and launched into 'Margaret's Waltz' on the fiddle, the closest he could get to 'Marta' I guess. Jesus, do all women's names start with "M" around here? Her trucker friend, whose name was Bob unless that was just the name of the Husky truck-stop shirt he was wearing, invited her to dance and the floor filled quickly following the couple's lead in the most elegant movement that bar had ever seen I'll wager. It was getting to be a freaking love fest in there. Holy.

I don't think Miles was too sure about what should happen next. Should we break the spell and go back to the old hits? We all looked at the set list we had prepared and nothing seemed like an obvious follow-up. Just then a large woman in stretchy jeans, an oversized plaid shirt, and, yes, those same bleach blonde curls that we've been seeing every night, climbed right up onstage and commandeered Dougie's mic.

"I've got a story," she yelled into the mic, causing a blast of feedback with her loud volume. This time it was the crowd, not Miles, who offered her immediate encouragement. Dougie motioned to her that she didn't need to shout, and she began:

"Some of you folks know me. I'm Jeannie Croft, from Croft's Crafts, remember, over by the old post office? Well, we closed up about a year ago, in case you didn't notice. We tried our darndest but we just couldn't compete with Walmart. You've probably noticed even some of the newer stores in the mall are closing. Now I'm not making any judgments here, but I know it was hard for you to resist those great prices they were offering, but for crying out loud that stuff you were buying was all low quality too, made in sweatshops in China when a lot of my products were made right here in Canada by people with decent jobs working for decent wages so of course we couldn't compete. I paid a decent wage too, and now the folks that work at Walmart can't even afford to buy stuff in their own store since their pay is so low and they're all part-time jobs too. Now I'm not blaming you, honestly, but sometimes keeping things local, keeping mom and pop shops in business, where you get good service and they know their customers by name, that's got to be worth more than saving a few bucks on cheaper sweat pants, isn't it? I lost everything and I GAVE everything I had to that place thinking I was going to get back in loyalty what I gave in service to this community. If we ONLY buy junk that's made overseas, you're going to lose YOUR jobs too. Don't you see it? And it's not just me that will be left with nothing. We all lose, but oh no we just let them waltz in here and we rolled out the red carpet for them too."

Old Jeannie started to cry. Suddenly everyone felt really uncomfortable. Her story was personal, but she was hitting us all hard with guilt which wasn't exactly everyone's idea of a night's entertainment at the bar. Walmart was probably the Numero Uno shopping destination for the majority of them. They obviously liked Jeannie, but if I was reading the room correctly, it didn't look like they were willing to be dissed for that. Miles was looking very agitated, since this was something he never tired of ranting about as we drove through towns that had been killed off by those bullies from Arkansas. Dougie went over and put his arm around Jeannie and Miles jumped up to his mic and wound up for the pitch.

"Two Kinds of People in this World, Jeannie. Folks who shop at WalFart and decent folk who..." Just then MG cut him off. That was a bold move. She must have recognized that we had crossed a line that wasn't ready to be crossed yet. She could read a room too, and it was dense reading material at that point. We were still just a band. This was still just a bar. We had a job to do which didn't include changing the world. Yet.

"Thanks Miles," she barked in the most chipper voice she could manage. "Golly look at the time! And let's have a round of applause for Jeannie here. That took guts, Gal, and we appreciate it. And I have a special announcement to make. Drum roll please, Drummer."

I obliged, not knowing what was up. MG continued:

"Tomorrow night was the band's night off before their big show in Winnipeg opening for the Buffalo Gals!" Some half-hearted cheers went up as the tension in the room was wearing off.

"But I'm pleased to announce that I spoke to some lovely folks here from Portage La Prairie who have invited us for a special barn concert tomorrow night. Of course they can't handle too many, and it's BYOB and BYOS, that's bring your own story, so if you want the address, go see that nice fella, name of Roy, at the back by the door. Wave Roy!"

Roy waved.

"And don't forget, Miles will have Jeannie's special song

ready for then, right Song Doctor Gerber?" Miles looked P.O.'d about her interruption but he gave the thumbs up.

"Let's hear it for Jeannie!" There *was* applause, a bit tentative at first, but she cajoled and romanced them into a genuine round of appreciation. "And if you can't come you can look for it the day after tomorrow at Miles 2 Go Dot Cee A! Now fellers I think you have one more special number for these fine folks don't ya"?

Jeepers. She was talking just like Miles, not a punk kid that had only a few days before been thrown off a grunge band bus! We all looked at each other with thought-bubbles all ready to burst but empty above our heads. First off, MG had not asked us about the gig in Portage. Second, what was our 'special number', anyways, and third, WTF?

Miles took a moment, conferred with us about a last tune, seemed to decide the only choice was to embrace the moment, stepped to the mic and said, "Well, thank you Miss MG, which I believe stands for 'Misbehaving Gal'. Yes it's last-minute but I hope to see some of you in Portage La Prairie tomorrow, And I'll sweeten the pot a little. He was too shy to get up here but Brendan down there by the shuffleboard table told me an interesting story before the second set. What he said was kind of the opposite of that 'Dreamin' of A Dream' song that I was so pleased that you enjoyed." Marta and Bob Whooped.

"Brendan says he is just back in town, do you guys remember him? He'd moved way down to Brampton, Ontario, to try to distance himself from *this* place enough to find *his* dream, and after trying out what he thought would be the good life there, he realized that he just wanted to come back here and get a fresh start. This place has a hold on him for better or worse. You can make your dreams happen wherever you are, right? And after all Brendan and Brandon are pretty much the same thing, so you might as well embrace it, 'eh buddy?"

Someone got a chant going alternating, 'Brandon' and 'Brendan', then believe it or not, despite Miles' little lecture earlier, we launched into a raunchy reprise of 'Burning Rubber'.

Chapter Thirteen

Nelly-Belle Tells

I could hear their finale from out in the lot. We automobiles are always skeptical about the wisdom in actually burning rubber, and to hear it twice in one night from a band that said they hated the song? Mercy. It must have gone well though. Normally those guys are out the door as soon as they get handed the cash and the gear is packed up. Yes, they still deal in cash mostly because of Miles' morning-after 'divvying up' ritual.

That night they lingered, and whenever the doors would open I could see them chatting up the locals like I've never seen before; and if the local people were anything like the local automobiles, they were pretty chatty. I couldn't get a stuck-up pimped-out 4 X 4 Yukon parked beside me to shut up about the load he could handle and the off-road adventures he'd been on. That don't impress me much.

When they were all safe in my arms and we headed back to the 'Worst Western', the gang just kept talking. They all talked at once, even Drummer, who mostly only talks to himself or to reporters asking him about 'life with Miles'.

It sounded something like this:

"What the fuck, MG! Who said anything about Portage la putain de Prairie"?

"That was awesome!"

"That was scary. Those bikers nearly turned on us!"

"Those bikers were pussycats."

"What was that 'last special number supposed to be anyways?"

"You had a night off anyway. What have you got to lose, losers?"

"Who said Pussy?"

"I like this story thing. Folks are into it. But shouldn't we somehow screen them first? What if they're all like that crafty bitch back there?"

"Shut up. She was the real deal."

"You're writing two songs for tomorrow night? What are you, nuts?"

"So now you've got us playing in barns?"

"I'm hungry"

"You're the nutbar around here"

"Why did you cut me off"?

"I was thinking maybe in Portage we could do more like a story circle"

That was MG and that got everyone quiet.

"A what?" the boys all said together.

MG had it figured out. "You know, more like a jam session with songs and stories. You could play one set with the two new ones, and then make it less formal, more intimate. I could set up my new gear to record the song, and maybe some of the stories too."

"So maybe this is that end of the music business you've been chasing, Miles", said Dougie. "How much money is in the story business?"

Drummer added, "Probably the same as the music business, Boogie; NONE."

"But it's a new direction, boys. Are you a bunch of prairie chickens? Bok bok fucking bok! Take a look at the direction you were headed before this story thing started. It's called south, dudes."

We were at the hotel then, though I noticed that Miles had taken us the long way back, past the Walmart and the street Jeannie Croft had apparently told them about.

Everyone piled out and went inside, except Miles, who just sat there holding my steering wheel for a long time. He flipped down my visor mirror and looked at himself for a while, then patted me on the dash and said, "Good night old girl."

Though there was tension around doing the Portage gig, by the time we headed there early the next afternoon, everyone seemed to be playing the same tune. Miles was pretty sleepy having stayed up to write *two* songs. Wow. He was sleepy but wired up. I think this overnight songwriting thing gave him a new sense of purpose that kind of energized him.

Spirits seemed up, probably because the take from Brandon ended up being pretty good. CD sales were awesome, and there were even a bunch of orders for the new song downloads that MG had created. She got us to stop at Staples on the way out of town and she printed up a bunch of download cards for her new operation. There was a bit of ribbing around doing this at a 'big box store' but it was a dose of reality. Staples had put the last family run stationary and print shop out of business.

This was the first gig that MG had really planned in her new role, so after some grumbling it was decided to let her have her way with it.

It turned out to be a real favourite of mine, though the boys seemed to think playing in a barn was hitting the bottom of the showbiz totem pole. It was the lap of luxury for me. We arrived at an old family acreage a few clicks north of town. They drove me right inside and used me as the backdrop of the stage. I was front and centre for a change.

The hosts were really fine folks, and they had invited their neighbours to chip in to make the event a special one. They had an old '52 International pickup, still running great, sitting under a tree so I knew they were good people. They drove the tractors and the manure spreaders out of the barn to clear some space. As you might guess Dougie made his usual joke about musicians and politicians just being human manure spreaders. They made tables from planks and a pot-luck supper began to appear as folks gathered. Jellied salads. Tuna Casseroles. Plump pies. Lots of plump little kids too, something we don't get to see much, and they played amongst the hay bales, some of which were co-opted for seating. It was a sweet early June night with just a bit of a chill in the air but the folks warmed things up pretty quick. The setting sun found its way through the cracks in the barn boards, sending beams of golden light across the straw covered floor. We were in that limited window for doing Canadian shows outdoors in rural areas. After the snow and the spring flooding, and before the bugs!

The boys did a really nice low-key set, leaning towards the old fiddle tunes and Miles' more country-style material, and I got to hear his new story songs. Jeannie Croft brought her family and they sure looked pleased as punch, though I never could figure out how pleased punch really got. I gather it had been a kind of controversial topic during the 'telling' the night before, but it sure went over big in Portage, and just like in previous nights there was a good contingent of folks who had made the drive to hear what Miles had done with the stories. Miles pulled off his two-for-one sale by going right into 'Back To Brandon', which sounded like a real hit to all who heard it that first time. First time of many it turned out. Two 'back' songs back to back.

James Gordon

Song 13: Back Before Walmart

Back before Walmart came to town
This was a going concern
On Fridays folks would come around
And spend their pay where it was earned
Well the hardware store was the first to go
Those prices just got way too low
Soon the other stores were closed
And the lights went out on main street

Whatever happened to our little town
Walmart has run it into the ground
Generation of hopes and dreams are all
Sitting down in a bank somewhere in Arkansas
Down in a bank somewhere in Arkansas

Well the storekeepers all knew all our names
And they knew just we wanted
But they could not win at Walmart's game
And now our streets are haunted by
The spirit of a town that died
They took our money and they took our pride
Took us all for a ride
Till the lights went out on Main Street

Whatever happened to our little town
Walmart has run it into the ground
Generation of hopes and dreams are all
Sitting down in a bank somewhere in Arkansas
Down in a bank somewhere in Arkansas

Made in America that's what they say
But the only thing that they really made
Was a profit large enough to take
The life right out of Main Street

Whatever happened to our little town
Walmart has run it into the ground
Generation of hopes and dreams are all
Sitting down in a bank somewhere in Arkansas
Down in a bank somewhere in Arkansas

Song 14
Back To Brandon

Let's go back to Brandon
I got people there
We had dreams and plans and
A little cash to spare
It was a place where a man
Could breathe some decent air
Let's go back to Brandon
It was better there

Let's go back to Brandon
I am feeling stranded
In the burbs of Brampton
This don't feel like anywhere
Things have got all out of hand
Why can't we just fix up the van
Let's go back to Brandon
It was better there

Let's go back to Brandon
Underneath that prairie sky
I know a man who's got a band
Said they could use a guitar guy
I bet that we could make a brand
New start if you and I
Headed back to Brandon
Before the tranny dies

You give up the weed, honey, I'll cut down on booze
We could have our seed money, what have we got to lose
Used to think those prairie towns were just dust on rust
But they're looking pretty good now since everything went bust.

Wow. A song with a van in it, and a transmission reference! Brendan was there with the girlfriend he had talked into driving back home with, and there was the usual town rivalry going on with folks saying he should have come to Portage instead.

After the break for dessert, they reconfigured into a kind of circle, a couple of rows deep. The boys and MG took their places in the circle and started to jam with some of the people who had brought fiddles, banjos, guitars and even an accordion, despite the objections of Drummer, who seemed to have been squeezed by one as a baby or something. I liked it. It sounded like I do in third gear heading up a slow grade.

Miles explained a little about what had been happening with the stories. He said he'd love to hear what everyone had to say. Folks out that way are mighty shy, so there was a bit of an awkward silence and then laughter because about half a dozen people started to talk all at once. Then to my surprise Drummer got in the circle with that big drum beater he brings along with him in case he meets a friendly drum circle on his travels, something he'd been getting into more recently even though he didn't know much about his own roots. He had the drum under his arm. (He says the drum is made with a willow branch, buffalo hide and stuffed with coyote feathers. That drummer, I can never tell when he is joking.) In his quiet voice that doesn't match his imposing size he said-

"Ok here's an idea for all you nice white people who aren't used to talking in a circle. Heh heh. This here is a talking stick. It doesn't talk. If YOU want to talk, it's here on this drum and you can hold it up meaning it's your turn to speak. Feel free to give 'er a little tap when you pick it up. This is a good spot to tell a story from anyway. When you're done, you can replace it, or hand it to someone who asks you for it."

He gave the drum a nice little flourish and set the beater on it. There was some nodding of approval and then it started.

Listening in from my prime spot, I noticed that it was the sharing of the stories that seemed to have more impact than the actual content of the stories. There was a reverence, a kind of holiness that everyone could sense, like I feel when a Rolls-Royce cruises by. Folks seemed honoured just to know they were in a space where they could be heard: a place where what they shared had value. We all want to be heard. That's why they have voices and I have a horn. Miles actually wrote 'We Want To Feel Heard' not long after that night I think, 'cause he started performing it at some of the Northern Ontario shows about a week later. Maybe just after Winnipeg, since he did that little trick of turning 'Portage and Main' into 'Pain and Main'. Ouch.

Song 15
You Want To Feel Heard

Standing on the corner of Pain and Main
Blown by the wind, soaked by the rain
Listen to the whistle of the midnight train
Singing that same old sad refrain

Down at the Drop-In, scraping up a meal
back by the tracks, trying to make a deal
Dude in black, tells you to kneel
Boots kick the dust, there's a flash of steel
Sirens wail, tires squeal
You're left with a hurt that'll never heal
This is your life, raw and real
Leaves you with nothing left to feel

But you want to feel held
You want to feel heard
You want to feel safe and reassured
You wish you could be
Loved unconditionally
You want to feel held
And you want to feel heard

High up in his golden tower
Looking down a mean man glowers
those who oppose him are devoured
He could crush you like you were a flower
he's got all the money he's got all the power
so why's he looking so sad and sour?
After all he's the man of the hour
He's got a heart still beats like ours

He just wants to feel held
he wants to feel heard
He wants to feel safe and reassured
He wishes he could be
Loved unconditionally
He wants to feel held
And he wants to feel heard

The Ark of the Oven Mitt

Rich man poor woman beggerman thief
Poet priestess pauper or King
Somehow deep down underneath
We all want the same thing

Not that the actual stories weren't valuable too. And there were a lot of them. Luckily those Manitobans weren't too wordy or we would have been there all night. If there was a common theme, I'd say folks talked about 'loss'. Loss of a way of life and a livelihood, loss of family and community, loss of hope; more basic things like losing the arena in the town they were from, or the local grain elevator. Losing a partner to cancer, a son to the oil patch. A young boy who I think really just wanted to hit the drum and hold the stick said he had lost his hat in the hay somewhere. After each story and during the exchange of the talking stick, MG would lead the group in applause or other vocal forms of appreciation.

"Right On."

"YES!"

"You tell 'em."

MG's patented 'whoo-hoos' were a bit much she realized and she toned that down a bit to reflect the gentle nature of the proceedings. Miles would nod his approval and make little comments, and some notes in that little book he carries around, reflecting on what he had taken away from each story.

"That must have been real hard, Ma'am," or "I know where you're coming from there, Mister."

When the circle had gone round, he expressed gratitude, but turned to MG and wondered aloud how he was going to pick one story to write a song about. "Let me think on that, folks. There's enough material here for a Broadway show!"

MG gave them the pitch about CDs, the 'Miles2Go' downloads, and the email list she was keeping. Miles told them about the gig the next night in Winnipeg, where they were to be the opening act for the 'Buffalo Gals', which seemed to illicit an equal amount of yeahs and boos. MG encouraged attendance by saying they wouldn't find out which story Miles turned into a song unless they came to the show or looked it up on the website, but it would be available as a download, 'a tune for a toonie' in a couple of days. Dougie seemed keen to wrap up with a couple of tunes, (he was the only one who seemed bored during the story session), so he started noodling on the fiddle but Drummer came into the centre to retrieve his drum, put his hand out to pause Dougie before turning to the assembly.

"Thank you for your stories. Thank you for honouring the talking stick."

Then he looked up to the big rafter beams in the barn, and the barn swallows dancing in the shadows.

"You speak of loss. I hear you. I know what it's like. I hope someday you learn, like I'm slowly learning, what it's like to lose a whole people. Your land. Your home. Your identity. Your future. To have your own stories taken from you. To be told you are worthless. I'm just learning some of the stories now, and they are dying out. The story of my people is harder to tell because the tellers are in pain and too few want to listen. Keep your ears and your hearts open my friends."

And with that he started to beat his drum and sing what he called an honour song. I'd never heard him do that before. He sang it through each time he turned to face each direction and his voice grew stronger each time and it hung in those rafters and the drum beat swirled around the barn until I swear you could hear his ancestors joining in.

He finished and there was a loud silence, then a bit of an awkward pause until Dougie started in to 'The Centennial Waltz' and folks started to get up and move about.

The boys finished up and for the second last song MG even did a number which was pretty cool. An Emmy-Lou Harris song I think. There was a bit more jamming, but it was late for farm folks, so everyone helped pack up and the crowd started to disperse. The host family had room in the house for everyone to sleep, though Dougie chose to sleep in the hay loft, muttering to himself about all the changes that were happening as he drifted off. I've always thought it was weird about Dougie that he was in a new place every day, but he really wanted everything to just stay the same. He might have picked the wrong job for that.

I happen to know which story Miles picked. Since I was safe and warm in the barn, Miles hauled a straw bale over to me, sat on it, leaned against my driver's door and started strumming. It felt good, and I was pleased that he had picked the same story I was drawn to. A love song, a topic Miles had been clearly avoiding since he had reached his 'heart-broke-about Maddie' quota. A young fella maybe in his twenties had taken the stick earlier and told about finding a good job in Calgary but his girlfriend wouldn't follow him there. He pointed at the night sky out the big barn door and said, "It's that derned Manitoba Moon. It tugs at ya somethin' fierce."

That song practically wrote itself, with Miles just nudging out the words gently. As he was working out the melody, there was a sweet violin sound from the loft and Dougie jumped down and came over to us while he played. I'll be darned if the two of them didn't share that straw bale and finish that song together. A first, I figure. I knew there had been tension between those two ever since MG came on board and the dynamics shifted a bit. And I also know that Canadian men don't really talk to each other about that stuff. It's an unwritten code. You simmer instead of talking then eventually you fight. In this case they created some music instead of talking, and by the time they both drifted off to bed I could tell that pretty intimate act of writing together did the trick, and they parted with a pretty sincere manhug. Dougie climbed back up to the loft and Miles headed to the house. I saw him pause at the barn doors and look across to the edge of the barnyard where a coyote stood silently watching.

It was a gem of a song. I can say that since I'm a songwriter now too. And boy, it could have been written about Maddie, so it must have spooked Miles a bit when he was wrangling the words all up in a bunch. Maddie had Manitoba roots. Did you know that? Oak Lake I think. Listening to the words, I was reminded that all those years of feeling Miles' heartbreak, and his kind of disbelief that she had left. He couldn't really have been totally surprised when she up and skedaddled. There were lots of obvious billboards up along that highway.

In the morning everyone woke up to the rooster crowing instead of diesel motors idling. I'll take the idling any day of course but I think the others appreciated the different kind of wake-up call.

Song 16
Manitoba Moon

Your eyes are miles from town, and they're the same kind of brown
As the wheat fields that surround your parents' farm
And it's as plain as the plains, that it goes against the grain
Trying to keep you any longer in my arms

Cuz that Manitoba Moon
It's hanging over you
And I know there is nothing I can do
All the stars up in the sky, will not keep you by my side
I'm going to lose you to that Manitoba Moon

I've tried so hard to keep you here, but it seems pretty clear
That the Red River runs through your veins
I don't want to let you go, cuz you and I we both know
That you won't be coming back this way again

Cuz that Manitoba Moon
It's hanging over you
And I know there is nothing I can do
All the stars up in the sky
Will not keep you by my side
I'm going to lose you to that Manitoba Moon

If I ask you to stay for a while, I get a half-hearted smile
And a silence as big as a quarter section
You've got those prairies in your bones, and when you say you're
bound for home
I know that's never going to be in my direction

Cuz that Manitoba Moon
It's hanging over you
And I know there is nothing I can do
All the stars up in the sky
Will not keep you by my side
I'm going to lose you to that Manitoba Moon

Chapter Fourteen

Drummer Tells

We headed to Winnipeg after a fine farm breakfast. Through the sprawl and the crawl past the malls into the downtown where we were gearing up to meet our fate as the opening act for the Buffalo Gals. Speaking of gears, poor old Nelly-Belle barely made it out of low gear all the way through the city. Even though there was general approval of MG's first booking the night before, there were clearly some mixed feelings about it, and about the night ahead of us. There was some excitement about getting into the big city and playing in a big venue again, but the prospects of 'playing second fiddle' to this all-image-no-talent outfit sure was putting Miles in a mood. 'Spice Girls with cowboy boots' Dougie called them. MG pointed out to him how outdated that pop reference was, but he didn't respond. Miles says 'New Country' is where rock and roll went to die. I hadn't heard of them, since Miles won't allow 'corporate country' as he calls it, on Nelly-Belle's radio, which was hardly working anyway, just like everyone else in the music biz. Seeing that we were going to share a stage, he allowed MG to dial them up on her new fancy device and we listened for a while. For once Miles seemed grateful that you could stream them for free. Normally just the mention of 'streaming' would launch him into a 'two kinds of people' rant. There were a lot of puking sounds and cries of agony from my fellow passengers while the Gals were singing, though Dougie didn't think what they were doing qualified as 'singing'. "That's mostly the producer running samples through a pitch rider," he grumbled. Not sure what that meant but apparently it was bad. MG seemed to defend their 'strong modern woman' stance though.

"So singing a song of empowerment while dressed in your dainties makes you a modern woman?" asked Miles.

"Well you didn't complain when I was only dressed in your T-shirt," said MG. Miles eventually made her turn the Gals off, and there was an awkward silence after that until the boys started to discuss the sorry state of what Miles liked to call 'Trashville USA'.

Me, I needed that bit of silence, still thinking about what happened on that farm, especially when I sang that honour song. I had never done that before, and to tell you the honest truth I didn't think I even knew the words. Is there a dishonest truth? Heh heh. Don't know where that song came from. I didn't even think about it. Just did it. I could feel the ancient ones guiding me along, a feeling that was strong on this part of the endless tour. Raised in foster homes, I never really got to learn about my own people, and I feel like I'm ready for more! Felt good to sing that song though. It was strange that no one said anything about it after, though MG came up and kissed me on the cheek and winked at me, like she knew exactly where I was coming from. Two misfits. Holy.

Chapter Fifteen

Nelly-Belle Tells

Miles parked me by the loading dock of the Centennial Concert Hall. I know that would have been poignant for him since that's where they'd always played in the 'Miles and Myles' days, when they had a big tour bus to park, but they were the main act then of course. Nevertheless it must have been a welcome step up from the Legion Halls. A real switch-up from this new thing the lads were developing.

I was feeling a bit vulnerable parked right beside the Gals' gigantic tour bus. The boys mocked it as being too ostentatious. Even though I felt their loyalty to me I could tell that they were envious. There were the giant faces of the stars themselves plastered on the side of the bus in an homage to airbrush technology. Perfect hairdos, perfect teeth, and their piercing blue eyes with photoshopped sparkles in them.

The bus itself was quite sleek and handsome I thought, and he was purring quietly to keep the Air Con on inside I guess.

"Hey," he said. Busses don't have large vocabularies.

"Hey," I answered, wittily, noticing that I was using my 'aw-shucks-I'm-just-a-little-ol-' girl-van'voice.

"What's that over there?" he said, looking at a car all by itself parked at the edge of the dock.

From the other side of the bus, another voice said "That's an electric car."

"Get out of Dodge!" yelled the bus.

"I'm not a Dodge, I am made by Mercedes-Benz," she said in the kind of snooty voice you'd expect from that company. "It's over there because it's charging from that charger station."

"How do you know?" I asked.

"Because I'm a Smart Car, dummy!" Sure enough she was. When I see them on the highway I always think they should be driven by Goofy or Donald Duck.

"More like a Smart-Ass Car," said the Chevy Cavalier beside me, demonstrating the droll tone that led them to being the only car named after an attitude, and a bad one at that. Almost as weird as naming a truck a 'Ram' or a car a 'Hummer'. Cripes Almighty.

"They're the future," said Smart Car. "And we're all toast."

"No shit," said the bus.

"No gas either," said the Smart Car. "Soon we'll be gone the way of the buffalo. No offence to your gals there Mr. Bus."

"It's Gus."

"You're kidding."

"Do I look like a kidder?"

I'd seen electric cars before, but the significance of it hadn't really sunk in. Smart Car went on, a bit too know-it-all-ish but it was informative.

"It's not just us that will be gone. How often do you folks visit the repair shop?"

We all confessed to frequent visits, even the Cavalier, though she said she could care less. At my age, I'm there probably once a month with some ailment or other.

"Well, think about it. The internal combustion engine is designed to fail, since the profit margin for the auto manufacturer is in service more than the actual sale. And it uses a fuel that we knew a generation ago was no good for us, but they couldn't resist the easy money from it. That electric car only has about 20 moving parts and apparently they never wear out. Car dealerships and the grease monkeys that work for them will be dinosaurs like us. I was just in Alberta. They are still operating on the belief that selling their dirty tar sands oil will keep them rich forever. Unless they get their heads out of that sand and invest in renewables, their economy will collapse."

Jesus on the Dashboard. Miss Smarty Pants was worse than Miles with the preachy rants.

"So why don't we just ban those electric cars? They're clearly bad for business," asked Gus.

"Well, some U.S. states have actually done that, because

they are slaves to the oil barons. And that's a key point. We are all slaves, and we won't be free or sustainable till we embrace the future of clean energy!" replied Smarty Pants.

"So the future is death for us, but life for the planet," I offered.

"You've got it Pontiac!"

"Actually I'm a Ford."

"Well," said Smart Car who turned out to be Verbose Car. "Funny you mentioned Ford. Not only was your founding forefather a Nazi sympathizer, he started, like others, with electric cars more than a century ago but saw bigger bucks by getting in bed with the big oil gang, which was just starting out. They've had a hold of us ever since."

We all looked at that electric car for a while in silence.

"It looks just like us," I said.

"Don't let that fuel you," said the Cavalier.

The show must have been over because just then the Buffalo Gals and their security crew ran down the ramp and jumped on Gus, followed by a crowd of autograph seekers who all looked like they were wearing the results of their Christmas gift certificates from Mark's Work Warehouse. There was no sign of my team.

I waited patiently, then got bored with that and waited impatiently for a while. That passed the time better. In the distance I could see the top of the St. Regis Hotel. Rooms were included with the gig so they had a decent place to stay for a change, though I knew Miles wouldn't like it because he couldn't park me right outside the door.

I remembered the last time we stayed there. Because it wasn't a motel, I was way out back by myself in a very cold parking lot. The band had quite an argument before they left me there after that gig. They were tired and grumpy, just like usual, and Dougie was pretty plastered which was usual then too. The argument was whether they should haul all of the gear up to their hotel room or not, it being so cold and late and all. Was Winnipeg safe? They had arguments about the parking lot being monitored by security cameras but Drummer wasn't buying it.

"I Know Winnipeg. Trust Me. Don't Trust."

They settled eventually on a compromise. They left the heavy stuff and their suitcases and took their instruments with them, Drummer just taking his precious snare drum, hoping for the best for the rest.

Sure enough at about four a.m. I felt someone grabbing my ass trying to break into my back door! As much as I had tried, I couldn't honk my own horn, and after much fumbling I heard a big crash and I'll be damned if my back window wasn't busted wide open. Ouch! A grizzled and smelly older man, even smellier than my back seat, who looked like a reject from gnome school, with about ten layers of clothes on, started rummaging around inside me. I thought at first that he was going to steal ME when he sat in the driver's seat but I think he was just trying to get further away from the cold blast of air he'd created by smashing out the window.

I could see him looking around first outside to see if anyone had spotted him, then inside at the prospects before him. I can't remember exactly, but here's what he likely would have seen:

*Cowboy shirts laid out over the back seat to dry. The Disturbers were drawn to the old school cowboy shirt as stage wear, even Drummer who always called it an "Indian" shirt instead.

"Those damn cowboys borrowed the idea from us!" he'd say.

'Laundry is for wimps,' was Dougie's mantra, and after the shows they'd peel off their sweaty shirts, change in the van, and leave them to dry till the next day.

*Drummer's drum kit. This took up more than its share of space, always a source of contention in the group. This, and the declining fortunes of the outfit, gave Drummer ongoing anxiety that he was the next to go.

*Three suitcases. The band had figured out early on that one large suitcase with enough clothes to last half-way through a tour with one laundry stop could stay in the van while Miles and Drummer each had a kind of 'man purse' with what they needed for overnight. Dougie had a plastic bag.

A box of band T-Shirts. Most of the time the boys seemed to forget to bring this in to the gigs, though they seldom sold any until MG came along.

Boxes of CDs, including unopened boxes of 'The Best of Miles and Myles' which Miles seldom wanted to sell, but that everyone asked for. They were probably still carrying a stock of cassettes then too. Me, I still had an 8-track player strapped under my dashboard, with a Flying Burrito Brothers tape permanently stuck in it.

Litter. Mostly Tim Horton's cups despite Miles' regular rants about this. Fast food containers, foil wrappers and bags. They seemed to leave their trash in me till there was no more room to sit down.

My section. Motor oil, wiper fluid. Anti-freeze. Jumper cables. Boy it was embarrassing how often I needed those, but it was usually after Dougie had left my dome light on trying to read directions. Fuses. A whole box of them. In the cold weather I seem to blow them a lot if the boys have my heat cranked. The manufacturers of the fluids I require more often in my old age seem to design their containers to hold just a little more than one fill-up, so my 'section' always contained nearly empty jugs.

Guitar and bass amps. Dougie and Miles were too cheap to upgrade these as the technology improved, allowing for smaller rigs, but at one point their vintage gear became hip and valuable, too valuable to leave in me I always thought.

The Rand-McNally North American Road Atlas. Yup. Strictly old-school when it comes to navigation.

Road snacks. Salt, sugar and fat. That's where it's at, as Drummer would say.

Magazines. Everywhere. They were like insulation. Miles usually had a book in his 'man purse', something too literary for the other lads' tastes, but it was strictly 'light reading' for the others. The 'girly' variety belonged to Dougie, and the others mocked him for it, but as the tours wore on I saw them sneaking their peeks too. Rolling Stone magazines seemed to be purchased just so they could lament the sorry state of contemporary music. Auto Trader, which always made me nervous.

A pair of ten-pound barbells. The lads at one point had aspirations about staying in shape, but I never saw them used. Miles actually said at one point, "Relax boys, we *are* in shape. Kind of avocado-shaped."

A life-jacket. No one knew how it got there, and no one seemed to want to get rid of it despite the shortage of space. It was a pillow sometimes, and sometimes Miles would put it on and say 'abandon ship' after a particularly bad gig. No one laughed at this anymore.

A stack of '8 by 10s'; pictures of the band that, when autographed, would stay on the walls at the clubs or in restaurants where they ate. That stack wasn't getting any smaller.

Three sets of snowmobile boots. These took up a lot of room. They never wore them, preferring their slippery cowboy boots in all weather conditions.

Three winter coats, nearly never worn.

Dougie's two basses. Miles always brought in his two guitars, an old Gibson acoustic and his Gretsch 'Country Gentleman' electric. Dougie was a bit lazier about his own gear, which is where we pick up our intruder's story again.

Our putrid perp found Drummer's stash of road snacks by the side door and started wolfing them down while he opened up the suitcases and searched through. He was hungry. He was cold! He grabbed anything that looked warm, then I could see him eying something that shouldn't have been there. The drunken Dougie had left both his basses behind. I'd often heard him boasting about the value of his 'good one', a Fender Jazzman from the early 60s that he often thought of selling for around 5,000 dollars when he was feeling broke. The boys always talked him out of it, but I also heard him say it was part of his 'exit strategy' to make first and last month's rent somewhere. Oddly enough, Dougie didn't mind leaving the bass in my cabin but he often thought it was too valuable to bring into the scuzzier clubs, which were becoming more common on their ceaseless tour. So, he had a cheap no-name bass that he also brought along. He had a little trick that he swore worked. He'd put the prize bass in a cheap soft-shell case and the worthless one in the fancy Fender 'California Girl' bass case. (Tan on the outside. Pink on the inside. Hey, I never said the boys were always politically correct with their 'road language'.) The backseat bandit spied the crappy case, opened it up, then did the unexpected; he set the fancy-pantsy bass that was in it aside and started stuffing the case with the clothes he hadn't actually put on and the snacks he hadn't gobbled down. He opened the passenger door and threw out the case and followed after, presumably because the rest of my insides were covered with glass. He had on Dougie's parka, left behind even on this coldest of nights, and he stopped to admire himself in my side mirror before hightailing into the bushes behind the lot.

I shivered till the boys arrived in the morning. They did an inventory, cursed a lot, and decided that nothing of any actual value was missing. Dougie seemed a bit grateful but mostly quizzical about his missing case but his intact bass. Drummer said, "Well, I wouldn't be caught dead with any of our grimy old suitcases. I'm not surprised." In Winnipeg, in the cold, clothes are worth more than gold apparently. Hey Miles, there's a song in there! That incident convinced the boys to stick to the motel routine, and I think this return visit to the St. Regis was the first time they had deviated from their plan, though I had heard them say they could leave their gear in the hall till morning.

Meanwhile I'm still waiting and it's really late so I'm getting worried about a repeat vandalization. I reckon 'vandals' got their name from dudes who broke in to vans. Dougie also called Miles' summer flip-flops 'vandals' cuz he only wore them while driving me. Where could they have gone? The boys, not the footwear. They were the opening act so they should have been done a long time ago. Gus the Bus and my other loading-dock buddies had all headed off.

After what seemed like hours, my driver door opened and Miles climbed in. He was looking pretty rough, even for a guy who just looks rough naturally. I could tell that he remembered that same night long ago that I just told you about because he looked around, taking stock, then wrapped my steering wheel in his arms and started to talk.

Miles can confide in me, and no else it seemed, and it was clear there was a lot on his mind. I respect the special relationship we have, so I won't reveal all his personal thoughts, but basically, he kept going back to one line: "Nelly, darlin', I think I'm done."

He talked about the gig a bit. Even though they played "Manitoba Moon" which I happen to know was a damn good song, some old hits, their novelty crowd pleaser "It's In The Middle", about the city's status as 'the middle' of Canada, and despite the fact that they played their asses off and brought MG up to join in one number, no one was interested or paying attention. What they were offering was so far removed from the 'New Country' of the Buffalo Gals that the audience just didn't relate. They were nearly drowned out by the crowd singing 'Buffalo Gals won't you come out tonight' in an attempt to get their heroines out earlier. Miles told me that he didn't figure any of the Portage La Prairie folks had made the drive in to hear the new stuff, but he blamed that on the ticket price, and I guess it didn't help matters when he went into one of his onstage rants about it.

"Nell Old Girl, all I said was 'Two kinds of people in this world folks; those who can pay eighty-five bucks to see this spectacle and those poor working people like I've been talking to lately, who will never have a budget for something as frivolous as what you're being ripped off for tonight'. Was that so bad? I was just being honest, though honesty has taken a vacation I guess."

Ya I bet that rant went over big. Besides you could tell how humiliating it felt being the warmup act when 15 years before, 'Miles and Myles' were headliners and on a roll. He was glad they had fired Kirk the Jerk, or he would have been fired right then, but really, Kirk was just trying to give them a chance at a 'comeback'. He DID speak to me about the interesting roll they were on with these recent gigs with the instant story songs and all, but it felt to Miles like a kind of 'cute' thing they were doing instead of just quitting like they should. He also told me that he was very affected by how many of the stories he'd heard in the sharing sessions were about losing something important, changes that weren't for the better. Miles was feeling their loss, *and* lost himself. His nightly joke about chasing the end of the music business wasn't really a joke at all of course. After their set, Miles had taken off and started roaming the streets until he found his way back to me. The band must have been looking for him, but I pictured Dougie and Drummer, or 'Drum and Dummer' as MG had taken to calling them, telling her that he was a big boy and he needed to do this now and then.

Eventually Miles grew silent, gave me a slap on the dashboard and headed out, presumably to the hotel, leaving me there 'til the load-out the next morning.

Song 17
Winnipeg: It's in the Middle

Maybe there's no mosquito shortage
And it gets a bit breezy down at Main and Portage
The weather gets a bit extreme
But Winnipeg's every Canadian's dream

It's in the middle, (Winnipeg); it's in the middle, (Winnipeg)
Not too big, not too little
Not on the left, not on the right
It's where Canadians like it at centre ice
It's in the middle, Winnipeg's in the middle

Well at the edge of town you got your tall grass prairie
Two seasons, winter and road repair
You got your Royal Mint, got your old Fort Garry
It's In the middle, right in the middle

Got your Golden Boy, got your Guess Who too
Got your Neil Young, Got your Winnie the Pooh
Got your two big rivers running right through
Right in the middle, right in the middle

You got bugs in the summer got mud in the spring
At Bird's Hill Park hear the folkies sing
Winnipeg has everything
It's in the middle, it's in the middle

Vancouver's too hip, Edmonton's too square
Saskatoon's Ok if you've got long underwear
St. John's is kind of rocky, Halifax has got no hockey
Montreal's naughty. Toronto's kind of haughty
But it's safe in the centre, come to Manitoba
Where it's far enough away from either coast
You know you love it, let's embrace the spirit
Come to Winnipeg, come on let's hear it

Chapter Sixteen

Drummer Tells

Holy Smokers, that was some night in Winnipeg.

We all exited stage left as fast as we could after doing our 'warm up' act, which seemed to leave everyone cold.

Miles was the first out the stage door, not even bothering to pack up his gear when usually he fusses over his stuff till he's the last one loaded out. Dougie and MG did this for him and then took off to try and find him cuz he had trouble written all over his face, with very bad penmanship. Me, I'd seen that look before and figured he was just going to let off some steam, then have his usual chat with Nelly-Belle. I know I know, he thought nobody knew he did that, but I've seen it a dozen times. Me, I talk to my ancestors. Miles: a van. Whatever butters your bannock.

I was nabbed outside the hall by three big Cree dudes who figured I could benefit from seeing a different side of Winnipeg than you'd get at a Buffalo Gals concert. More like Loserpeg. I tagged along and they walked me around 'their side of the tracks' a while; showing me the underbelly of this place where I'd misspent some of my youth, the things that never show up on the tourist brochures. The group grew as we walked, collecting folks along the way. They took me to their hideout under a bridge right by the 'Forks', which got its name from the place where the Assinaboine and the Red rivers kiss and make up. A sacred gathering place that is now a hipster 'boutique' haven. My new friends thought it was called the 'Forks' cuz it was where the colonials stuck the last fork in Louis Riel's dream of a Metis Nation.

We talked; they smoked, and shared stories and some pow-wow songs. I pretended to know those songs. A tiny teenaged girl, with a lined, worn face and sunken eyes; a sign that she'd likely been through a lot in a short life, arrived with the results of her late-night dumpster-diving and she shared her winnings all round.

"I'm Clover. Move over!" she said as she plopped down beside me.

"Drummer," I replied. "Just Drummer". I asked about her name. She gave her only smile of the long night when she told us that her mom named her that because her dad used to always say, 'Someday we're gonna be in clover, honey', which actually is a kind of honey, eh? MG looked that up later on her thingymabobber and said that 'in clover' meant 'to live a carefree life of ease, comfort, or prosperity.' Ya right.

"Worked like a fuckin' Lucky Charm, right Drummer Boy?" she said before burying her head in her torn jeans jacket. Many of their stories would rip your heart out, which I guess is what my ancestor warriors would do to their enemies sometimes but heh, what's a little organ removal between tribes? One tough kid named Mose with a face all scarred up from being in a fire on his rez told tales between his coughing fits about his sister's suicide, gas sniffing, alcoholic parents who abused him, the racist attacks and police harassment when he came down to the city. I knew about these things but hearing him speak about how it had affected him directly made it hit harder. I never told them that I was adopted out to a white family when I was a baby and have no memories of the rez.

It turns out they had gathered there not to show me around, but to 'hold space' for Clover who was in a bad way. Three of her friends had suicided in the last three months and she was just barely holding on to this troubled earth. We helped her through the night and when I told the Disturbers the story, after they calmed down from *their* night, Miles wrote that 'Hey Clover' song, just as if I was one of the folks sharing stories that could be turned into songs. That was huge for me. I felt like Miles actually heard me, which he didn't always do, especially when I was trying to keep him on the beat.

Song 18: Hey Clover

Hey Clover
I see you're over-
Whelmed by it all
Don't forget
We can be your net
To catch you should you fall

We know what you
Have been going through
It's not hard to understand
That you've had enough
Life's too rough
But we're here to hold your hand

Here at the Forks where two rivers flow
You have a choice, which way will you go
When you've been driven to the edge of life once more
We'll help you drive those ghosts out of your head
Where the Assiniboine joins with the Red
Clover there's still so much here to live for

You can't see that now
And we know how
It gets when the darkness blinds you
But if you give in
You'll let those ghosts win
And the hope that's there can't find you

We've all seen
Winnipeg can be mean
It seems like no one cares about you
But we're all here
To fight your fears
And we can't picture a world without you

Like this bank holds the river in its arms
We're holding you; we'll keep you safe from harm
We're beating our drums, we're singing you a song
Now there's a little crack of promise in the light
Just a little longer you've made it through this night
Hold on Clover hold on!

I'd had a hint of it back at Portage, so somehow the stories I heard by the Forks made the ones I've been hearing from the well-meaning white folks along the road seem like real 'first-world' problems. So you're upset that your town is going through tough times and the local store closed? How 'bout going to that store and being told you are not welcome to shop there? Sad that the local school closed down and your kids have to be bussed to the next town over? How 'bout being yanked out of your parents' arms and being thrown into a residential school where they suck the Cree right out of you and leave you with nothing, if you actually survived? I had heard the stories before, and they always seemed to conjure up memories for me that I couldn't really have had. For some reason the tales shared that night changed me. From the inside of a van or on the drum riser in a club, you can easily forget what's going on out there.

I felt connected to those guys under the bridge in a way that I hadn't really been feeling for a while in the band. As dawn came up I figured I better check in with my crew, and I said goodbye to my new friends and headed back to the old. When I got back to the hotel MG and the boys were having at it big time. It sounded like the 'Big Time' was what they were yelling about too. Miles knew the 'big time' train that the Buffalo Gals were riding on, and he felt stuck on a siding somewhere. MG was pitching a new direction that would pull them off that siding, and Dougie just seemed to be randomly yelling, so I knew his late-night search for Miles had been interrupted by a search for a bootlegger.

I am just the drummer, so I beat it. Heh heh. Found a nice greasy diner breakfast then headed to the hall to retrieve the gear and found everyone already sitting in Nelly-Belle looking like a dog's breakfast. Why does a dog's breakfast always have to look bad anyway? A little garnish here and there maybe? MG was in the driver's seat, which was a big shock and I don't shock easy. Did she even have her driver's license? Yikes. I climbed in. Her idea to get us down the road and out of town fast wasn't quite as dramatic as it might have been since you could tell she didn't really know how to use a stick shift.

No one said shit, even though that's a word that usually starts every sentence when Dougie is talking.

Chapter Seventeen

A rusty dusty van heads east out of Winnipeg. Late morning. A thin sun over a fat highway. The van lurches and sputters as it reaches the edge of the urban sprawl. Patches of prairie pop up between townhouses. Warehouses loom like cliffs above the flat land. Pancake Houses offering a meal that accurately reflects the landscape. Car dealers. Strip Malls. Now some actual farmhouses. If you look closely the lurching is because the van has a new driver. The usual one is in the passenger seat, his head in his hands, and the two in the back look like they are trying to sleep between the grinding of gears. The driver is young. Female. She's driving, and she seems driven too, intent on propelling the occupants towards Ontario and Mecca: Toronto.

The prairie starts to look as patchy as the van. Gradually it gives way to scraggly forests, first poplar, then pine, spruce and tamarack. Crossing out of Manitoba the landscape turns to rocks and lakes and scrubland, only occasionally interrupted by mining towns where there is no mining, railroad towns where there is no railroad, and other settlements where there is no hope. Truck stops where the big rigs idle in the lots while the drivers eat truck-sized breakfasts. The van keeps up a steady pace, stopping every night in front of taverns or Legion Halls. It will take longer to cross this bleak landscape then it would take to drive across most of the nations on this scarred planet.

Kenora. Atikokan. Dryden. Wabigoon. Ignace, where the time zone changes while still remaining somehow lost in time.

The ramshackle houses that dot the edges of the tired towns tell the story of their owners' struggle for survival in the harsh environment. Pickup trucks in the driveways with 'For Sale' signs on them. A disparate selection of services offered to passersby as everyone scrambles to make ends meet: Car Repairs. Smoked Fish. Well-drilling and Income Tax. Septic Tank Pumping and Palm Reading. Usually an ongoing yard sale. Haircuts and Bait. 'Handyman Hank Hangs Here'. 'Indian Souvenirs and Mortgage Brokering.'

Beside each house and shed you see the entire history of the owner's vehicles spread in a line. Cars, trucks, tractors, snowmobiles, trailers. You never know when you might need a spare part.

Nipigon. Marathon. Thessalon. On and On.

Every hand-painted sign tells a story. Stories that are being repeated in saloons and halls to the occupants of the van when they stop for the night, and it's some of those story-tellers and story-listeners with little to stay behind for that end up following the decrepit van along the highway the next day. The growing caravan snakes along, competing for the two-lane blacktop with logging trucks and motor homes.

Song 19
Highway #17

Like islands lost in a frozen ocean
The towns of Northern Ontario
Spread out along an icy coast
I'm tossed on a snowy sea
On Highway #17.

My windshield's just got one defrosted spot
As I pull out of the parking lot
This map's a game of join the dots
I know cannot be won

Driving downs towards Thunder Bay
Through Dryden, Wabigoon, Ignace
The miles of empty space erase
My senses one by one

Like islands lost in a frozen ocean
The towns of Northern Ontario
Spread out along an icy coast
I'm tossed on a snowy sea
On Highway #17.

From Nipigon to Marathon
Sault Ste. Marie to Thessalon
Through Iron Bridge I travelled on,
Blind River, Espanola

Through Sudbury and Sturgeon Falls
I tried but I just could not recall
Why I followed this road at all
It's swallowed me whole

Like islands lost in a frozen ocean
The towns of Northern Ontario
Spread out along an icy coast
I'm tossed on a snowy sea
On Highway #17.

Chapter Eighteen

Drummer Tells

We got back into our rhythm after a while. I'm not sure what kind of deal MG had made with Miles, since I could tell he had been ready to bail on the whole thing. Somehow, in coming on summer, Northern Ontario starting weaving its magic spell and things seemed to go back to the pattern we were in before the 'Peg. After a couple of shows, Miles took charge of Nelly-Belle again, after she got a whole new clutch put in at Dryden. He got his groove on again writing songs from the previous night's stories, and he pumped out a few more along that road, since songs were always his therapy.

"Farther Along" was written then too, based on our tour through there the year before when we were having a tough winter. It didn't come from an audience member's story but boy, everyone seemed to relate to it. You could tell that Winnipeg had left him frustrated that the band wasn't 'farther along' in their career and that was weighing on him when he was writing it. At the same time, new things were happening that still kept him feeling like something was just around that next bend. Maybe getting out of the prairies was good because now there were *actual* bends in the road.

Song 20
Farther Along

Well in the fall the lonesome tamaracks stand silent and so still,
Scattered golden over those cold Atikokan hills.
Driving down from Dryden, through the new fallen snow,
You know somehow I thought by now I'd be farther along the road
I thought I'd be farther along the road.

In the clear reflection of those frozen northern lakes,
I ponder my direction, wonder at this path I have taken.
All those years of wandering, what have I to show-
You know somehow I thought by now I'd be farther along the road
I thought I'd be farther along the road.

In a highway cafe the waitresses face shows a trace of your sad
smile,
Reaching out to me across those long and lonesome miles.
Once I figured there'd be bigger things for you and I,
But the more I try the more I find I'm falling farther behind

I've been around these pulp mill towns too many times before,
Though I swore in Kenora I wouldn't go back any more.
It's not that I don't like this life- it's a good one I suppose,
It's just somehow I thought by now I'd be farther along the road
I thought I'd be farther along the road.

When Miles would get that songwriting juice flowing, it was amazing to watch. It really made him come alive, and also made you notice how 'un-alive' he had been. When a song was done another one would pop out right after, fully formed and ready to be sung. He called those his 'afterbirth' songs.

Dougie had plenty of wildlife and road kill to call out so he kept himself occupied. "Moose. Moose. Porcupine. Coyote. Naked Roadie. Just Kidding."

MG was frustrated by the lack of Wi-Fi signal across the north, which is kind of like a magic talking stick I guess, cuz once she had it there was no stopping her. When she grabbed it she would whoop and slap Miles on the back and report on how many people were getting into the song downloading and following the tour. We were news. At each town where we'd stop, do a show, and collect a story, *we* were a story to the local press. Yes, some of those places still actually had newspapers. Newspapers were nearly extinct too. Don't get Miles started on that. *And* if I don't mind beating my own drum a bit, I was a bit of an attraction there. Northern Ontario was dotted with lots of reserves and 'townie' Indians. To some of these folks I was someone who 'made good' in the music business before the explosion of Indigenous bands started happening. I always felt kinda weird about that, growing up in white households. A white guy with brown skin really. I was like some kind of pioneer to the Disturber fans, even though the actual pioneers were the ones responsible for the deplorable conditions my people live in to this day. You know me, I don't like attention, but it didn't feel too bad, heh?

By now our shows weren't really shows at all. We had collected enough 'story songs' that we pretty well just did those. People were getting familiar with them on the 'Miles2Go' web thingy, so they'd ask for them. Miles would talk about the tellers behind the songs, and that would just stimulate more stories from the crowd, and boy were there crowds, even in towns that normally couldn't even field a baseball team. Sometimes we'd be booked into a bar but the club owner would hear about what was happening and we'd be switched to the curling club or the community centre or even the salt barns from the Highway Department. Whatever they could find. We had figured with the long distances and all between gigs that no one would follow along, but up in that country ya got a pickup truck ya might as well use 'er, right?

Around Nipigon, home of the 'Nipigon Nylons', the nickname for the wool work socks women wear most of the year there, the caravan following along had taken on a life of its own. They were having their own 'tailgate parties' outside the halls or at the edge of town. Folks would get out the barbeques and the lawn chairs, and they were swapping food and stories all on their own. One guy in an old mail truck started selling 'Gerber Burgers' and 'Drummer Sticks'. Dougie was out of luck I guess. We were getting to be a sideshow to our own show. When they started selling 'Miles2Go' tee-shirts, MG put her cowboy-booted foot down and demanded a piece of that action. We'd join the party after the shows sometimes and were always welcomed as heroes. In those parts there were often fiddlers who would join Dougie in some tunes too. The rule seemed to be 'stories first, then tunes' and the stories could go all night. No one needed them turned into songs anymore, it was the act of telling them that mattered, but Miles' songs were kind of the glue that held the whole thing together.

MG loved the whole thing. She was in high spirits as things grew. Her energy kept things positive and it seemed to gradually shift Miles over away from his thoughts that he was no longer relevant in the show business. Soon she was out in the parking lots organizing the 'camp followers' too. It was a gift she had. Miles was really drawn to that quality. I guess we all were, but I could also tell that sometimes it made him kinda wistful since that was a gift that Maddie had. Has. She's gotta be still somewhere out there.

It was getting pretty bizarre leading a long line of vehicles along the highway, and a bit embarrassing too, since with three middle-aged men in the van we rarely passed a pee stop. Nelly-Belle wasn't the fastest van on the road so there was a bit of a jam-up sometimes. Being in the front still, we tried to carry on as best as we could in our regular touring pattern.

That pattern always included 'Juanita's Diner' in Iron

Bridge, a little town as tough as the rusty structure it was named after.

Juanita's was one of the last of the highway truck stops that hadn't been taken over by one of those big chains. That's why we always went there. Juanita herself was always at the cash register, holding court, dishing out change and wry observations. Wry on Rye is what you got with your runny eggs at Juanita's. Long may they run too. Fiery and curvy, always with a gyspy-style headscarf , she seemed to fulfill the dual fantasy of every long-distance trucker: a mother figure *and* an object of desire. These days it was mostly the 'mother' part that won out, but she could still turn heads while promoting the pie selection. She made everyone feel like part of a big family, which is what everyone wants, really, and if we all felt like that away from her run-down diner then Robert would be your father's brother.

As we walked in from the parking lot we must have built up Juanita's 'legend' status a bit too much, cuz MG seemed kinda disappointed when it looked pretty much like every other joint along the Trans-Canada. We were disappointed too, since Juanita herself was nowhere to be seen.

As soon as we got in the door the truckers all gave a good wolf-whistle to MG. The truck stops, construction sites and bar-rooms were the last bastion of the wolf-whistle, but you'da never guessed it was an endangered tradition by the enthusiasm of those 'good buddies'. MG shut them down pretty quick.

"Chill out fellers, I know you've got trucker bellies on ya, so you don't have to keep sucking them in all the time when a gal like me graces you with her divine presence. That goes for you 'Disturbers' too, right?" We all looked guilty over that, and our digestion was a bit better for the rest of the trip.

We took a booth near the kitchen, and as MG looked over the menu, (we knew it by heart), Miles shushed us and said, "Hey, hear that? Isn't that Kenny Ford?"

"Sounds more like Blake Chesney or George McGraw to me," said Dougie, who thought all country singers sounded the same just like we thought his fiddle tunes all sounded the same.

"No, no, not on the radio, back in the kitchen. Listen! Back there calling out the orders!"

"Who the fuck is Kenny Ford?" said MG with her typical sensitivity.

I answered: "Why, only the best Canadian songwriter to come out of the '80s." At this point Dougie kicked me under the table and I smoothly added, "Except for Miles Gerber of course."

"You never heard "Young Suzette" MG?" I asked. "Kenny wrote that and Miles and Myles covered it; had some real success with it, and it was kind of a foreshadowing of the kind of work Miles is doing these days, right Miles?"

Kenny was known for writing songs after eavesdropping on conversations, like any good writer I guess. They're all thieves really, but more like Robin Hood. Robbing stories then giving them, disguised as songs, to the people.

Miles ducked behind the counter and stormed the kitchen. The whole diner heard him yell out, "Kenny Ford! What's a huge international rock star like you doing in a dump like this?" Kenny hollered back, "Miles Fucking Gerber? I could ask you the same question, pardner!"

Kenny came out, dragged by Miles, threw his apron to a pimply dishwasher kid and said, "Cover for me Angelo, I got some old friends here," before joining us at our booth. It was quite a squeeze since he'd filled out some since we last saw him, but despite the hair-net he was sporting, he still was a commanding figure. I doubt he was commanding five figures a gig anymore though. Heh heh. With his chiseled face, piercing blue eyes and slightly folded frame he looked a bit like Miles on steroids. Kind of a Canadian Johnny Cash, though Canadian cash is worth less, of course. There was a tribal resemblance that MG clearly noticed.

After some classic Canadian-guy back-slapping and shoulder jabbing Miles introduced MG as our new 'Manager and Merch Girl'.

Kenny roared, "Well darlin, these dudes are unmanageable and no one buys merch anymore so that's a pretty sweet gig you got there! And hey, is that the famous Nelly-Belle out in the parking lot? Wow, I figured she would have packed it in by now, but I thought the same about you losers!"

Turns out Kenny, who we used to cross paths with regularly out on the 'Trail of Tears and Beers' was having the same problem as the rest of us in the biz. Running out of road and hope. While he was wondering about what kind of future lay ahead, he dropped into Juanita's diner and shortly afterwards, into her welcoming arms. He was just as bitter as Juanita's coffee about the way artists were being treated these days, but he'd found something here that felt like a good place to press the pause button. Make a new life. Literally new life. Juanita was off that day since she was, as he described it, 'in the family way'.

"I got knocked out of the music biz and got the boss lady knocked up at the same time," boasted Kenny. "I can tell you think I'm slumming it in here, but why is slinging hash less worthy than slinging a guitar?" He was looking pretty comfortable in his new grease-covered skin, and I could see Miles looking at his old friend with a touch of envy even though Kenny had broken the unwritten showbiz code that said you were never allowed to quit, you just had to keep believing that the buffalo were returning, that you'd be back on top with one more hit. I think looking at Kenny made the rest of us realize just how stupid that rule was.

So of course Miles had to include Kenny in his collection of story songs after that. He was starting to be called the story 'harvester' and it was a bit ironic that Miles' song from Kenny's story gave *us* a real boost when MG put it out on that Miles2Go thingy. By that point a lot of the live shows with the new songs were being filmed for YouTube as well. "For Free" was Kenny's story, and he's *in* the song, but you can tell that this was Miles' excuse to make a kind of political statement about the state of the biz.

Song 21
For Free

Guess I don't look like my album covers anymore
But every now and then I still get recognized
They say "hey didn't you used to be that Kenny Ford?"
 I say "I still am, do you want that with fries?"

If I serve you a coffee and a butter tart
In this run-down diner you expect to pay
But if I serve you up a song that comes straight from the heart
You expect me to give it all away

You want me to cry
You want me to bleed
And at the same time be the flavour of the week
Doesn't matter if I
Got mouths to feed
You want me to give it all away for free

They say "Hey I hear you all the time on Spotify!"
I tell them "honestly I really am quite thrilled"
It doesn't seem to mean a whole lot if I
Tell them that won't really pay my bills

I find myself saying "Hey Pal you
Used to put a little value
On what folks like me are working hard to do
We tried to raise you up out of this shit
Cheer you up a little bit
Give you something that was real and true
Is it too much to ask for a little back from you?"

You get a refill on that java if you want some
In this joint you get a bottomless cup
But it's not a bottomless well us writers draw from
It takes a little help from you to fill it up.

I wish that Miles had that "For Free" song in his pocket in the diner that day. Instead, after Kenny started getting razzed by the regulars for abandoning his line-cook duties, Miles jumped up onto the counter and started into one of his patented rants. "Two kinds of people in this world, Kenneth. People who care about our creators, our story- tellers, our culture keepers, our songworkers, and selfish assholes like too many of us have become."

"Here we go," we all said, even Kenny, who whispered "He still does this, eh?"

"It's worse than ever," me and Dougie said in unison.

Miles continued despite our glares.

"You don't even know what kind of a national treasure you have, modestly working away hear at Juanita's! This man," (that man was now back at the grill trying to catch up since Angelo was floundering), "This remarkable gift of a man, has been carrying forward your voices, your tales, your worries, your dreams, for a generation with his amazing songs, and what does he have to show for it? Maybe a share of the tips at the end of a long day. He's just about the last of a dying breed. Why are they dying? Because pirates like you think you can just take what he's offering, what *we* are offering, for free. Just because the corporate rip-off technology you are crazy for allows you to steal doesn't mean you SHOULD, bozos! How would you like it if I asked you truckers to ship your asses all over the country for nothing?"

"It's pretty close to nothing these days," called out one nervous diner.

"When you steal something, think of who you are stealing from! This is a good guy. He deserves some respect." Miles was winding up.

"Unlike you," shouted another trucker. "Sit the fuck down."

Miles looked ready to go for that dude, when he got tackled from behind by Kenny himself, to a round of applause.

"Breakfast to go, maybe fellas, and you m'lady?" he said, picking Miles off the floor, and promising to stay in touch while hustling us out the back way through the kitchen, filling a bag with Juanita's famous butter tarts as we rushed towards Nelly-

Belle.

"You almost got us fucking killed, Miles," snarled Dougie.

"You mean by going into the music business?" answered Miles.

Me, I didn't say anything. A real specialty of mine.

There was a real party going on in the parking lot and along the shoulder of the highway. The Miles followers were having a communal smorgasbord, waiting patiently for their leaders to carry on towards Espanola. They were all following MG's tweety-thingy now so they knew where we were headed, but still chose to follow behind.

Things were pretty quiet in Nelly-Belle the rest of the way.

MG broke the silence by saying to Miles: "Bad Bandleader! Next time you have to stay in the car! It's just another week till we hit the Horseshoe in Toronto, boys. Try to keep it together till then, kay?"

Chapter Nineteen

Nelly-Belle Tells

I don't know what happened at that diner in Iron Bridge, but my passengers were very quiet about it after they jumped into me looking like they were being chased by hornets.

I'd actually been having a great time myself in Juanita's parking lot. The 'Miles2Go' caravan was growing by the day as word spread. It was coming on summer and more people were able to tag along for something cool to do, I guess. They were all very friendly and when the driving stopped, the party started. I had a lot of other autos to chat with, including a handsome black Jetta whose name actually was 'Otto'.

Folks would gather around, sometimes with us 4-wheeled ones in a circle around *their* circle. We shared stories just like the 'passengers' did. Ours were mostly road stories of course, and we'd compare repairs, dents and accident tales. Not that different than humans I guess, but not as whiny.

We headed east towards Espanola, another pulp mill town, and the 'gateway to Manitoulin Island'. We were booked into the 'Ranch'. You guessed it. A country bar, that still had a stripper night where they advertised 'Tuesdays: Ranch Undressing'. Har Dee Har.

Miles was still riled up from his visit to Juanita's, and I got the gist of it when he pulled out his guitar and started writing "For Free" right then. Drummer said that he had captured his old friend Kenny Ford's story perfectly, and used the back of the driver's seat to beat time with his ever-present drumsticks. Dougie had the harmonies in the chorus and bridge figured out in no time flat, (well, 4/4 time and Bflat). He didn't pull out an instrument since he was sticking to their 'practicing is for wimps' stance. The song made its debut at 'The Ranch' along with the latest story songs from Thunder Bay, Sault Ste. Marie and other stops along the way. I know I know, I missed a few.

There's too many to tell you about. I hope Drummer is filling in the details for you.

"For Free" seemed a bit cathartic for Miles and he loosened up a bit, so MG felt safe filling them in on what she'd been doing with her fancy devices. She'd already booked a tour of the maritime provinces starting almost right after the Toronto date. The boys always liked it down east but it was hard to make a buck there. Not that they were making a real buck anywhere. For one thing, there were fewer bucks to go round, but also because down east they had so much fine music of their own that they didn't need imports like the Disturbers. MG said it would be a perfect next step since Miles was now catching all this attention for catching the mood of the nation through the Miles2Go phenomenon. And what better story-tellers than the Maritimers? *And*, she said that the distances between gigs are pretty good, so it would be easier for the new fans to follow the tour like they'd been doing, and easier on Nelly-Belle.

The lads didn't seem to be able to think that far ahead, so they kind of ignored her. Miles seemed leery about 'the Ranch', mentioning 'that incident' from last time. MG asked him about it but he said she wouldn't want to know.

"Remind me. It doesn't have a mechanical bull, does it?" he asked Dougie. Those creepy mechanical distractions from the music on stage seemed to be his measure for 'Turbulence Ahead', which co-incidentally was the name of the warm-up act a few nights back.

"No, Miles. You've got enough bull yourself to spread around that joint."

We pulled into Espanola a lot later than scheduled. It wasn't my fault really. Miles knew that my oil light didn't work and that I required frequent checking. He usually stayed right on top of that, but was clearly distracted. We had to make a pit stop in Blind River after I started coughing and wheezing. Of course Blind River was famous for a mention in the Neil Young song "Long May You Run". The boys would often sing that for me as we chugged into town, since it's about a car, and we always hoped that I wouldn't repeat history by breaking down there the way Neil's hearse did. Mr. Young of course also mentions Northern Ontario in his song "Helpless", a sentiment we often felt a kinship with along that long and winding road. Oh wait, that's another song.

Well, wouldn't you know it though, there I was, holding up the show probably at the same garage where Neil had to give his hearse a death sentence. Spooky. I lurched in to the gig although I could tell that Miles was worried about me. He's sweet. I ended up right beside a big reefer truck. His motor was idling to keep his cargo cool. Pee U. His name was Mack, which was just as predictable for semis as 'Ranch' was for country bars.   He was from California, which kind of grinded my gears a bit. Hadn't seen that place in a few years. That's where most of the cars go around topless.

I asked him what he was carrying.

"MP8. 505 Horsepower. 1860 Torque. Wave Piston. The Works," he said with a drawl, since he had been assembled in Hagerstown, Maryland. That was mighty impressive. Those brash Americans want to get right down to what's under the hood, but that's not what I wanted to know.

"I mean, what's in the trailer?"

His answer wasn't quite so cocky. "Broccoli," he said, almost apologetically.

I stifled a giggle.

"I can sense that you think that's amusing, Missy," he said, "but it's no joke."

"Well, I didn't mean to laugh. I guess big ol' you and a bunch of vegetables seems a bit, well, incongruous. And besides, we grow a ton of broccoli right here in Ontario so what brings you all this way, stranger?"

"Don't get me started" he said, and then he started.

He talked about how it costs truckers like his owner more to haul that broccoli than he gets paid for trucking it, what with the price of gas and all. Kind of like Burt raising his sheep. He said, "It's a losing game. *And* the goddamned 'go local' movement is slicing into business in a big way because people don't like the frigging carbon footprint of the food we haul. The only footprint I'd like to see is the bootprint on the asses of all those foodie activists who are putting us out of business!"

"Besides," he continued, "with climate change and the drought in California sucking up all their water, and the folks wanting to buy local even if it means they can't get everything all year round, basically I'm driving myself into extinction.

Weren't we all.

We were chatting away when I felt something weird in my nether regions. In the rear view mirror I could see a stream of oil leaking out behind me.

Uh Oh. Incontinence. How embarrassing.

Chapter Twenty

Drummer Tells

Espanola always sounded like a nasty version of the Spanish Influenza to me. And there's no cure. The place did seem kind of under the weather too.

MG was busy ringleading. I was ringfollowing. There was quite a crowd gathered in the parking lot of 'The Ranch', including a TV crew from CTN. We were still news apparently, except it looked like the caravan was more a story than we were.

MG noticed that the lot was full but the club was not. This was not cool with the Ranch manager. He looked like every bar manager we'd crossed paths with in the last month. A cross between an undertaker and a stevedore.

MG smiled her killer smile at him and said, "What if we just put this operation outside, and you'd have way more thirsty customers to serve. It's such a fine summer night, darlin." For some reason MG was back to her southern accent, which she used when she wanted to get males to do her bidding. She needn't have bothered. They always seemed to do that anyway.

"Honey," the manager said. "You're in Ontario, the province with the most anal liquor laws in the country. Maybe the world. We can't sell booze outside. We'll lose our license."

They worked out a deal. She asked him if he had a roll of drink tickets anywhere. He did, from when the place was rented out for wedding receptions. It somehow made me sad to think that newlyweds with their future spread out in front of them with hope and promise would choose a place where every carpet stain had a story that usually involved an arrest, but hey. In those parts you couldn't be too choosy, I guess. After a bit more manager wrangling, MG went out and stood on Nelly Belle's roof and got me to lay on the horn till she got the attention of the throng.

"Hi everyone! Welcome to the hauntingly beautiful 'Ranch'. Espanola's finest!" she yelled.

"Espanola's only, you mean"! shouted back a caravanner.

"Whatever!" she said back. "We're delighted that you all came. One small problem. There's more of you than will fit in this fine club, and Bart, our extremely handsome bar manager says that you can't park here unless you've paid the cover to the show. We'd love you to stay and enjoy the Miles2Go experience, and Bart the Sweetheart says we can move the show out here if you just buy a ticket and display it on your vehicle dashboard." This was obviously news to Bart but it looked too complicated to contest the matter.

"Now this remarkable waitress in those daring Daisy Dukes, Linda here, will come around and give you a ticket in exchange for one of those nice Green Queen twenty-dollar bills!" Poor Linda looked like she hadn't stepped outside the bar since the '80s. She also looked like Bart had forced her to wear those too-short shorts and heels in order to keep her job.

In short order the gear was outside on the porch and the show was taking shape. MG had something else up her sleeve. Some of the caravanners had their guitars and the odd banjo, (they're all odd), and had been following Miles' lead, writing their own songs that captured the feel of the 'Miles2Go' movement, which by golly it surely was by now. She organized a bit of an open stage despite Miles' abhorrence of the concept. The TV crew loved this and it helped spread the 'movement's' message far and wide. I watched these performers with the boys. Some of them were pretty good and they'd sure captured the spirit. Miles seemed to like it after his earlier grumblings. Being imitated can be lawsuit material or it can be flattering. Miles took the high road on this.

When our turn came, we started strong with a couple of our so-called hits and then launched into the brand-new "For Free", which seemed to boost CD sales without the scolding this time.

'Story Time' seemed to go better than the songs themselves, with everyone cheering on the tellers. Several of those who shared their tales were interviewed for the TV too.

The show seemed to naturally drift into a jam session, and tents started to pop up around the vehicles. They weren't going anywhere. Bart could see the advantage in offering the washroom for the night and breakfast in the morning, and suddenly it was a festival.

Towards the end of the more 'formal' part of the proceedings, Miles thanked the crowd and, seeming a bit confused, asked MG where the next stop was.

She took the mic and announced, "Friends. We're all in this together now. Can you all meet at 10 in the morning out in front of the Manitoulin Welcome Centre out there at the turnoff? We need to plan our future together!"

"So you're managing the audience now too?" said Dougie, sounding as bitter as that morning's coffee.

"I'm facilitating a collaborative process, Dougie," she said, with that cheek kiss that kept him in line and still smitten.

The Ranch still had a band room, a holdover from those days I was telling you about before. Those days were gone, but out of respect for heritage I guess, the room had been untouched and uncleaned since the golden age. One week in that room would have done us in for sure, eh? Holy Smokers it was rough. We were pretty bushwhacked though, and MG slyly said she had another 'option' for the night. The three of us were too tired to even wonder what that meant.

Chapter Twenty-One

Nelly-Belle Tells

All I remember was feeling my bodily fluids draining out of me. My life passed before my headlights. A hard life, yes, but I felt loved and I had a sense of purpose. Who could ask for more than that? I was part of a team.

I had visions of being born at the Oakville plant. Shiny and new rolling off the line. Birthed by workers with good jobs who cared about me.

Dirt roads. Open highways. Driving along the beach in Tofino. The wide open prairies. Keeping watch over the band outside the motel rooms. Protecting my precious cargo along icy roads. And always, Miles' hands caressing my steering wheel and talking to me long into the night.

Suddenly I was awakened. I was moving and a stranger was behind the wheel! Had I been stolen? Carjacked? Van-jacked?

I heard voices. I was being towed! How humiliating!

Gradually sorting out the chatter, I learned that I had passed out after a major oil leak. Caravanners with mechanical know-how—which describes anybody along the northern Ontario Trans-Canada route really, do-it-yourselfers all of them—were underneath me and under my hood, sussing out the problem, and I guess it was bad news. It was Sunday morning too. No garage with an emergency room. The whole gang was moving over from the Ranch to the Welcome Centre just back up the highway a ways.

Nice of them to take me along.

The verdict wasn't good. Pretty much a heart transplant, though I was still aware, still feeling a desire to rock, but mostly to roll.

There was no sign of MG although she was supposed to be in charge of this operation. I could tell that the boys hadn't seen her either since last night, even though I heard Dougie say that they sure had lots to talk about.

The parking lot was buzzing with people. There was a sense of confusion. Now me, I like a parking lot. It's like a motel for me, but the two-legged ones, that's not as much a natural habitat so some looked ready to blow.

The Disturbers were standing around chatting with caravanners, even the ever-shy Miles, but looking around for MG. I used to know a cute van named Cara by the way.

The CTN RV pulled up. A camera person jumped out and started to set up. Then the reporter, Roxy, who had clearly gotten the job because she looked like every other female on-air reporter is required to look these days, (blonde, twenty-something, generically attractive in a kind of sanitized way, powder blue pant suit, a walking cliché, you get the picture), emerged with MG in hand. They gave a long movie-style embrace and a kiss that melted my tires.

"Holy Shit," said Dougie.

"Ditto," said Drummer and Miles together.

"Look what I found, boys!" MG beamed. Roxy patted MG's butt but put her hand on her lips to signify that, in her employment situation, probably mum could be the word for a while.

"Holy shit," repeated all three eloquent band members, who had found an appropriate expression and were running with it.

Drummer and Miles looked as deflated as my left rear tire. Another road fantasy gone down the drain. Dougie looked as if that tire had blown up in his face, a face that seemed to be trying on some appropriate expressions, but had given up and just went for the 'stunned' appearance that was kind of a default position for him. Trying to recover, he whispered to his mates, "Maybe she goes both ways!"

MG overheard and cracked, "Dougie, I ride the highway, not the Bi-Way. Sorry."

The boys were quiet after that. As for me, I say whatever puts the gas in your tank is alright by me.

There was a commotion as another caravan of trucks started to pull into the already crowded parking lot.

Dougie: "It's a bloody circus".

Miles: "Tell me about it."

Dougie: "No I mean, it's actually a circus."

Miles: "No kidding."

Dougie: "No. Not kidding. Over there. Regardez-vous. Are they joining us?"

Miles: "May as well, they'll feel right at home".

Dougie: "Do circuses have a home?"

Miles: "Do musicians? We certainly don't need any more clowns."

Transport trucks. Some RVs decked out like gypsy caravans, (though I heard MG schooling her pals about how 'gyspy' was really a racial slur so we have to stop using it, even though that's often what they call travelling musicians. The language is tricky these days, especially for automobiles). A couple of tired looking midway rides. Everything emblazoned with what I'm guessing were once bright reds and blues with faded signs that proclaimed 'Sycamore Sister's Sircus and Clown College'. One faded but elegant trailer all decked out fancy-like had a sign that said 'Madam Claire Voyant: Mind Reader, Fortune Teller, and Futurist', and since the operation had apparently fallen on hard times, a smaller sign tacked below that added 'And Manicurist'.

"Sisters!" yelled Roxy and MG, still arm and arm.

"Sisters?" muttered most of the rest.

"Death defying feats and gender stereotype bending at the same time," said Roxy, "My kind of circus!."

Some of the circus folk emerged sleepily from their vehicles, looking, well, like circus people, though denim rather than spandex seemed to be their fashion statement of choice.

MG disengaged from Roxy and climbed up onto a converted bread truck that advertised 'Ty Dye the Hippy Fry Guy' and his specialty: deep-fried parsnip and plantain chips with black fly sauce. Lucky vans don't eat food. Sheesh. MG had a megaphone now and she got everyone's attention:

"Ok fellow travellers. Sorry I'm a bit late. It's wonderful to see everyone here, and a special welcome to those who have just joined us." There was some bicycle horn honking from the circus section of the lot. "I have a few announcements, then I'd like to hear from you all."

"What are we, chopped liver?" said Dougie to Miles. "We're not the centre ring in *this* circus anymore it feels like."

"Shut up, Morrison," said Miles.

MG continued, "I want to thank Miles Gerber and his Excellent Excrement Disturbers over here for inspiring this exciting journey that we are all on." There were cheers and applause, with car and bicycle horns added in. The boys waved meekly but looked worried, as if this was their retirement speech coming up.

"And a bit of news. Looks like Nelly-Belle here is in critical condition."

I was? What?

"The band's next gig is actually in two days, at the legendary Horseshoe Tavern in Toronto. They'll have to leave Nelly-Belle behind until she can get back on her wheels again. Would anyone volunteer to drive the band down there?" Many hands went up. "Thanks a bunch. Could you go over to talk with Miles about this? Nelly-Belle is his sweetheart, so he'll be pining for her, but he'll be ok. Right, boss?"

Miles clearly didn't know what to say. He looked pretty overwhelmed. It was like his rad cap was loose and you could almost see steam coming out of his ears.

"Now here's the thing, though. I'm wondering if it makes since for us all to make the trek into the big city. What do you think?"

There was much chatter amongst the crowd.

A young woman with a baby on her sturdy shoulders piped up to say, "Do you mean we should all go home? I just joined at the Soo and I'm kinda getting into this!"

There was more chatter and confused looks.

"Not at all," said MG. "Here's what I've been thinking!" She held up a bunch of brochures from the info centre about the **Wiikwemkoong Cultural Festival,** which she said was more commonly known as the **Manitoulin Pow Wow.**

"Folks," she continued into the bullhorn, "We can't just keep driving."

"Why not?" shouted some of the throng in almost unison.

Roxy chimed in with her news reporter voice which automatically made everyone listen, "Well, for one thing, the ecological footprint of these vehicles is unsustainable." She smiled and handed back the megaphone to an admiring MG.

"What the?" said more than one quizzical caravanner. A burly guy in biker leathers and a red bandana shouted, "I think what that little filly means is that gas ain't cheap anymore."

"That's not what she means at all," called out another.

Chaos developed wings and flapped around for a moment, or maybe it was just the dust coming off the gravel in the parking lot.

"What Roxy is saying," continued MG, "is that we are building something beautiful here, and I figure it would just flower and blossom all the more if we stayed put for a while and really dreamed about where this could all lead. You've been chasing Miles for miles. You've caught him. Maybe we could try letting others come to us for a while. Now, Manitoulin island is a very magical place, as many of you know."

From the chatter in the crowd it didn't really look like there was many of them who knew. One loud voice complained that there was only one 'Timmies' on the whole island.

"Time to read from the brochure, Roxy," said MG, handing back the megaphone.

Roxy knew a thing or two about reading a script, you could tell, and she made the kind of dry text sound like a late-breaking news story:

"Manitoulin Island is unique in many ways – it is the world's largest fresh water island. It has more than a hundred inland lakes between its shores, and many of those lakes have islands on them! There are more than two dozen small settlements, First Nations and towns spread out across more than 160 kilometres of Boreal forest, lakes, rivers, shorelines, escarpments, and meadows. The people and the communities have emerged through a history as colourful and complex as any in Canada – from the fur trade to free trade, from the Ice Age to the New Age"

"Who wrote that? Margaret Backwood?" muttered MG.

Roxy continued: *"Our history shows through at every turn, from fossils to lighthouses, under these same stars, with Native and non-Native communities across the Island co-existing like nowhere else on the continent. As a result, it is a place of stories."*

That perked everyone up. "Stories!" That was a buzz word for the Throng.

"It says here that, *'The Manitoulin Island lifestyle continues as it has for generations – in close mutual relationship with the environment and resources of the land. It is a peaceful and spiritual place. It is a place of important community knowledge and traditional skills, and a place where this knowledge and these skills are shared openly and generously'."*

"Sounds like us!" shouted the Throng, almost as one.

MG took back the megaphone and the focus of the crowd.

"Now Roxy tells me she has a friend with a farm not far from the Pow Wow grounds. The Sycamore Sisters here are thinking of setting up their tents and such there, and we could make an awesome circle out of our flotilla here. We could rest and restore and share stories in the LAND of stories!"

Roxy again: "You'll love my friend Maxine, and she'd welcome you all if you helped get her hay crop in!"

"Her name's Maxine?" called out an incredulous crowdster.

"Yup. Maxine Yasgur"

"Are you fucking kidding me?" could be heard by many of the older hippie-types in the throng.

"Nope. Who's In?"

Chapter Twenty-Two

Drummer Tells

Well, things were changing faster than I could think. I figure Miles actually hired me because I wasn't going to overthink things; that and I could count to four and I had my own chopped down drum kit that fit into Nelly's Belly without much trouble. Speaking of trouble, I had been mostly staying out of it.

A lot to take in. The band heading to Toronto with someone else driving us in a vehicle that wasn't Nelly-Belle? MG leading her tribe to the promised land? Maybe MG stands for Moses Goddess or some darned thing. I dunno. Where did I fit in to all this? Why am I asking you, Bic?

To be honest, the way things had been going, Miles didn't really need me that much.

When he'd been doing these instant songs, everyone was really listening closely; I was feeling like a distraction as they're pretty much ballads that just needed brushes or hand percussion anyway. Any fool could do that. Not just this fool.

The parade to the farm sounded interesting, and I'd been enjoying all the camp followers, but really, all I could think about was that Pow Wow. My new friends back in Winnipeg really talked a lot about Pow Wow Power. I didn't tell them that I had never been to one. They seemed to think that was how you could connect to your people, find your sense of place and purpose, and recharge your batteries. We were heading that way, and it was just getting set up that very day, so I figured that was some sort of sign, eh?

There actually *was* a sign in the Welcome Centre beside a picture of the Pow Wow that said, I kid you not, 'Drummer Wanted'. Well, we all want to be wanted I guess, so I gathered up my courage, my backpack, and my hand drum and went to tell Miles that I'd catch up with them when they came back from Toronto. Don't remember making a choice for myself before. It felt good!

Miles and Dougie both gave little speeches about how we couldn't separate the band, and how badly they *did* need me, ya da ya da; but it was a pretty lame pitch and I could tell they knew that I was right. They were already loading gear into the fan's van, who was being a little too helpful. Never fuss with another man's stuff on the road. They'd head out soon and get in a night early to do interviews the next day, all laid out by MG on an actual itinerary. We gave the usual awkward Canadian man-goodbyes, and a few repetitions of 'take 'er easy', which actually passes for affection in their world which maybe wasn't going to be mine soon.

Unaccustomed as I was to being right, I headed out to tell MG, which was tougher cuz *she's* tougher. She made a deal. She'd help me get there if I promised that I'd return to the 'fold' as soon as I was done, and share the experience with the growing gang. The promise was sealed with the kind of hugging that left me both appreciative and wondering why guys can't do that, though it felt a little different, maybe better, now that she had shown her rainbow colours. She looked at me, misfit to misfit, and said, "Drummer do you think I know what I'm doing here"?

I answered with the same question, "Do *you* think you know what you are doing?"

"Not at all" she said, dropping her eyes to her boots and looking for a sec like a scared teenager, which maybe she was underneath her tough-chick surface.

I answered: "Well, then you are just like everybody else, so you'll be fine!"

On MG's suggestion I went looking for some clown to drop me off on the way to whatever-the-hell she had up her Manstead's little-old-lady-blouse sleeve. I guess she was having a laundry crisis too. Not that she was ever really lady-like, or old, and she was little only in height. A giant in every other way.

The procession out of the parking lot was stalled for a bit while the van containing Miles and Dougie paraded around with grand celebration. They were waving queen-style from their host's van, which actually was a Dodge Caravan. Circus folks on stilts and unicycles were waving banners. What was left of the circus band was attempting Miles' "Continental Drift". Two bikers out front escorted the van out onto the highway towards Sudbury. The whole nine yards. Well, maybe eight. It was as if two devotees had been chosen to be thrown into the volcano known as Toronto as a sacrifice to the gods. I had figured that the TV crew would follow them since they were supposed to be the story, right? But Roxy and company seemed to be following a bigger story now, though no one was sure what it was. The CTN motor home, with MG barking megaphone orders out the window, headed south down Highway #6.

I was tempted to sit in Nelly-Belle after she got loaded onto a circus flatbed truck for the journey, but it didn't look too safe the way they'd tied her on with binder twine and some mic cables. As promised, I found the 'clown car' and was welcomed in with a rousing, "Always room for one more!"

As we got underway, I was thinking of you, reporter guy. I guess I blew it. Sorry. Having said I'd document the trip for you, I was about to miss one of the crucial parts. The press was apparently already billing their Horseshoe appearance as the 'culmination of a triumphant adventure', an important statement about our current society, blah blah blah, where the stories and songs collected would be shared for an eager national audience. You'll have to piece it together yourself, Bic, unless a miracle happens and the boys decide to tell you themselves. By the way, I ran out of cassettes back aways, but MG had me talking into her fancy-pantsy digital recorder. She did some transferring so you should get this somehow or other. She even gave me the loan of this 'Zoom' contraption I'm talking ever-so slickly into right now. Yee Haw. Do I sound like some sort of techno guy or what? Hope you're ready for all this. Holy. I think you unleashed something in me. And from what I'm learning about my heritage, being leashed is a real sticky point. Thanks buddy.

That led to the next thought. I was headed for my own adventure at the Pow Wow, but you didn't want MY story, right? I said too much about my visit to the 'Forks' probably. Did I get permission from Clover and Mose and those guys about sharing their story? No. Dammit all to bloody hell. And who'd want to know about that? And besides, if I reported about the Pow Wow, I'm not sure what I could tell you. I'm learning about my past as I go. And one thing I NOW know is that I cannot pretend to speak for my Indigenous sisters and brothers. I can only tell my own story from my heart. So I'll catch up with you a bit later on. Are the boys returning to Manitoulin after their gig, or are they continuing east towards the mecca of story-telling, the Maritimes? Wow, now your story has suspense to it. You're welcome.

Chapter Twenty-Three

Nelly-Belle Tells

I was dual exhausted, and after humbly accepting the fact that I was not moving under my own steam, and grumbling a lot as they winched me up onto the back of the circus flatbed, which looked like it was steam-operated, it was actually kind of nice up on top and near the front of the parade. If you want a bed by the way, flat is always best I'd say. It was kinda comfy up there and I could see for miles. But not Miles. That felt weird.

I didn't like the way they tied me on to the truck. I was never that into bondage, and of course I've never enjoyed guys crawling around underneath. I'm a modest gal, really, but once we got rolling I started to enjoy the view in my rearview mirrors. Well, mirror. Musta lost one when they were jostling me around.

The caravan was getting longer all the time. We autos measure distance in car-lengths, and I figured there was about seventy-five of those; a couple dozen just from our new followers in the circus. Or were they leaders?

I could see:

About 30% pickup trucks. I never got the popularity of the pickup in the north country. They're empty most of the time, and like whiskey, they shouldn't really go with ice. Pickups owe their popularity to gravelly-voiced narrators on slick TV commercials pumping up the macho nature of those beasts, even if their main use is to pile 4-across into the cramped cabs to drive kids to school. Don't get me wrong, I've met some nice pickups in my day. If you had met that silver-tongued Silverado in Camrose like I did, you'd know the other reason they called them pick-ups.

Rez cars. A bunch of them. Beater Buicks and Pontiacs mostly. Unsuited to their environment but cheap and you can drive along any northern highway and find replacement parts easily. Why do we like to name cars after the Indigenous peoples displaced by car-loving settlers? Pontiac, Dakota, Cherokee, the pretentious 'Grand Cherokee', Comanche, Aztec, Winnebago, Cheyenne, Apache. Sheesh.

SUVs. Always thought that stood for 'Substandard Urban Vehicle'. Whatever it means, most of these ones were older models since our gathering wasn't really attracting the income bracket that you need to be in now to buy a new one.

A few compacts, which I always thought was a verb describing what happens when one of those tin cans gets in an accident.

Not too many vans; we're a dying breed, especially this one.

The circus vehicles: trucks, buses, and trailers, most of them looking like rejects from that Mad Max movie I saw at the drive-in. They had once all been painted the same reddish colour but now rust was the predominant look. The flotilla included the caravan's only 18-wheeler, an ancient Mack that folks were saying contained the big top tent.

I know I know, you probably want to know who was *in* these vehicles. Well, humans all look kind of the same to me. This Miles2Go crew was mostly misfits, freaks, rejects, outsiders; my kind of people that the new circus folks fit right in with. Now that I wasn't being driven, I could see that *they* all felt driven. I could feel their energy, though mine was low. They were on some sort of mission, and although they didn't seem to be sure what it meant, for many of them that was a new and welcome feeling.

The flatbed started to talk to me once I got settled in. He coughed a lot when he spoke. I wondered if there were girl flatbeds. Times are changing. He had a gruff voice that seemed to emanate from his gearbox. Friendly truck bedside manner. He was older than me I bet, though I couldn't see his face.

"Folks call me Clutch," he said, "and you'll see why when we hit that next hill."

He explained that his 'bed' was available to me because he used to carry the 'cup and saucer' ride on his back from the carnival part of the circus. Some ways back they'd sold it for scrap to pay for gas. It was too quaint for kids to want to ride these days anyways. If you are paying money for a ride, apparently now you want to see at least a possibility of death. Sad days for the carnival and circus biz. Not so different from the music biz I guess. People used to go to the circus for the sense of wonder it created. Now they're getting that on a little screen in their hands, and they 'wonder' why circuses exist.

"We're trying to find a good end for it all," Clutch said, which was Miles' story too.

I could see the 'Clown College' sign on the back of his cab. I asked him about it.

"When Claire Voyant took this thing over," he said, "we were looking for any angle to keep afloat. You have to diversify. Our clowns were serious about their craft, and despite the disinterest from the new generation of screen-gazers they would give classes when we'd stop in a town. We only got the towns that were too small for the Ringling Brothers, although I hear they are going tits up soon too. Sad. Clowning was an ancient art form for humans, and for cars. Remember the Lada? Total clown car. The whole deal is based around turning what's 'normal' upside down. People laugh when we see that, but it's often that kind of laughter that hides their uneasiness. Clowns seem jolly but they have sad faces. Everything about them is exaggerated. They are anarchists and disrupters, which in my view we need, so we can reinvent the steering wheel before we all go off the rails. Ok, mixed metaphor there. Flatbeds aren't poets. Clowns are not so subtly pointing out how silly humans are by pushing 'silly' to a dangerous level. By playing 'the fool' the two-legged ones recognize how foolish *they* are too! Kids understand clowns because they don't have a fully formed view of 'normal'. That's why they laugh and cry often at the same time."

I told him about the recent journey The Disturbers were on, noting similarities to his crew, and since stories and songs have become the common currency of this tour, I asked him if he could tell the tale of his outfit.

"Funny you should say currency," Clutch said with a real

grind in his voice. "When Claire bought the operation from the Sisters she got it for a song! Isn't that the currency of the band you are dragging around?" He went down into an ominous-sounding low gear for a bit and continued: "The Sycamore Sisters were a high wire act in the days when that was the centre piece of any circus. By-the-by Nelly-Girl, are you into Etymology at all?"

"No, I'm afraid of bugs," I replied, trying to wiggle my wipers a bit coquettishly.

"Har har," bellowed Clutch. "A circus was originally any circle where magic happens. Humans still gather in circles if they want to tap into the mystic. There used to be four sisters until one fell off the wire right in front of a big crowd one night in Toledo. That gave the remaining three: Sally, Sadie, and Sarah, the heebies *and* the jeebies, and they preferred to get high in other ways rather than head up a rope ladder. That was the '60s after all. They started to run the show rather than be in it. They bought the whole operation from their dad, Seymour, who had been a real pioneer in the 'human cannonball' shtick. Remember that? The gals' mom Stella used to get all their marital conflict out by blasting him across the three rings twice a day. Hauling that cannon around was hell at the border and Seymour's nerves were shot anyway so they sold the whole rig to Hugo Zachini. Without the high wire and the cannon, the circus was down two big draws, but for a time the gals did well as kind of an alternative circus. Precursors of that French-Canadian outfit I guess. They were a kind of hippy circus, with the accent on artistry and beauty and peace and love and all that crap.

Madame Voyant joined towards the end of that lost decade too. Her mind-reading act was pretty convincing, and her stage presence was undeniable. She could hold the whole crowd enthralled by picking random audience members and revealing their whole story. I know she had tricks of the trade, but I ain't tellin,' Nelly. That would spoil the magic. Have you seen her? I think she drew a crowd just for her striking appearance. Half angel, half devil, half trickster. Ok my math ain't too good. She's in that trailer behind us that's decked out like an old horse-drawn caravan. She doesn't come out much these days. I don't know what the deal is.

Anyway, she helped the Sisters a lot, and she bought *them* out when they retired, though they kept the name. It was Claire who initiated things that were politically correct but tough to sell. She banned animals for starters. Then she made the whole operation a co-op, and insisted on a living wage. They even unionized. Up until then most of the characters in the carny side of the show made their real money with side hustles that she thought gave the outfit a bad name. She was right, but along with everything else we're kind of just doing this out of habit like your band, right? Claire seems to be thinking a lot about 'transitions' and maybe that's where we're both headed now. Hold on, sharp corner ahead, and some clowns tied you on kind of slap-dash!"

We were getting close. The parade pulled up in front of the entrance to the Pow Wow. After Drummer squeezed out of the clown car, I could see him thanking his driving companions, and follow the line of vehicles until he climbed back inside me for a bit. This held up the show for a while, but I could hear him talking fast into that new trendy recorder he borrowed from MG. He scooped it up, climbed out, slapped me on the arse and checked once more to make sure his drum kit was safe inside me. We all sent him off with a horn tribute, though there was no one to honk mine. I saw him walking uneasily towards the mystery that lay ahead. It was very dramatic watching him go, then he spoiled the moment. Maybe cold feet, I don't know. We could all see that the Pow Wow was still getting ready. Teepees going up. Booths. Folks gathering. It looked a bit like what we had going on actually. It looked so cool that we lost a few of our bunch who drove in to see if they could help. Whatever it was, Drummer turned around, recorder thingy in his hand, and ran up to MG and Roxy who were canoodling outside the media truck. He looked embarrassed, especially when MG centred him out and announced over her megaphone: "Drummer here figures he should see where we're setting up camp and all, so he knows where to find us after the Pow Wow, or maybe that sendoff you gave him was so nice, he wants to do it twice!" He scowled since that last part was just to get his goat, which was one of her hobbies. He climbed in with MG and Roxy for the last little leg of the journey.

Just a few more clicks and we eased our way down the farm lane. Maxine was at the entrance guiding us in, a real earth-mother type with wild curly earth-brown hair, overalls and rubber boots. She was full of welcoming joy, but you could see that she was wondering if she was getting a bit more than she had bargained for.

Maxine had mowed a big field in preparation for our arrival. MG had leapt out of the media truck and was standing in the middle of the field, encouraging everyone to gather their vehicles in a circle. Not too big. Not too little, just like the Winnipeg song. The crew boss from the circus, a tall and graceful woman named Sam, with a long ponytail in a braid that would put an actual pony to shame, seemed to take charge of logistics. She looked more like a dancer than a tent putter-upper, and it turned out she was both. She marked out where the big tent would fit and used rope to indicate where the two smaller tents would go beside the big top. So they *had* rope! Why had they tied me to Clutch so haphazardly then? As soon as that thought had passed through my spark plugs Clutch seemed to break ranks and headed straight across the middle of the circle. Waved off he took the turn a bit tight and a bit fast and I broke free and I rolled out of Clutch's clutches and landed butt first on the ground. Ouch! It was a soft landing though because about twenty pairs of strong hands were there in an instant to guide me into an upright position. Sam looked at MG, nodded, and MG announced, "OK, Nelly-Belle here is how this 'Miles2Go' adventure kept rolling, so she's in the centre ring". Sam motioned the crew to place the centre pole right up against my left side. I was honoured by the great vantage point, but a bit reluctant to be relegated more to mascot than contributor. In a remarkable show of organization and collaboration, the big top went up in no time flat, with all hands on deck. Clutch bade me fondue and joined the circle of vehicles around the giant tent. There were a lot of them, so

MG and Sam reconsidered and it was decided that after lunch there would be more of a 'campground' setup organized over by a grove of spruce trees set back from the main field, since many of the caravaners had their own tents or campers to sort out. More of a village arrangement. Made sense. I noticed that the 'Claire Voyant" trailer got dropped behind the grove, off by itself a bit.

Turns out one of the side tents was the 'Yes You Canteen'. The two food trucks following the tour, Ty Dye and the guy with the Gerber Burgers and Drummer Sticks, along with a popular soft ice cream rig called 'Killa Vanilla', got nestled in beside the canteen, and as if by magic, circus magic, a late lunch for about 100 appeared with contributions from Maxine and everyone who had something to offer. Pot luck style. I could smell pot too, and everyone felt that good fortune was shining down upon them that day. A circus clown duo called 'Cher 'n Dippity' blessed the meal with mock pomp and ceremony and everyone settled in to eat and to get acquainted. Drummer shared the meal, remarking that when they said the Pow Wow had Indian food, he thought they meant samosas. Ha Ha. Now, with less pomp and a somewhat awkward circumstance, he took a ride out of the camp and headed back up the lane.

We were there. But what did that mean?

PART TWO

Chapter Twenty-Four

Bic the reporter tells, until further notice.

Holy Hanna.

It was after midnight I remember. I was just ready to fall asleep after catching the first set of a Corey Hart show downtown. My laptop dinged. I'm a slave to that ding. My editor says always leave your device on. There's always a chance it could be the next big story.

It was from an email address called 'MG@Miles2Go.ca' which had me intrigued. The subject heading just said 'From Drummer' and it had a huge mp3 file attached.

I had pretty well forgotten about that cassette recorder I had given Miles Gerber's drummer, after getting frustrated that Miles himself wouldn't talk to me. The magazine wanted me to do one of those 'Where Are They Now?' stories. Normally I'd tag along with a tour for a bit to get the scoop, but Miles said a quick no to that. I don't blame him after seeing their 'tour bus'. What a joke. That 'nostalgia' about 80s and early 90s music actually was why I was at the Corey Hart show too. The magazine thinks that stuff sells copies. Corey also blew me off. I suppose if I were Miles I wouldn't want to admit that he fit into that nostalgia category. After all, he was still out there grinding it out on the bar circuit. Once you've had a major hit, you've always got a gig. It's just that the gigs get crappier.

Turns out Drummer had followed up for me. And how. Christ, this wasn't an article, it was a bloody book! I'd heard a bit from another reporter who had been following Miles' recent activities, but hadn't thought much of it. I started listening right away. I knew I had to catch up with them even though I'd seen that they were due at the Horseshoe in two days. The story was clearly now centred on Manitoulin, so I caught the first flight to Sudbury after getting a sub reporter to cover the Toronto gig. I listened on the plane and then in the back of a cab. The cabby couldn't believe I wanted to ride all the way to some unclear destination on Manitoulin, over 100 clicks away, but he was game. This would surely blow my limited budget. Do you have any idea how broke the magazine biz is these days? Worse than the music business! The driver asked what I was up to, and when I told him about the Miles story he said he knew about it and started singing, "Burning Rubber", Miles' worst song IMHO. He said he didn't mind taking me since the winter before he had picked up a kid with a guitar who climbed into the cab and said, "Nashville or bust!"

"Goddammit I took him! Took me fifteen hours. Always wondered if I'd hear him on the radio one day. Maybe I played a part in making his dream come true."

Uh oh. A talker. I apologized, said 'homework' and put my headphones on. I was hooked and desperate to get on with the rest of the story. I was sorry I didn't have the budget to arrive by helicopter. This tale deserved a dramatic entrance. Actually I guess I *was* part of the tale since Drummer addressed me a few times. The weirdest thing was now and then there'd be a different voice, but it just sounded like Drummer using what he thought was a female voice, and the voice claimed to be their van talking. You never know. Stranger things have happened in show business. And if you happen to be reading whatever comes from this, if you want to hold on to the story that it really was a Ford talking, I don't want to be the one to turn the wick down on your lamp. As I got into his rhythm I noticed that 'Nelly-Belle' would often speak if Drummer was uncomfortable with talking about something, or if he hadn't actually witnessed part of the tale and he was just speculating. It was pretty cool but it made me curious about Drummer himself, though he modestly presumed that I wouldn't be interested in *his* tale. The story was peppered with song references of new material that didn't sound commercial but certainly sounded relevant. Good for Miles. Like many, I had written him off after Maddie Myles left years ago.

We sped through Espanola, passing The Ranch, just as I heard Drummer talking about it on the recording. As if by magic, and magic certainly is a part of this story, the tape ended and there was a ding on my tablet with another message from MG and the last little bit of the recording which basically gave me enough to direct the cabbie to our destination. We passed the Pow Wow site. Mighty impressive. I almost stopped to see if Drummer was there—I was using the fast-forward button a lot on the file now—but chose to keep going after two young Ojibway kids looked me over and said, "Are you guys going to the Hippy Days? It's just down there a ways," and they pointed southwest a bit. Sure enough, there was the sign at Yasgur's Farm. Ya no kidding. On the mailbox someone had tacked on a note that said 'It's down here. Whatever it is.'

I wasn't the only one inching down the laneway, which looked pretty torn up from all the traffic. Poor Maxine. Folks were still arriving, drawn by word of mouth and no doubt the twitter feeds of the hipper participants in this journey. My driver, Mohan, turned off the meter, rounded things down to a flat rate, drained my credit card, and then said maybe he'd stick around a bit.

There was a huge tent already up and I'm guessing from Drummer's description that the decrepit disabled van in the middle was none other than Nelly-Belle, limousine to the stars and soon-to-be legendary storyteller. Everyone was in a smaller tent finishing up a big communal lunch. I hadn't had breakfast. A really efficient, friendly crew was gathering everything up as folks were making their way out back to where a big campground was getting set up. There was a real festival vibe to it, which was something I knew a bit about, having written that well-received article about Guelph, Ontario's legendary Hillside festival called 'Why Can't It Be Like Hillside All Year Round?'

A tiny but mighty young woman with a megaphone was just telling everyone that perhaps the rest of the afternoon could be spent setting up the campground and getting generally settled in.

"Let's meet again at sundown. Right around Nelly-Belle," she said in a voice way bigger than you'd imagine. I presumed this was the now-famous MG in the same boots and Disturbers

T-shirt described on the recording, although now she was wearing a CTN ball cap instead of the cowboy hat she had used to her advantage back on the prairies. And there were those remarkable eyes that Nelly-Belle had mentioned, a stark contrast to the kind of brown mixed-race skin that I always thought would eventually end racism when we all looked like that. She certainly had the magnetism that had been described on the tape. No wonder she was in a position of command.

I recognized Roxy. We'd done press junkets together in the past. I wondered how CTN had let her follow this story. I headed their way and turned back when my reporter spidey sense told me that I might do better if I was anonymous for a while.

There were nods of agreement after MG's announcement but some looks of confusion from the growing crowd. A large bearded gent with an 'I'm With Stupid' T-shirt on, although Stupid his or herself was nowhere to be seen, struck the only note of discord I'd heard until that point. He shouted, "Hey Lady! Who put you in charge!"

MG paused a moment, looked around, and said "Well, I guess that's on the agenda for the meeting tonight!"

Wow. Agenda. Meeting. I could see that those two things weren't necessarily on the 'agenda' for a lot of the Miles followers. As I roamed the grounds, my cab driver Mohan took off across the field towards the trucks after saying, "Hey, there's my old buddy Clutch!" Oh I get it now. Clutch was the driver not the truck! That Nelly-Belle. Honestly. I could see that most of these folks were probably just looking for some summer fun, like a car rally or a pumped up version of the Miles Gerber Fan Club, and all of a sudden they were charter members of, of what?

I wandered, and wondered, and realized I was totally exhausted. 'Dual exhausted' as Nelly-Belle had so eloquently put it. There, I was starting to believe in her. Everyone was busy but chilled, something to aspire to. The largish tent that was *not* the canteen turned out to be a kind of office. There was a generator in there. I guess the circus was used to plopping down anywhere. They even had an ancient printing press and they were already handing out flyers; invitations to what had been upgraded from a 'meeting' to a 'Solstice Selebration'. It was not just a celebration, it was a festival of alliteration:

> Sycamore Sisters Sircus
> and the
> Society of Story Yellers
> Solicit your Sharing Sircle Attendance
> at a
> Solstice Selebration
> Se Soir at Sunset
> Surrounding Sister Nelly-Belle.
> BYOI (ideas), BYOS (stories) BYOFFF
> (flashlight, food and fluids)

That sounded cool, though I was pretty sure we had missed that actual day by nearly a week. It was a lovely afternoon. Young folks with guitars gathered under trees near what was turning into a little village. Folks in circles building campfires, sharing stories, which was, after all, what seems to have brought them all here. They may have not yet quite known what they belonged *to*, but there was certainly a sense of belonging. I guessed that many of these people were looking for something to believe in, something to hold on to. Yikes, I'm glad Miles is the songwriter, not me. I was starting to sound like a Phil Collins song, and I heard that Miles had a 'No Phil' rule on the van radio.

Maybe the fatigue was sending me into easy listening mode, so I looked for a quiet spot to lie down and found it in the back seat of Nelly-Belle her good self! It was just as described: messy, funky, smelly, but at this point it also felt like sacred ground. After all I'd listened to from the cassettes, I actually felt 'held' there.

I slept deeply, apparently the rest of the day, for I was awakened by tittering and whispering. There was the whole congregation, 'cause that sort of felt like what it was at this point, gathered around on blankets, chairs, and in the back, bleachers from the circus collection. There was applause as I emerged. I took a clown-like bow and took my place near the back, where reporters are supposed to be. I think Roxy and her cameraman/driver Don recognized me from where they had mounted the camera on top of their truck, but they let me be. A clown, a stilt-walker and a 'little person', as we call them now, led a parade of the half-dozen or so actual children in the group who looked like they had been having fun making instruments and raiding the circus costume trailer. MG and Maxine came in last and climbed up onto Nelly-Belle and MG began to speak into a mic plugged in to the circus' antiquated but functional sound system.

"Good people, and clowns," she began, to applause. "If you haven't officially met her yet, this is Maxine Yasgur, and she's the badass babe that is kindly hosting us on her beautiful land." There were mighty cheers and bicycle horns.

Maxine had a small voice but everyone shushed for her.

"Thank you everybody. I'm thrilled to have you here, although Roxy didn't tell me there'd be quite so many of you!" (More cheers and horns. Those horns were going to get tiresome soon). "You are welcome to stay as long as you like, as long as I get some farm help, and you're gentle with this land."(Much enthusiasm about that!) "You know with the wacky weather that seems to be the new way, it looks like I won't get a first cut of hay for a spell, but there's plenty more to do. You'll find we've got rocky ground but we do with love in this short growing season what we can't do with the soil we ought to have!"

"Yes, this is my land but not really. I want to acknowledge that we are on unceded Indigenous territory here. We are grateful to the Ojibwa, Odawa, Potawatomi and other Anishinaabe peoples who have been good stewards of what they call Spirit Island here. I wish I had the right words for this, gosh, I hope I didn't get that wrong. Everyone who could be speaking to this better than me is over at the Pow Wow. I urge you to check it out and if you do, please offer your thanks."

Big applause, hooting, and yes, horns. Ouch.

"There's no wrong way to say things here, sister," shouted a young woman on the bleachers. "You spoke from the heart, and that's one of the things that brought us here honey!"

Ok, you can just assume that there was a lot of applause and cheering after just about everything, all right?

A tall, thin but strong woman who was introduced as Sam, the one Nelly-Belle had mentioned, climbed up on the van. Three of them up there now. How much could Nelly-Belle hold? I wasn't the only one concerned. The sea of bodies parted and made room for Clutch and his flatbed to edge into the centre of the action. On the truck was a gaggle of some of the same young folks I had heard jamming in the afternoon. Earnest second-or-third generation hippies representing that new alternative old-timey acoustic genre that made up with sheer quantity of keen members what they lacked in actual musical quality. They were playing a fiddle tune as they rode along, and they lurched to a stop when the truck did too.

Sam thanked them, and she climbed on board with MG and Maxine to everyone's relief.

"Look! We have a real stage now!" hollered MG, who had genuine hollering skills.

"Yes, we're celebrating Summer solstice tonight," Sam began. "I want to invite the Reverend Dippity to join us with a few special words".

Dippity seemed to be recognized by all. He was in full clown regalia but with an oversized minister's collar and a huge book that said 'Real Good Book' on the outside. Listening to him speak took a bit of getting used to since he looked silly but his words were serious. I caught sight of the 'I'm With Stupid' dude who seemed to be appreciative of the collaborative effort instead of it being the MG show as he had feared earlier.

"My friends," Dippity began with a mock evangelist's voice. "Today the sun is as high as it can get in the sky."

"And I'm as high as I can get Rev!" shouted a potential troublemaker near me, in the back of course, where troublemakers dwell. Dippity was winding up in a melodramatic tone, "And we're all high on fellowship and love tonight, ain't we brothers and sisters? This is when we celebrate the light.

The light within and the light without.

"And Bud Lite," crowed my heckler neighbour.

Dippity ignored this and continued. "A new awakening. A new beginning, and it seems so fortuitous, verily, even FIVEtuitous that we are gathered here on this night of promise and hope for good things to come our way. Times are hard, but I feel a softness here, an openness. Do you feel it too?" (Canadian-style polite cheering). "I said, do you feel it too?" (A little more raucous response.) He got what he needed with one more try. The band saw their cue and launched into a fast reel that had everyone clapping and dancing until all could see that MG was ready to speak.

"Thanks Dippity and thanks, Band. Awesome. You guys got a name?"

The banjo player, a dude with an Edwardian beard, peaked cap, plaid shirt, suspenders and pants that could have been borrowed from the clowns, stepped forward and said, "We're Highway 17 and we're named after Miles' song, not the highway. We're here to learn from Miles and you fine folks about how we can all find a way to live our best lives, leave something good behind, while leaving no *one* behind, plus do some good pickin' along the way."

He ended with a little flourish on the banjo, that same lick that seems to go along with that old 'shave and a haircut, two bits' line.

MG said, "Gosh, thanks, er, um.."

"It's Dylan, ma'am."

"Of course it is," she said before continuing. "I think Dylan put his banjo-playing finger on something I wanted to share with ya'll. He took the words right out of my foul mouth really. We're all here together on this beaut of a night 'cuz we want to share, we want to learn, we want to have some fun, and we want to figure out how we move forward in a good way. That's our common story, yet we all have our own stories that shaped us and brought us here. Am I right? What we've all been experiencing I think is that by sharing those stories, singing these songs, we are growing, we are finding our voices, we are making choices. So far we've just been following Miles along this road, and now that we've paused we are all wondering what comes next. We're followers but we can be leaders too, right? And we have a shared desire to know what that kind of leadership looks like, including that little matter that came up earlier about 'who's doin' the talking'. That's what I'm hoping we can dig into a bit tonight. I'm hoping we're all in this together, and first we have to figure out what 'THIS' looks like. Wadda ya think?"

MG was starting to sound a bit like an old western movie where the townsfolk meet at the church and decide how they are going to get a posse together to go after the cattle rustlers while the sheriff was off chasing train robbers. I could tell she was struggling a bit with wanting to bring folks together and move the conversation along, make some plans and set some guidelines, without looking like the 'boss lady' as I'd heard some people refer to her earlier. Dylan leaned over and whispered to her.

"Go for it, darlin," MG said. "This isn't all about me talkin' at ya, right?"

Dylan said, "If I may, I think this ditty addresses some of what you were just sayin'. We all want to know how to live our lives in these uncertain times, am I right?" He launched into "How", which I gather was one of his originals, though you could tell there was a Miles influence on it musically. The lyrics were a little more political than Gerber gets. I had wondered if politics was going to make an appearance under this big top. The song had an easy chorus so there was some great singing along.

Song 22: How?

We're staring a hurricane in the eye
Temperatures and tempers are running high
Banks and wells are running dry
How do we live our lives?
Do we just take the money and run
Move to the country, buy a gun
Wait for the day of judgment to come
How do we live our lives?

If it's all, if it's all, if it's all coming down,
Tell me how, tell me how, do we live our lives now?

Do we go after the consumerists
The ones who got us into this
Show them another way exists
How do we live our lives?
Do we try to keep our footprint small,
Could we make a farm out of that mall,
Is there anything we can do at all?
How do we live our lives?

If it's all, if it's all, if it's all coming down,
Tell me how, tell me how, do we live our lives now?

Do we abandon this sinking titanic
To our leaders who just say "don't panic"
Or do we try to go local, green and organic
How do we live our lives?
Do we confront the climate change deniers
Quit preaching only to the choir,
Crank it up just a little bit higher
How do we live our lives?

If it's all, if it's all, if it's all coming down,
Tell me how, tell me how, do we live our lives now?

Do we get in our cars and just drive fast
Until we run right out of gas
Do we go out in a last plastic blast
How do we live our lives?

Suddenly everybody wanted to talk at once. MG had dashed into the back of Nelly-Belle and reappeared with a drum stick. She held it high before speaking again: "Wow, thanks Highway #17. That pretty much sums it up. Now I can see that this has stimulated some ideas from a bunch of you, so can we use Drummer's drumstick here as a talking stick? He showed me how to do this back along the road aways. Ask for the stick if you want to talk, and if you don't have the stick, well then don't talk, OK?"

There was a round of approval, yet some grumbling too about that being both hippy *and* dippy. One older gent in overalls got hold of the stick and said, "It's just like that young man said about 'sinking Titanic'. If feels like we've got something good going on here but out there in the worried world it DOES feel like our ship is sinking. It ain't the Titanic though, I'm thinking . Look around you, everybody, it's more like an Ark we've got going here except it's people of all kinds weathering out a storm together waiting to see where we land and how we can start over with something new".

The talking stick rule was broken quickly when a dude shouted out, "Ya brother. It's a Narc!"

A bit of a panic ran through the tent, especially from the area where the scent of weed was wafting from.

"Holy Shit," laughed MG. "An Ark. Oopsy".

The guy with the stick protested. "Hey I've still got the stick! I wanted to say that it's like an Ark, but who's the Noah around here? Miles? Is it you, young lady?"

Sam the Circus roustabout was still on the flatbed, and she asked for the stick before taking the mic and saying, "That whole Noah thing was a bit of an entitled male construct if you ask me. I bet Ms. Noah was cleaning up a lot of animal poop while Noah was lounging on the top deck, not the poop deck. Noah sounds kind of negative anyway. Maybe we should have a 'Yes-ah' instead of a 'No-ah'.

Laughter rippled through the crowd and everyone starting chanting 'Yes-ah' together.

Sam went on: "Here at the Sycamore Sircus we're a co-op and we make all our decisions together, it's non-hierarchical, collaborative, and at the same time we take guidance from our elder, Madam Voyant, who is kind of our spiritual leader, yet if we're moving towards something new, we want, in my view, to get away from a 'leader and follower' model. Claire is here but she's keeping a low profile. I know she's kind of our ring master but she doesn't like being the centre of attention. I know. Weird huh? She's showing that it's possible to have a ringmaster, without a ringleader! She's more like a facilitator. Leadership doesn't have to have the look of a 'boss' or have a corporate model. We all want to contribute, to offer up what superpowers we have to 'save the world' like in comic books, and sometimes offering leadership skills is one of those powers. Leadership doesn't have to mean control. Speaking of comics, our esteemed clowns here will tell you that you need to turn things upside down sometimes to get a better look at how to make the change we need. And sometimes when you turn upside down all the change falls out of your pockets! We need change! I'm excited that we can be whatever we want it to be, and maybe this is an opportunity to ease into something new. Let's see what emerges, OK?"

I could tell that Sam's speech went right over the heads of most of the attendees, but MG took the stick with a gesture of appreciation and said, "Thanks for that. Facilitator. Cool. And thanks to you, sir, for that Ark analogy. I'm liking that. A shelter from the apocalypse, the storm that's coming, and with all this worry about climate change, floods are going to be part of what we're dealing with, you bet."

A little girl wearing a tiara and a tutu gestured for the stick and her mom hoisted her onto the flatbed. The girl proudly took the stick from MG, looked up to her, and said, "What is an Ark?"

A nerdy guy in a tweed jacket who looked pretty out of place there but was an example I suppose of all the different 'species' gathered in the 'Ark' handed MG his phone and gestured for her to read. "Well, sweetie," said MG. "It says here that it's a 'vessel or sanctuary that serves as protection against extinction', and extinction means that if we can't land this Ark somewhere safe, we won't be around to see you grow up tall like me." That got a laugh 'cause MG wasn't that much bigger than the kid. This was tough stuff for a kid to hear, but the mom held on tight and assured her there were lots of friends here who would make sure everything was ok. The nerdy guy borrowed his phone back and quickly directed MG to read the next bit. She scanned it and said, "Cool! There's also the Ark of the Covenant, ya'll know about that, right? Says here on this nice gent's phone," After asking his name, she said "Solomon? Seems appropriate n'est pas? It says on SOLOMON's phone that it was 'a wooden chest which contained the tablets of the laws of the ancient Israelites who carried it on their wanderings in the wilderness. Well, we don't have tablets and laws," -

"YET!" shouted a stilt-walker.

"Yet," repeated MG, "but we HAVE been wandering; and what we DO have is a growing collection of songs and stories that are starting to shape who we are and who we'd like to be! I hope we can spend more time if you can stick around for a few days to chat more about that 'who we'd like to be' part. We don't have a wooden chest either I guess." She was interrupted by two clowns who plopped what looked like a pirate chest on to the stage, and as they emptied out coloured scarves and theatre props from it, the crowd roared.

"Wow! OK we've got a chest, and we don't have a temple to keep it in but we've got Nelly-Belle over there to keep our treasures safe. Wadda ya say? Can we really call it the Ark of the Covenant? Would that be sacrilegious?"

"What did you call it?" asked a little boy clinging to his mom.

The little girl offered help to her brother, saying, "I think she said the Ark of the Oven Mitt."

A spattering of giggles erupted, but the crowd could see how serious the little girl was, so then there was a rousing roar of approval. MG said, "I love it. Shall we have our first vote? Who likes it? It could be the name of this whole operation!"

I think the little talk about the clowns looking for change by turning things upside down had an impact, and helped with the spirit of the evening. Also that sense of fun *and* the sense of renewal which is where the solstice talk started. There was instant unanimous approval for their accidental new name. The band could sense it was time to dance! The fiddle player stepped to the front and hollered, "Thanks, little girl! I'm lovin' it! Welcome to the Ark of the Oven Mitt!"

He cranked up 'Turkey In The Straw'.

The dancing commenced. The soft ice cream truck honked its horn as a way to announce they were open for business. The horn actually sounded quite a bit like 'Turkey In the Straw', and the party was underway. MG kind of knew they were done talking for the night, though I could tell she wanted to have a more formal closing out ceremony. I saw another circus roustabout come to the front of the flatbed truck and signal to Clutch who started her up. He climbed out of the cab and hoisted the hood. The roustabout clamped a pair of cables to the battery, plopped a strange-looking gizmo on to the truck and suddenly the music stopped and there was a gasp of wonderment from the crowd. The ceiling of the tent was filled with sparkling stars and flashing lights that rotated around, creating a kind of heavenly sphere. Then Dippity got back up, this time holding up an ancient boom box. He turned it on with a dainty white-gloved hand and I'll be damned if we didn't start to hear Miles the man himself singing that strange atypical song that he and Maddie had performed when they were guests on the Muppet Show back in the late '80s which ended up being kind of a kids' classic; nothing like their other work. "The Waltz of The Fireflies" filled the tent and in the air above ballet-dancer-fairy-firefly creatures climbed a series of silk ropes suspended from the grid at the top of the tent. The joy and surprise on everyone's faces made me remember that in my haste I hadn't packed the magazine's camera! We all got a glimpse of what the Sycamore Sisters thing was about: magic. They had found a wondrous way to send us all into a remarkable solstice night, where the real stars were just coming out as if to mimic their imitators.

James Gordon

Song 23
Waltz of The Fireflies

When the marshmallow moon
Floats high in the chocolate sky
That's when the whippoorwill whistles a tune
for the waltz of the fireflies.

By the banks of a looking glass lake
In a grove of invisible trees
That's when the fancy dressed fireflies
 take to the air on the lingering breeze

Dippin' and divin'
Waltzing and jiving
The fireflies flashing their taillights
 in time to the beat of the cricket guitars.

In the bull-rush ballroom
The frogs turn up the volume
They croak out a song as the fireflies
wink to the twinkling stars

Chapter Twenty-Five

Before begging for leftovers at the canteen and heading back to Nelly-Belle to try to sleep, I walked around the farm trying to take it all in. It was sort of a combination 'bush party', festival, circus of course, and refugee camp. Maxine's farmhouse was a bit of a hike and seemed to be off limits but I guessed that might change, especially with the latrine issue for the growing population. (The Circus had just three of those ubiquitous blue 'Johnny-on-the-spots' with them and they were planted now at the edge of the campground.) Maxine also had a well-used barn that I bet MG and company already had their eye on. Our hostess did have a water tap not too far from the canteen. Not ideal but of course no one knew what the scope of the Ark would be.

Campfires burned here and there with keen conversations and jam-sessions around them. As a music critic, I've always been fascinated by what songs have become a part of the standard campfire repertoire. Neil Young for sure; some Beatles but they often had too many chords for the amateur; always "The Weight" by the Band, even though I don't think anyone really knows what it's about; "You Ain't Goin' Nowhere" by 'the real' Dylan; some Miles of course; occasional Stones sung that day by a group that looked they were more than occasionally stoned; John Prine; Hank Williams; Lightfoot; always "Wagon Wheel" these days; too few women writers but some women performers, and though there were young people, almost nothing written within the last 30 years. Maybe there's another magazine article in that, if the 'Maple Leaf Rag' makes it through the season.

I suppose a lot of these folks have been following the 'Miles2Go' journey for a while. Most of them looked well-equipped and in it for the long haul, or for a summer vacation at least. I must have looked like a city rube since a family sitting in front of a camper van offered me a blanket as I drifted back to my makeshift lodging. I passed a solitary woman in a long cloak, hood up so I couldn't see her face, who seemed to be inspecting the grounds. I wondered if that was the mysterious Claire.

I fell asleep listening to the campfires crackle, the guitars strumming softly as folks seemed respectful of the young'uns , and a lone coyote with a melodic howl in the distance. I thought that farther off I could hear the drums from the Pow Wow tapping into the rhythm of this island that was really growing on me.

A little too early in the morning I was woken up by the slap of a piece of paper on Nelly-Belle's windshield. Another missive from the printing press in the office. Who was doing this? This was the start of a remarkable organic process where Ark tasks seemed to happen spontaneously, though you could tell they had been planned carefully and not done in isolation.

The Ark had its own logo now - a nice plaid oven mitt looking a bit like Gumby trying to make a peace sign. The text in an old circusy font offered this:

Pour Votre Consideration Aujourd'hui

Soon as you can get there:
Community Breakfast at the Yes U Can-Teen
Bring what you have, The Lord of the Fries can fry 'er
Tai Chi @ nine by the pond
Clowning Workshop @ 10 on the easterly bleachers
in the Big Top
Lunch. One p.m. sort of sharp, to put it bluntly
Hands off Maxine's chickens
Work Crews' sign-up sheet on the Community Board
in front of the Office Tent
Volunteer Crew facilitators wanted:
Get a badge by the clown car
Work Crew Options: (Add more if you can think up any):
Sanitation Environmental Sustainability* Logistics *
Making an Arking Lot

*Energy: How To Power This Operation Up
With A Low Footprint
*Programming and Fun-Making *Housing * Organizational
Structure
*Farm Labour Crew: Make Maxine's Day
*Financials: How Do We Pay For This?
*Long-term visioning:
What in the Holy Heck are we doing here?
*Discussion: So, how DO we live our lives now? @4
@the Flatbed Stage with Solomon
Afternoon Field Trips: Pow Wow visits and supplies
In Little Current
Or just CHILL
Sunset Gathering at Nelly-Belle with crew reports
AND THE BIG NEWS
Live Streaming of Miles And Dougie from the Horsehoe
@ 9 PM in Maxine's Barn!
Lost and Found: One Clown Shoe: Size 28

Wow! And what? There was a pond? I missed that somehow. I wondered how this handout would land with everyone, but I noticed that at the lineup for the 'Spiffy Biffy,' as the bog was now called, and at the water tap, folks were sharing it, laughing at the silly bits, and making plans together around some of the items on the list.

I headed to breakfast with nothing to offer but a healthy appetite with a side of curiosity, and the decision to make myself known to MG as the sender of the audio files and to Roxy as the only soul I knew there. The gossip at the canteen, (where there was a donation jar for losers like me who had literally brought nothing to the table) was that Roxy and her camera guy, Don, were leaving the next morning. Everyone wondered what MG was going to do. Neither of them was to be seen.

There was a kind of twisted bugle call that filled the air. I followed the sound to a pair of those ancient ballpark-style loudspeakers that were on the front of the biggest circus truck, supposedly to attract a crowd when they arrived in a town. I recognized the voice of Dippity, sitting in the truck cab talking into what looked like a CB radio mic. He rattled off some announcements that sounded like the kind that Radar would have made on MASH.

"Good morning, campers! I'm your Arker Barker, Dippity. I'll keep this short, but not as short as 'Stretch' my sidekick here."

"Howdy," said Stretch with a voice that led me to believe he was the little person we'd seen in his hobo clown getup the day before.

Dippity continued, "I hope you all got your copy of the oven-fresh flyer this morning. If you didn't, it's up on the community bulletin board. If you are around tomorrow we'd like to deliver the news to you by text, since that old printing machine is a bit of a draw on the power here, and well, we're trying to leave a light mitt-print right? There's a sign-up sheet on the board for that too, and thanks to Maxine the Magnificent there is now an extension cord running from her farmhouse to the back of the canteen with a power bar, not the edible kind, where you can charge your phones up. Woah doggies! I can hear the stampede already! Take 'er easy: there'll be two lines soon if anyone else has got some more cords we can string together. After all we want two of everything on the Ark, eh? In the Lost And Found department we found the clown shoe already thanks, and Stumpy is grateful to its discoverer. He only had the one. Marge Fielding wants us to know that she has lost her desire to be a dental hygienist, and she's open to suggestions. She'll be the one gazing wistfully at the sky over by the pond, and Mrs. Isabelle Duchamp says she has lost her ability to finish a..."

The broadcast ended. I could tell they'd be back.

On a hunch, and skipping clown class, I headed towards Maxine's barn, which was in a state of elegant decay, yet still functional and welcoming. The CTN truck was outside, as I'd guessed, and MG, Roxy and Don were setting up the live streaming operation. It was a working barn, with hay and farm equipment and one horse in a stall. Cream coloured. The horse, not the stall. According to a sign above the stall the horse was named Buttermilk, but that could have been the name of the stall. Oops! I was sounding like Drummer again. Could have been a circus horse if the Sycamore operation still used them. I could see why they were adapting the barn for this use though it was much smaller than the big top. It had a nice wall to project onto and no centre pole. It looks like they had raided Maxine's collection of bed sheets for the screen.

I saw Roxy. She was hard to recognize out of her polyester newswoman outfit and her corporate make up. She looked like a regular person except for that network-issue blonde hair, partially hidden by a straw hat that shaded her pleasing high-cheek-boned face. She recognized me though, and came running over for a warm embrace that was more enthusiastic than I would have thought for someone I didn't know well.

"Long time no see," she yelled.

"Hey, you know that's a racist imitation of Pidgin English right, miss PC? You know where you are, right?" I followed with a laugh and another embrace, but I wasn't totally joking. Those few of us left in the journalism hustle have to be very careful these days. Too careful if you ask me, but no one asks me anything.

"That's why I remember you. Still a total pain in the ass, eh? And I presume YOU know where you are. You must be the only guy here wearing a suit jacket. Loosen up a bit there buddy! How's the Rag Tag Mag Bag going anyway?"

"Terrible. How's the cheesy network gig going?"

"More Terrible. That convo is worth a bevy sometime Bic." She introduced me to the others, and MG was thrilled to hear that I had received Drummer's files and more thrilled that their content had lured me here.

I told her that I had actually been assigned to cover Miles' show in Toronto so I was grateful that I could do it in this way. We discussed whether my presence should be revealed to the Arkers or not, and there seemed to be consensus around waiting a bit on that. I asked her if I could interview her at some point , and she cryptically replied, "I'm guessing that after tomorrow night the interview will go a bit differently, so hold on to your steno pad 'til then, pardner".

I helped by arranging hay bales into seating for a bit, then wandered off looking to check out the rest of the activities going on. I ran into Mohan my cabbie who was carrying an unruly tangle of extension cords towards the farmhouse.

"You still here? Wow!"

"This is a lot more fun than driving around Sudbury, let me tell you!" he said. "Besides, I've delivered a few folks over to the Pow Wow already. I wouldn't miss this for the world, and I'm thinking that the world is going to be missed soon too if we don't start looking at more of this cool alternative shit. Can you help me string these cords together? Not nearly enough power around here. They don't call it 'Little Current' for nothing, bro!"

As we worked we passed the Highway #17 band around a still-smoldering campfire. They were working out something with the Circus orchestra, (just a three-piece group but they had cool Sgt. Pepperish outfits). I think they were going to be the warm-up act for Miles and Dougie's livestream.

I guessed that things like this were happening all over Mittville, as some were calling it. You'd never believe that what we were seeing was only one day old, but then again the Sycamore crew were experts at creating an inviting space from nothing. All over, people were seeing what needed to be done and taking initiatives, chipping in or making sure they were getting what they needed out of the experience.

As we toiled with the cords Mohan told me HIS story.

"Back in Bangladesh most of my family were doctors and lawyers and such. No work for me though, the black sheep son, so now I'm in the Promised Land driving cab, which was supposed to be just so I could raise some cash to get a real education and a real job. Ten years later and my family back home is still waiting for me to raise the money to bring them here."

His journey in between made for the kind of Canadian story Miles would love and I suggested if he could stick around awhile he could tell it to him. Conversations like this were happening all over the farm; you could tell there was a hunger for that kind of sharing. Speaking of hunger, I asked Mohan if he'd take me into Little Current for supplies. I was the least prepared camper on the team.

He said, "It's on me, pal," and we set off together after collecting some orders along the way. We gave a lift to a crusty guy who said he was from the Soo. He told us he was hitching a ride out and leaving his family back at the Ark.

"I just came along 'cuz my wife's the one who told Miles that story about trying to make do after the mines closed in the Northwest. She's really into this but it's really not my thing, and I left our huskies with a neighbour. So I've left her with the pickup to get back, which hopefully won't be too long. She'll need it more than me. She says she's just waiting for the return of Miles the Prodigal Son or some crap like that." Mohan asked what his thing was, and the guy, who's name was Dawson, admitted that he didn't have a good answer.

"Dunno, but it feels like an alien planet to me here, I mean folks are real nice and all but seriously, an Ark? Christamighty!"

Mohan told him a version of what he'd said to me earlier, "Well, we'll have to find another planet for ourselves if we don't start rethinking what we're doing to this one, and I am finding that this kind of 'rethinking' is my new thing!"

The rest of the ride was quiet. I noticed that down the farm lane there was the same amount of traffic heading in as heading out, and a kid with a reflective jacket had taken up the task of directing the coming and going. It looked like 'Mittville' was sorting out its population organically as it became more clear what it was all about. More were arriving, drawn to what they've been hearing, replacing those Dawsons who felt like outsiders. There WAS more clarity but I kind of liked that there was still an element of mystery as to what was actually happening. We all had our oven mitts on, and something fresh baked was emerging from the oven. I always have loved the smell of fresh baked ideas.

Chapter Twenty-Six

We returned a couple of hours later with a cab full of supplies and two young hitchhikers who looked like they were expecting to arrive at Woodstock; perhaps they were in some ways. There was clearly a net gain in the population, and the infrastructure was stretching to capacity. The campground had expanded, and was now divided into two sections delineated with two funky signs. One said 'Party People' and the other said 'Stick-in-the-Muds'. With the cars coming and going it was getting a bit muddy.

It didn't exactly look like the itemized activity list was being observed too closely, but I felt like it had just been a list of suggestions, and there were lots people in clumps chatting and planning. In the distance I saw MG and Roxy coming out of Claire's trailer. I wondered what they had been cooking up.

A small crew was collecting garbage. Good idea. They had vests that said 'Gang Green' on them. Maybe it was just me, but the 'cute factor' was getting to be a bit much.

I left Mohan to sort out the supplies, since the reporter in me wanted to see who came to Solomon's 'How Do We Live Our Lives Now? 'chat. He had a nice diverse group gathered by the pond, who had followed a bristol board sign with an arrow that announced 'Where is How? It's Here Now'. Remind me to never go to Bristol. I'd be bored.

Dylan was there, since he had written that song that I presume he had shared again, and they even had a flip chart going.

Here's the gist of what I heard. None of it was new to me, but maybe if was new to them that was a good thing:

The way we live our lives now, as a species, clearly isn't working.

What the 'Oven Mitt Experiment', (O.M.E. on the flip chart), is demonstrating is that we have strayed from being guided by a sense of community, family, personal interactions, caring, sharing, etc. and instead corporate greed has taken over. It's all about profit; the bottom line; and that greed has led to a huge income gap. There's no more middle class, and those who are shoved farther and farther to the bottom feel more and more helpless while that one percent at the top stays there through the exploitation of people AND of the planet. This 'experiment' was, without being really planned, designed to see if we can learn to relate with one another in a new and different way that puts people before profit. Fair enough.

We need a major shift, but how can folks here under this tree affect that change? Up to that point the talk and the flip chart had been filled with broad strokes, the big picture. Solomon himself said that what was lost in this discussion was how to move forward on an individual level.

That's when the talk turned to something closer to what they were there for. People got up and told stories of how they were trying to manage personally with all the changes. We'd all heard these concerns and observations before, of course, but hearing each person in that circle be given the chance, on Solomon's invitation, to describe their own situations and aspirations became very powerful even to jaded me. One very exotic-looking South Asian woman, who I think had been one of the graceful circus 'fireflies' from the night before, offered a unique perspective.

"Where I come from, if we had sat under a tree, which is where meetings often happened because trees are good listeners, and we had spoken some of the things we are addressing now, the police would have slaughtered us all and thrown our bodies into the river. We are complaining about our plight, yet we have a certain level of freedom, maybe less than we think, but some nonetheless. Yet we are people of privilege, despite our differences. Until no one is left behind, until there is equality in race, gender, and economic status, until it feels like we are working together, not against one another, until we are looking out for our dear earth first before taking what we need for ourselves, then we are a lost Ark that will never find a safe shore."

Some stories were more specific, like this one from a middle-aged woman who said she was following the Miles movement nearly since the beginning.

"I lost my job when the company that everyone in town worked for moved overseas somewhere. The town died and I guess we died a bit inside too since we couldn't see a way forward. That's when young people turned to drugs and older people turned to booze, to dull the pain instead of finding cures for the ailments that bring us that pain".

The mom of the kids who coined the name of this adventure said, "With my kids, we're trying not to be consumers of the crap that's made overseas by the corporations like the one that left your town. If we continue to buy their crap, then they'll keep making it, and the growth-for-growth's-sake mentality that is driven by this new kind of 'capitalism on steroids' is not sustainable. We are the victims of this system, but we hold the solution. We bitch about our governments, but we voted for them. When we say we always get the same governments it's because the same people are voting for them. People won't vote unless they think their vote matters, and that they matter. When we don't think we DO matter we lose everything. We can vote those assholes out but first we have to show what we are advocating for, not what we are against. That makes people nervous I think, to think of how we'd adapt to a new system. We are afraid of change but we know we must, right? But friends, look around, this feels different, doesn't it? Governments are not for us anymore, they're puppets of corporations, and corporations only care about us as consumers, not as people. If we don't feel like we matter, then we lose our own sense of our value and place. We CAN make that stop if we raise awareness about what's happening, right?"

She was a bit preachy. I'm allergic to preachiness, but she really was speaking from the heart.

"Education is important for all this then," Solomon said, trying to summarize. "I was a teacher 'til the cutbacks happened here. Of course education is a first step but our system is now designed to keep us stupid. Only stupid people would vote against our own interests like we do!"

A short, earnest man with a Quebecois accent jumped up

and said, "The stories I'm hearing here and on this trip are often about loss. Loss of faith, identity, our communities, our jobs, blah blah blah. No offence, but 'been there done that'." His exaggerated air quotes emphasized his clear agitation. "Can we please talk about what is possible to gain by living differently? The things we've lost that I'm not hearing about are compassion, empathy, caring and kindness. Ou sont-ils allés? Maybe we lost them because we are just trying to survive. I want to hear more about how to get that back rather than mourning what is gone."

The crowd was engaged, but it was heavy stuff; maybe more than any of them had bargained for. Solomon sensed a restlessness, and said, "OK. How can we wrap this up in one phrase or thought that I can bring to the sunset session tonight?"

The firefly woman came forward, took the marker with a graceful and grand gesture wrote, "Love Is All You Need".

Wow. That was the take-away from all that? Excuse me, but 1968 called. They want their trite slogans back. This ragtag bunch was an interesting combination of hippies, fans, activists, partygoers and, yes, clowns. If they could somehow all get on the same 'ark' then there really would be hope for us all. Somehow in the context of this instant festival thingy, 'love is all you need' didn't sound quite as cliché. Maybe it just got me going because love has not been seen around my lonely condo-life in a while.

That summary was a cue for group hugs all around, and the workshop dispersed, with Dylan leading a parade back towards the canteen with a chorus of that old Youngbloods song that went 'Come on people now, smile on your brother, everybody get together, got to love one another right now'. Spare me. The gathering was devolving into a series of old pop song clichés. I lean towards a cynical journalist's skepticism, but these folks were not being ironic about it. You'd never get away with sappy stuff like that now, but there's a genuine sentimentality I'm noticing about the sixties, when there did seem to be hope and promise in the air, and the feeling that we could make a difference. It was a simpler time when you could speak your truth, before we all got jaded like me in the '80s. This stuff would have made my millennial hipster friends in Toronto throw up. Too hippy right? But in one day I was learning to suspend my disbelief since these folks seemed to be the real deal. I was ready to get a Mitt and get in the game. I was ready to try a little kindness with my morning coffee, though this morning at breakfast someone pointed out that coffee has a horrible footprint so we needed to get over it! It looked like I had missed my chance to check up on the other crew meetings and break-out groups, but judging by the smiles and the friendly chatter along the way the afternoon seemed to have been a success.

As we headed around the pond, towards the barn and back to the canteen tent, a more elaborate parade spontaneously formed itself, which comes naturally when there are circus people about, I suppose. Our group led by Dylan and Solomon folded into the grand parade. Dippity said that 'The March' is what circus folk called the parade, though he told me that the Sycamore Sisters called it 'The April' as a kind of inside joke, since to them that sounded more feminine and less militaristic. In Drummer's narrative the circus sounded like it was a cast of thousands. I began to notice that there was really just a couple of dozen of them, and being a co-op they all played multiple roles. The procession was led by the stilt walkers and the ragtag band, and I recognized some of them as being also clowns, carnies and 'kinkers,' which is what the acrobats and dancers called themselves. Any job where you'd have to stretch to get out the 'kinks' before getting down to business. Only Claire seemed to be just Claire, though Sam cryptically said, "You never know who is behind the masks and the greasepaint around here."

We picked up other Mitters as we wended our way, and it became clear that another committee had spontaneously formed itself. A sign committee. Each sign was hung from a vintage circus banner, the kind that would have formed the banner line luring the townies into the magical world under the big top, and each had the new Oven Mitt logo. Spies must have been strategically placed at each afternoon session, as the signs reflected some of what had transpired at Solomon's gathering as well as others. They seemed to come in pairs, just like a good ark I guess:

'Decolonize'

'Semicolonize;'

'Divest'

'Digest'

'Be Kind'

'Be Kind of Nutty'

'Leave the Oil In The Ground'

'Unless it's Olive Oil'

' Eat The Rich: They Are Delicious With Soy Sauce'

'Feed The Poor'

'Feed the Rich To The Poor, though they are kind of oily'

'Praise the Glory of Stories'

'Amen' 'Ah-Woman'

'We heart Manitoulin AND Womanatoulin'

"I knew you were going to say that"- Claire Voyant

'Stories are our currency, and we're rich'

'Close the Income Gap'

'Don't buy the Gap's Crap'

'Let's break bread together: Love is all you Knead'

And more practical ones:

'Miles And Dougie Live-streamed Tonight Only: 9 pm in the Barn'

'Dinner in the Canteen 5 pm. Or Not'

'Ark Angels wanted for Latrine Duty. Lousy Pay. Can you dig it?'

'Gather under the Big Top at 7. Be there. Or Not. That's cool too'.

Like that. They were fun but hardly needed as Dippity, and sometimes MG, were on the squawky loudspeaker often. I noticed right away as the meal was commencing how much larger the population of 'Mittville' had grown just since the morning. The tent was busting at seams that had been fairly busted for years, it seemed. The tent flaps were open and the diners spread out on straw bales supplied by Maxine and her crew. Maxine herself stood on a picnic table and provided a welcome and a land acknowledgement. A request came from a beanpole young man in overalls who I recognized as the Highway #17 gutbucket player.

"Should we say grace?" Dippity removed his raggedy top hat, looked solemn as a clown can get, and said, "Well, folks, if I may be allowed to offer my own variant of the famous 'Clown's Prayer' I'd be tickled pink!" To nods of approval, and some tickles from Stretch, he began, "As I stumble through this life, help me to create more laughter than tears, dispense more happiness than gloom, spread more cheer than despair. Never let me become so indifferent that I fail to see the wonders in the eyes of a child, or the twinkle in the eyes of the aged. Never let me forget that my total effort is to cheer people, make them happy, and forget momentarily all the unpleasantness in their lives. Never let me forget the kindness offered by you all in sharing this meal with a poor fool like me, and never let us forget that breaking bread is the finest way to begin a conversation around breaking new ground."

Cher, his clown routine partner, squirted him with a mustard bottle and joined him to say in unison with mock gravity, "And let us not forget that every good meal ends with a food fight! Amen!"

MG gave her patented cowboy hat whoop at that, and announced, "OK folks, it's country style cookin' tonight!"

"What country would that be?" said Roxy beside her, who now seemed to think she was part of a new comedy team inspired by Cher 'n Dippity themselves.

"Why lots of different countries except Turkey and Chile tonight 'hon! Let's hear it for the amazing help of the good people in the newly formed 'Grub Hub' who are coming around with platters with the bounty gathered from this afternoon's panty, I mean pantry raid." With that Roxy slapped MG's butt and Cher slapped Dippity with a large fake fish. "We've got a feast fit for a king."

"That'd be me," said a tall guy with a fedora whose name apparently was Tom King. "But I'm willing to share if you direct me to the machiatto bar."

MG continued after looking confused about that: "Y'all got

the memo about bringing your own plates and cutlery, right?"

"Oops," said Dippity, resulting in a bigger fish slap and some groans, but things seemed to soon be in order and the food was a wonderful mixture reflecting the diversity of the Mitters.

The food fight was glorious and started before many had finished their meals. Two young twin sisters named Karen and Sharon, who seemed to lack the empathy that their names suggested, fought fiercely to the last bun and were declared the winners. Their trophy closely resembling the love child of a coffee pot and a toaster. Highway #17 had forgone the food fight, except for the initial 'salad toss,' to set up for welcoming in the diners to the evening's proceedings, and started playing tunes on the flatbed under the big top. They now billed themselves as "Superhighway 417" since they were growing as much as the general Mittville population. They were a classic hippy line up of guitar, mandolin, fiddle, banjo, gutbucket bass, djembe and accordion. They all sang, sometimes actually sounding harmonious, other times, well, not so much. They were joined by the circus band, consisting of sousaphone, trombone, cornet, glockenspiel and marching drum. Their membership seemed to change whenever I heard them, which was a little too often. Hey, I'm a music critic by trade and temperament. My ex would say that the emphasis was on the 'temper' in that. Of course there was a wild-maned woman, probably about seventeen years old, in a long swishy skirt with a tambourine. I've been to festivals where it looks like those skirts were issued with the ticket She was also contributing sign-language translation when there were songs. They made a riotous but engaging sound, and they succeeded in drawing everyone in for the evening's activities.

They finished with a flourish, and a rosy-faced woman, who turned out to be named Rosie, climbed up to the mic on the flatbed stage and said, "Evening. I'm Rosie from the Governance Committee."

We had one of those?

"This afternoon we decided to have a rotating chair for these 'Sunset Sessions'. So here it is!" A wheelie office chair appeared on stage and two dancers picked her up and twirled her around on it.. She caught her breath and said, "So I'm it tonight, you poor things. I'll do my best and MG here is going to do a little coaching as we go."

Rosie was quite riveting. She did a good job of facilitating a summary of the days' proceedings. Each committee had someone get up with a sheet of newsprint to briefly explain the results. She wrapped up the proceedings by inviting up Dylan with some of his crew, who got everyone going with a song they had written that afternoon as a kind of team-building exercise.

Song 24: We Can Do This

I still find myself down at the wishing well
I still drink from its healing waters
If we have a hope in hell,
To leave something for our sons and daughters
It's that our true spirit will prevail
To bring us back from beyond the pale
Don't you weep and don't you wail
We can do this if we try

We can do this We can do this We can do this if we try
We can do this We can do this We can do this if we try

Here we are we're on an ark
We're looking for the light
In a world that's turning dark
Let's seize the day back from the night
Working in community
We can sail this ship on a gentler sea
To a place of possibility
We can do this if we try

We can do this We can do this We can do this if we try
We can do this We can do this We can do this if we try

If we have all hands on board
For the epic task at hand
Combining forces we could move towards
A vibrant reborn land
When hope leaves us behind we grieve
But together if we all believe
That we can overcome this tyranny
We can do this if we try

We can do this We can do this We can do this if we try
We can do this We can do this We can do this if we try

Get up stand up, don't give up the fight
Get up stand up, we can make this wrong a right

MG closed out the big top proceedings with an invitation to grab a bag of popcorn at the canteen on the way over to the barn for the live stream of Miles' show. A perk of having a circus kitchen.

Chapter Twenty-Seven

As everyone headed to the barn, led by a torch-juggling clown, there was excitement, patchouli, and either weed or skunk aroma in the air. I could never figure out why those two smells had a similarity. These parades were getting really epic, and I suppose kind of a microcosm of the life of Miles' band, where the journey was often more significant than the destination. The last few weeks had been a long parade of vehicles following the tour, and now the tradition carried on with a better carbon footprint and a more creative quality.

I called my buddy filling in for me at the Horseshoe to see how things were coming along there. He told me that the show might be a few minutes late because Miles had figured he'd get paid extra for the live stream, and when the management pitched him around the fabulous exposure he'd get he had replied, "Why does everyone seem to want me to expose myself?" It looked like things were smoothed out though, and he tipped me off to a surprise; their original drummer Buck Skins was on the riser sound checking as we spoke.

Back at the barn, there were, as always, kinks in the system getting the live stream going but the CTN truck had the satellite humming. The crowd was gathered and excited. Half the gang seemed now to be in the ever-growing house band, which was now known as the 'Arkestra'. Maybe changing your name every so often was part of the new vision. They did a bit of a warm up show, with Dylan leading the throng again with another brand new one, "Manitoulin". That guy was matching Miles' productive output, if not the overall craftsmanship, but in that regard I think he'll catch up fast with all the inspiration, perspiration, and what looks like a bit of macho competitiveness.

Dylan, who seemed to be cultivating an early-Lightfoot look with his vest, boots and curly mop, introduced it by saying that it came from that morning's listening session. He motioned to his friend Derek, who had shared with their group his desire to find the tools from these Ark sessions to somehow make his year-round life away just as rewarding an experience as he was finding here. Lots of appreciative nods for Derek, who was onstage playing ukulele, though he seemed like a nice guy anyway.

Song 25
Manitoulin

Well tonight in my mind's eye
I can see us side by side
We are laughing, we're somewhere up on Manitoulin
Time is finally standing still
In my dreams I know I will
Play that scene over and over in slo mo

Why must a moment like this always seem stolen
And who are we stealin' it from?
If time's like a river that just keeps on rollin'
Let's roll with it together as one

Well I know I always say
Just give me a few more days
And I promise, I'll get all of this work done
But I'm fooling myself
There's always something else
And I know you've figured that out by now

Now we're on Lake Manitou
Blue water, red canoe
We should get someone to take a picture of this
'Cause it happens so seldom
I called the office to tell them
That I'm going off-line for a while

Why must a moment like this always seem stolen
And who are we stealin' it from?
If time's like a river that just keeps on rollin'
Let's roll with it together as one

Roxy signaled to the Arkestra that the live feed was ready, and the band found seats in the hay mow. With exaggerated flourishes, jugglers tossed bags of popcorn into the crowd, reminding the recipients to save some for the obligatory food fight, and everyone turned their attention to the big screen.

A red-tail hawk has settled in to the top of a lone pine tree, looking down over a scene that until recently was an ideal spot to scout for supper: a field where the nice farmer seemed to raise him a fresh crop of mice every year. In the last few days the field has been overrun with two-leggeds and four-wheeleds.

A coyote, silent and nimble, sees that the humans are gathered inside, so she wanders through the new settlement, observing close up what she has been watching from a distance all along. She senses the hawk above her. They have come to an arrangement.

Where a deer path once led from the copse to the pond, a wider trail that carries humans and automobiles is carved into the hay stubble. It already looks as if it has always been there. A sign with an arrow pointing towards the pond announces 'Felicity Freeway'. Yes, coyotes can read signs.

Branching off from the freeway are side trails, each named for what lies at their terminus. 'Boujie Boulevard' leads to a circle of upscale, though worn out, motor homes, each with awnings extended, barbecues at the ready, patio furniture surrounding propane-powered fake fire pits. 'Eclectic Avenue' is a mixture of tents, lean-tos and tarps, beside older cars that have been recently yarn-bombed. 'Dilly Dally Alley' ends at a grove of spruces with blankets sheltered by the branches. Long strings of Christmas lights lead the way to 'No-Hate Ashbury', where the 'Calm Zone' is situated. Another sign states 'This is not the Party Plaza. To find that, listen for the bass guitar'. 'Sycamore Street' is lined with circus vehicles and bunkhouses, behind the Big Top tent, surrounded by the 'Yes You Canteen' , where Coyote finds some nice snacks. Then the First Aid tent, and beside that a smaller tent with a sign that said 'Second Aid: We're trying our best'. A trailer is labelled 'Bank: Closed.

Always'. On a striped tent are two signs: 'Office'and 'Onice'. Coyote groans quietly at that one.

Through an archway made of recycled junk and hay bales, with a sign that says 'Ark of Triumphs' , another path leads to campfires, and talking circles, though coyote had never heard a circle talk. Music could be heard in the distance up a small hill, where a golden light leaks out of the cracks in the weathered boards of an old barn. The whole barn vibrates with an energy that feels welcoming to Coyote, but she heads farther up the hill to the only other light on, above an old caravan. There coyote cocks her head to the hawk above, and sits down in the grass to wait.

Chapter Twenty-Eight

After a delay which didn't seem to bother the barn crowd, the screen, which had just been showing an empty stage with the backs of the Horseshoe audience, came to life with the entrance of Toronto DJ and MC Gary Straight.

"Good evening everyone, and sorry for the delay. Actually, I'm not sorry really. This is, after all, Queen Street, where there is a municipal bylaw that states that a delay is required to maintain our hipster status. A special welcome to our live stream guests tonight, and to our servicemen and women overseas listening to the big broadcast tonight on short wave."

There was no reaction to this from Gary's crowd or in the barn. I see Gary a lot at Toronto events, and that was a typical response. He continued, "Who's up for some nostalgia at the Horseshoe tonight? Who here remembers Miles and Myles? Well, you are in for a treat, folks. After a long tour we're delighted to bring back to this filthy stage the next best thing. Please welcome Miles Gerber and the Shit Disturbers!"

Great applause from the barn, and it seemed pretty enthusiastic in Toronto too, but the boys didn't come on right away and I'm guessing they were reluctant to take the stage after that introduction. How would you like to perform after being called the 'next best thing'? Finally, we saw them take their places, with Dougie mock el-kabonging Gary with his bass as he passed him.

In seeing them I realized that Drummer hadn't really talked about their physical appearance much, I guess because he has to look at their mugs everyday, and because he figured they were well known to the public. In old promo shots of Miles in the M and M days he fit that '80s pop look pretty well. Big hair, padded shoulder pastel sport jacket, that moody gaze at the camera favoured then. Looking at them both now I realized that Drummer was teasing them a bit when reporting to me. They were probably both in their 50's but looked pretty good, I thought. Dougie wore a cowboy hat that probably hid his thinning hair. Miles's hair was salt and pepper now but it gave him a distinguished look that fit his legend status. They both had cowboy shirts, jeans and boots, and in fact looked like they could have been brothers. Their bodies, not as saggy as Drummer had hinted at, showed a lot of wear and tear but they were still holding together all right. In covering the 'where-are-they-now' beat for the magazine, I've noticed a cool thing. Once artists of a certain age hit the stage, the magic kicks in and they drop about twenty years. Dougie was just as compelling a performer as Miles. They commanded that stage. A bit larger than life. Looking at Miles I could see why Jim Cuddy from Blue Rodeo once told me that he and Miles sometimes were mistaken for one another. Sharp jaw, keen eyes, and a kind of boyish charm that has lasted long past 'boyhood' for them.

They launched right into a revved-up version of "An Hour West of Lonely" which actually was a modest hit from the Disturbers' first album just after M and M broke up. You could tell this certainly wasn't going to be a Myles and Myles golden oldies show, and in the barn no one was expecting that anyway.

With the song done, and hearing the positive reception to it, you could tell that Miles had chosen the high road without moping about Gary's nostalgia crack, and he was going to make it about the music, not the baggage, (though ironically 'An Hour West of Lonely' was clearly about him missing Maddie after their break-up. Interesting choice.) The band sounded great. Miles and Dougie bowed with the applause and immediately welcomed Buck officially, saying it had been twenty years since they'd played together. Despite his best efforts to look mildly, but not tragically, hip, Buck looked as if he'd spent those twenty years in an accounting firm.

Looking cool but not quite settled in, Miles continued. "Thanks to you all, I'm honoured to be back here, and it seems appropriate that the Shit Disturbers should be playing the best damn shithole in the country! And thanks for that introduction, Gary. I guess. I didn't realize that they still let you on the radio."

Ok, he got his little dig in. Tit for tat. You could see him relax a bit.

"Seriously, I totally understand where that kind of intro comes from. I'm not here to judge, but to maybe show that I have something new to offer, otherwise I wouldn't be shlepping around putting up with this guy anymore," nodding his head at Dougie. "Ladies and Gents, my sidekick, who often does kick me in the side, Dougie Morrison!" Dougie was ready with his fiddle, and he launched into a quick tune that got the barn dancing and the Horseshoe toe-tapping. Miles was a pro. That was well-timed to get everyone on the same page, on and off stage.

After Dougie took a bow accompanied by a little jig, Miles carried on. "Some of you might be here because you've been hearing about what's been happening on the road with us lately." The barn exploded in cheers. "I've learned so much about this great but struggling nation and all it really took was a bit of listening. I highly recommend it. These aren't just to keep your glasses on. (At this Dougie came over and flapped Miles' somewhat prominent ears). Tonight I want to use this opportunity to share a little of what I've learned, and it's something you might miss here in the Big Smoke 'cuz we can get pretty caught up in the gears of our own machinery. Folks, people are hungry for connection. Connecting through community and family is the glue that keeps us all in one piece, and without it you can see things unravel. The world out there is spinning faster; it's hard not to fall off. We need each other to hang on to. Out in the hinterlands where we've been hintering for years, hardly ever landing, folks aren't just statistics about job loss and this loss and that loss. They often DO feel lost, but they haven't gone anywhere. I'm here to tell you that they are not lost. We just haven't gone looking for them. They have something to offer us if we'd just listen. They have names and craggy faces like Dougie here, though usually not that ugly, and most of all they have stories that have real value. We need to hear them if we are to understand our common journey. I've been deeply honoured that so many of you in such a short time have entrusted me with those stories, and allowed me to bring forward your voices through song. It's given me a renewed sense of purpose. A sense of self. Dougie, you probably thought it was my full-time job to sit around feeling sorry for myself."

"You gotta go with your strengths," said Dougie, who was clearly restless to play, so he motioned to Buck and they started into the groove for the next song on the set list.

"Thanks buddy," said Miles, as he got his guitar synced with that groove. "More about that later. But enough about me. It's time to share some of those stories with you tonight. This one goes out to my new family who have been following the song-trail, currently up to who-knows-what on Manitoulin Island." There was a huge ruckus in the barn as the trio launched into the first bars of "The First November Snow", better known as "Burt's Song". Over the intro Miles called out, "Here's to you Burt. You got this ball rolling."

The Toronto crowd seemed to be into what was happening as much as the Arkivists. Miles rolled through much of the new repertoire in the order in which they appeared, so that we got a sense of the evolving narrative. I hadn't heard the songs, but through Drummer's audio journal I heard of them. He couldn't do them all of course. The collection was now more than could be contained in a concert. At one point he paused and invited up Lewis, who I guess had driven them from Espanola to Toronto in record time.

"Lewis Maclean here did us a big favour, filling in for the lovely Miss Nelly-Belle when she became ill. Of course on that drive you get to talking about driving, and he told me the story of how he recently had to arrange the removal of his father's driver's license as the old guy has got the Alzheimer's pretty bad. Those licenses are a real sign of manhood for us Canadian dudes, so I know how rough that must have been. So Lewis, this new one is for you. It's bus fare for your excellent service. Fresh baked out of the oven here in the Horseshoe's so-called green room". Miles sang "Angus Maclean" which sure put tears in the eyes of everyone at the barn. Makeup was running down the cheeks of the clowns. That was a keeper for sure.

James Gordon

Song 26
Angus Maclean

On that awful day, they took my license away
Might as well have taken me out back and shot me
Bit by bit they steal, everything that makes me feel
Like a man, time has tracked me down and caught me.

Well the auctioneer, he's on his way here
To take everything except my pain
What am I bid, how much to get rid
Of one old man named Angus Maclean

Their gonna take me away, to that old folks' place
Put me in a hog pen to die in
And when they try to say, Angus it'll be OK
I still got enough upstairs to know they're lying

Well the auctioneer, he's on his way here
To take everything except my pain
What am I bid, how much to get rid
Of one old man named Angus Maclean

You can't separate the land, from an old farmin' man
We're made of the same damn dirt
Might as well auction me, then maybe we'd
Know what an antique like me was worth

One more trip into town, on this old David Brown,
Don't need no license for that
Then we'll sit in the barn, till they auction off this farm
And we're sold off together for scrap

Wow. Miles could clearly drop a good song at the drop of a cowboy hat now. The response was a good indicator of the simple magic in the Miles2Go movement. A very basic story that seemed personal, yet everyone could relate to it, and after the applause, audience members were sharing their own related experiences around the aging process that we all face.

Miles was on a 'new song' blitz. "If you don't mind indulging me a bit, here's a song I wrote after hearing a common theme running through a lot of the stories, which have been about what we've lost as a society. I'm here to tell you that we can grab a pitch fork and a lantern and take this country back!" They jumped into "We Owe It To The Pioneers" which was a good singalong. Kind of anthemic.

Song 27
We Owe It To The Pioneers

If they saw their squandered legacy, we would surely be ashamed
All they worked for all those years for we have given it all away
To the bankers and the bureaucrats and to the Conrad Blacks
We owe it to the pioneers to take this country back

For the miners in Cape Breton toiling deep beneath the ground
Who never even made enough to buy the coal that they found
To the dust bowl farmers starving in their cold tar-paper shacks
We owe it to the pioneers to take this country back

Take back the spirit that was captured in the canyons of concrete and glass
Give it back to the lakes and the mountains, and to the prairie grass

For the migrant workers harvesting their crops with calloused hands
Who thought that they had made it to a fair and an honest land
To the labourers who cleared the swamps and laid the railroad tracks
We owe it to the pioneers to take this country back

For the women in the textile mills and the canning factories
All those who dreamed some day they'd find respect and dignity
For the natives on the Fraser drying salmon on their racks
We owe it to the pioneers to take this country back

Take back the spirit that was captured in the canyons of concrete and glass
Give it back to the lakes and the mountains, and the fields of prairie grass

And for those who scratched a living from this frozen rocky earth
Who thought they'd made it where you were not judged by your net worth
Canadians who have fallen in between the corporate cracks
We owe it to the pioneers to take this country back

The show was becoming a religious experience, ironic for an old heathen like Miles.

It looked like he was just getting started. He turned to Dougie and said, "Dougie my man, my old side man, my old pain-in-the-side man, there are two kinds of people in this warped old world."

"Here we go," shouted everyone.

"People who are always pointing out our differences, like me, and those who are focused on what we share, how we really have to be on the same side if we are to survive, thrive, revive, jive and drive on! So I hereby retire my 'two kinds of people' rants and offer this instead. We are all just people. There has to be only one kind. One very kind kind. I was wrong."

Song 28
We're On The Same Side

Under the same beautiful moon
Under the same star-filled sky
Do you think that me and you
Can leave our differences behind

We're on the same side
Human beings on a cosmic ride
Watching the comets glide
Up above
Tell me why oh why
Must another day go by
Living in a world that's not guided by love

I really think we can get through it
With a wonderful joining of our hearts
If you really look in to it
We're really not so far apart

Sometimes it's hard to understand it
It doesn't make any sense to me
If we share this same delicate planet
Why can't we all just agree

We're on the same side
Human beings on a cosmic ride
Watching the comets glide
Up above
Tell me why oh why
Must another day go by
Living in a world that's not guided by love

Since we're all in this together
Let's look at the possibilities
Let's take a look at whether
we can shift society

So we're all on the same side
All on the same side

Pretty trippy hippy if you ask me, but I'm a jaded old journalist, and of course it went over big time in the barn. How the hell was Miles pulling all these songs out of his arse? It looked like an addiction now. He wasn't done. He had been on autopilot too long. He was on fire now. He blazed on: "Because we've got this live stream thing going on, I want to give an extra shout-out to Canmore Alberta in case there's anyone tuning in tonight from my hometown."

Ok, there was a small seismic disruption in the barn and in the Horseshoe at the same time here. At the Ark, full of Miles followers', the consensus was that no one had ever heard Miles mention his own past before, preferring to hide behind characters in songs or borrow other people's stories. Most of the barn-folk seemed to have their own opinion about where he was from, based on place names referenced in songs, and the fact that he was known to have lived with Maddie while they were big news in a modest place behind Kensington Market in Toronto. As a supposed investigative reporter I'm embarrassed to say that I didn't know his origins either.

There must have been lots of side conversations going on at the Horseshoe then too, since Miles shushed them and said, with an impish grin, "What, I never mentioned that?"

"You never even told me, Miles," said Dougie, looking wary.

"Sorry Pal, I was just trying save you from having to tell folks you were from Mississauga." Big laughs on the Toronto end there.

"Not true, and what would be wrong with that?" Dougie threw that in to mollify the suburbanites in the crowd.

"Anyway, maybe all this storytelling has made me think about roots more. My daddy was a coal miner there, and when the mine closed when I was a kid, it changed him. Changed the town of course too, from a working town to a tourist town. My dad's miner buddies couldn't dig in the ground anymore, but at the Canmore Hotel, where we played many a time, eh boys?, they'd gather, spitting bitter tales about being left behind in the world, but bound together by common memories that always got them through the hard times. I grew up listening to those storytellers, wondering what their point was, not realizing that those tales were all they had left. I finally figured out that they helped me along this road I've been on ever since I left school and headed to a flop-house just up here on Huron Street. It's just this last little while that I've started to appreciate the value of what those miners had, a bond created by their shared experience, and an understanding of what my dad went through that made him as hard inside as a lump of coal. Dad, I wrote you this song a while ago but tonight's the first time it's felt right to sing it. It was waiting for its turn, and I didn't realize 'til I passed that old spot on Huron that this song is more about what I'm doing now than what I left behind. Dad was mining for coal, and I'm mining for songs, which can be worth more to us than gold as we hold each other through the scary times ahead. While you were kicking coal dust off your boots, I was throwing song dust on those tales. It's thirty years too late, but I love you, Pops Gerber. Hit it boys!"

A smooth show biz segue was missed there because the band didn't know the song, but Buck got a groove going and they launched in. I had made my way over closer to MG.

She leaned over and said, "Mining For Songs. Holy Marketing Opportunity Batman! That would make a great logo on a T-shirt!" Always the merch girl. "That dude is mining for his soul too, eh Bic? Holy shit."

Song 29
Mining For Songs

I don't miss the mining, I don't miss the coal
Though they say that the dust somehow sticks to your soul
But I miss my mine buddies and the stories they told,
This isn't the town I remember

They closed Marra's Grocery, and the hardware store too
Places where you'd always get a 'how do you do'
These days it's out with the old and in with the new
This isn't the town I remember

So tell me a story, sing me a song
Keep those old stories alive
That's how we know that we're where we belong
That's how this town will survive

Monster houses go up, mostly for the weekenders
High-toned rich folks, big city spenders
SUVs lining Main Street, fender to fender
This isn't the town I remember

Flashing their money when they come around
It's hard to turn those developers down
When they tell us what they think is good for this town
This isn't the town I remember

So tell me a story, sing me a song
Keep those old stories alive
That's how we know that we're where we belong
That's how this town will survive

If you dig for those stories, go mining for songs
Gather old friends and family to sing right along
You'll find the real treasure this town's sitting on
And this will be the town you remember

Holy shit was right. The pandemonium was overflowing to the point in the barn that they had to get a new pan. That last chorus was already being sung again like it was 'Auld Lang Syne' or something.

"That's it! That's fucking it!" shouted MG as if Miles could hear her.

Then it happened. Drummer had alluded to this in his recording. It happens maybe once a show. Someone at the Horseshoe yelled out, "Where's Maddie?"

You could hear pins dropping, though I'm not sure why so many people had brought pins and why they couldn't keep them from falling.

Awkward pause.

Then, remarkably, Miles seemed to shrug it off and turned to Bucky. "Hey Bucky Boy, have you seen my wife?"

Bucky got his only line of the night when he said, "Last time I saw her I gave her a ride to the airport after a gig right on this very decrepit stage."

Awkward pause again, then Miles said calmly, "Hey Maddie, folks have been asking about you. Are you out there somewhere? You know how I've been writing all these songs really quickly after a dry spell caused by, well, you know...Well, here's one that took me twenty years to write. This one's for you."

Bucky and Dougie started an up-tempo groove that sounded fresh, so this must have been in the plan, and the lighting guy actually paid enough attention to give Miles a spotlight, and he started in with this:

Song 30
Madalaina

I made it a full-time job feeling sorry for myself
That's a job that doesn't pay
It didn't leave room for anybody else
They just got in the way

Madalaina, it took me way too long
To learn that you can't make things right if you've done nothing wrong
Madalaina, It's not your job to set me free
Madalaina that can only be me

I'd drag around my broken heart
So that everyone could see
I had self-pity down to an art
Poor me, poor me

Madalaina, it took me way too long
To learn that you can't make things right if you've done nothing wrong
Madalaina, It's not your job to set me free
Madalaina that can only be me

I'm reaching out I just want you to know
Madalaina- I'm ready to let go-o-o
Madalaina, Madalaina, Madalaina

It took about ten seconds for that one to sink in. Then Toronto and 'Mittville' both went ballistic with cheering and a genuine 'standing O'. The band gathered downstage, took a bow, and exited. In the barn, everyone seemed to be sharing the sense of release that came with that song, for Miles' years of pining seemed to be part of his mythology now. I could tell as a media man that that guy with the aw-shucks songwriter persona was using the first national forum he'd had in years to set things straight, and his audience seemed to get that. By the front entrance I could see that even the elusive Claire Voyant was smiling.

The cheering kept going in Toronto and Gary the MC got back up and said, "How 'bout that! Miles Gerber and the Shit Disturbers! Do you want to hear one more?" That was a pretty rhetorical question at that point. It took a while. I don't think Miles was milking it, he was probably deciding if they should go back or not. Eventually they returned, Buck to his drum riser and Dougie and Miles stood together at the centre mic. As the attention was shifted back to the stage Dougie said into Miles' mic, "Thanks everyone. That almost severed my humility cord."

Miles thanked the Horseshoe crew and even Gary. To Buck he said, "It's been awesome, Buddy, though I have to say I've been seeing another drummer. We'll always have Oshawa though, right?" Bucky tossed a stick at him for that.

Miles went on, "This is the last blast of this adventure for a while. Not sure what lies ahead, but with the help of Lewis over there we're heading back up tomorrow to Manitoulin to check out that scene. Sorry, Manager Girl, it looks like we'll have to put a pause on that Maritime tour for now. We love you down-easters though. There's a gathering waiting up on that island there of folks that are starting to feel like family, like home. We're gonna do two songs to close, one that we missed in the excitement 'cause we always want to hear one Dougie song, right?" This got less applause than it should have, but Dougie took it in stride and borrowed Miles' guitar, dropped it into a DADGAD Celtic tuning, (hey, I play a little guitar too, you know), and Miles grabbed the bass.

Dougie said, "Well Miles, thanks for this chance, and thanks for all the good times and crappy money along the way. I didn't mean to spring this on you onstage and all, but I've decided that I'm not making the trip back north with you tomorrow."

Miles kept his head down as the audience took an intake of air together.

"You see, we're talking about home here, and the road still feels like that's where I belong. That's my home. I know that sounds as crazy as a bag of hammers but it's real for me. It's getting harder to see where that road leads what with the state of the show business and all, and the fact that I'm getting to be a gent of a certain age, but I plan to have some fun looking. Me, I'm at rest when I'm in motion. So sue me bro. For you, I'd like to sing perhaps my favourite Miles Gerber song if you don't mind. This really could have been about me as well as you, and by the bye, not bad nautical imagery for an Alberta boy!" Then he signaled to Buck and they launched into "At The Whim Of The Wind And The Sea" with Miles joining in late but then singing harmony on the chorus. It was getting really Kumbaya-ish in the barn.

James Gordon

Song 31
At The Whim Of The Wind And The Sea

You would be wrong, if you said I was free
For I'm a slave to the fear of who I might be
If I lingered too long, if complacency
Whispered in my ear and got ahold of me

No one can tell where I might be
Far to the west, or on a warm easterly
I know not where you'd look to find me
For I live at the whim of the wind and the sea

A cowboy out on the trail, a gypsy on the highway
A sailor tossed on the ocean, they all would say
That through doldrum and gale, come what may
We're at rest when we're in motion
At home when we're away

No one can tell where I might be
Far to the west, or on a warm easterly
I know not where you'd look to find me
For I live at the whim of the wind and the sea

This did generate a genuinely warm response from the crowd even though the attention had been deflected from their hero, and you could tell that the barn dwellers really identified with it. After all, many of them had been in motion for a while now.

Miles followed up with "Isn't it Time To Go Home" as a poignant closer. This had become a regular set ender for him during his 'lost in the wilderness' years I'm told. I'd heard it before, but now that he had revealed that he really seemed like he had a home to go home to, it had a different feel. There was an irony here too. He would sing it, I guess, when he was wondering aloud what the point of being out there playing those dives was. Now, with the attention from his Miles2Go thing and what I'm modestly stating will come from the article I'm writing, he could have that revival and that renewed purpose if he wanted to reach out and grab it.

Song 32
Isn't It Time To Go Home

Tonight the crowd is smaller than a Canadian dollar
And we're only getting paid the door
But the expenses are low 'cause after the show
We get to sleep on the club-owners floor

I know they call what we do playing
But it feels like work tonight
Nothing we do seems to make it through
To the other side of the mics

Not another tune to carry. Jesus, Peter, Paul and Mary
Isn't it time to go home

I just don't get it, they raise the speed limit
But the towns seem farther apart
Though you're on it so often the road never softens
It stays just as hard as my heart

The audience is older, the winters are colder
And it's been years since I was warm or young
Just how long can you sing a song
Before it is all sung

Not another tune to carry. Jesus, Peter, Paul and Mary
Isn't it time to go home

Another beige motel, another meal from hell
Another fun-filled tour,
They never said that the glamour was dead
In the show biz brochure

Too many guys with guitars, too many wannabe stars,
So the money keeps getting worse
More and more I have to dig deeper for
The words to the next verse

Not another tune to carry. Jesus, Curly, Moe and Larry
Isn't it time to go home

At the end, the two old road warriors did a little better than the regular man-hug, and they headed off to who-knows-what. It looked like Lewis was going to get them out of there quickly, since Buck was already tearing down his kit.

The live feed came to an abrupt end. There was some milling about until MG got up and urged everyone to head back to their campfires for a bit to do their 'thang' since Maxine was keen to get the barn back to being a barn. Hoping that some would stay to help, she advised us that tomorrow would be a busy day.

"We are all pumped for the return of the prodigal Miles, bummed that Dougie isn't coming too, but understanding, ammaright? And BONUS, my loverly Mitt-mates, we get Drummer back too I think! There are some more morning activities that are going to show up as texts first thing at sunrise." There were boos to that, until she continued, "The sun rises at 10 around these parts, right? Get some sleep."

I saw her retreat into the CTN van with Roxy, and then a moment later their tech guy Don emerged with a blanket, looking for a place to spend the night. I would have offered the back seat of my luxurious abode, but really, I'm just not that nice a guy.

I headed back to Nelly-Belle and made some notes about the night's proceedings before turning in and then off.

Chapter Twenty-Nine

It's hard to sleep in when you are living at the epicentre of a movement. There was a loudspeaker on the pole that Nelly-Belle was nestled against. Dippity opened a crack in the dawn earlier than anyone was hoping for and announced, "Morning Mitters! Pay no attention to this announcement. Breakfast is on the griddle. Park your Arkasses over at the Yes You Can-Teen anytime, though late is preferable in this case. In the meantime, here's Cher to serenade you with a morning raga on the stomach Steinway, or the Arkordion as it's known around here. Hit it Cher. Ouch!"

Ok, Ok. I was up, and I peered out of Nelly-Belle's grimy windshield and saw the CTN truck pull up at the tent's south entrance. Roxy and MG climbed down, and I felt embarrassed to be witnessing their fond farewell, as the tech guy discreetly climbed in the passenger side door. Roxy and the tech guy had been with the story for close to a week now, so it made sense that they'd have to get back to reality. Ok, that was me showing my metro-bias I guess. This was reality too, right? Just a new kind. MG spotted me. She skipped over to Nelly-Belle, pounded on her hood and shouted, "Up and at 'em Mr. Ink Slinger. Let's go see what's shakin!" With that she gave a waggle and dragged me into the morning.

"You OK?" I asked as I grabbed my toothbrush and stumbled out of the van.

"No biggy," she shrugged, but I could tell she was lying, and had decided to make light of Roxy's departure as a way of getting over it. I gestured that I needed to get into the outhouse line up so she said, on the run, "Meet me at the Canteen. I'll grab you a breakfast burrito to go." I wondered where we were going.

When I caught up with her she was holding court, and two burritos, and laughing a little too hard and talking a little too loud. First symptom of heartbreak. I remember my own heartbreak strategy of trying too hard to not look heartbroken.

Glad I got over that, it didn't go with my carefully crafted 'who gives a shit' image.

"Time to make the rounds, dude. Follow me!" She took off towards the pond at a gallop.

It probably took an hour to make our way there. Everyone got a fist bump, a high five, or a hug; often all three, and it looked like a new Ark handshake was developing that was meant to signify two oven mitts meeting. Sometimes a tickle was added in for good measure. She knew everyone's name, though true to her style she had already developed nicknames for many. She'd start with a 'wuzzup?' or 'everything groovy?', then there'd be a plan made or a question answered before you knew it, or she'd say things like, "Hey you big muscly hunks" (to those who certainly didn't fit that label), "How 'bout scoring us some firewood this morning, eh?" To a willowy woman taping a cardboard sign to a fence post that said 'Massages in The Second Aid tent. Two PM. Ish. Pay What You Can', MG said, "Hey Fancy Francie! Nice bedhead. Who does your hair? Why don't you flounce it over behind the Canteen. Aren't you on washup duty this morning?"

"I am?" Francie looked confused.

"Well, you are now, honey!" MG cackled before she dished out a kind of hip check and dragged me along the trail a bit. Versions of this interaction kept going as we made our way, adding bum slaps, hair tussles or blown kisses to her repertoire. In a slight break in the action, I asked her if she needed to talk.

"Always, Senior Curioso," she said, then changed the subject quite deliberately so that I got the message. "Hey, what did you think of Miles' show last night, if that's not giving away some of your reportage?"

"Epic," was all I could think of at the time. "You?"

"Yes, I have my epic moments too. Ha ha. Seriously, Miles is a pro. He did his job, he aced it, right? Except for one thing. Those idiots forgot the only thing I asked them to do. Bring some Merch and plug the Miles2Go website!"

Oh right. Merch Girl to the core.

"It's gonna be interesting to see what happens tonight

when Miles shows up," we both said together, which earned me one of those hair tussles and a cheek kiss. Finally at the pond, newly christened 'Lake Inferior', MG pulled off her T-shirt, shucked her shorts, kicked her cowboy boots at me, and dove in. What remained of her clothing left little to the imagination, though I don't know why people say that. It certainly made me imagine more than I should have in that moment. She emerged quickly. You don't really want to hang out in Lake Inferior that long, trust me.

I like the way you relate with everyone here," I said. "The other night some people wanted to talk about that 'who's in charge' question, and you looked a bit tentative about that. It sure LOOKS like you are in charge today. Where are you at with that?" She was sunning herself on the bank before putting her clothes back on, so I asked while looking away, like you are supposed to do in the movies.

"Well, what you just witnessed on the walk over here was me showing leadership. I have come to understand that people look to me for that, and I want to offer it. I'm learning, like Sam said, to not be the boss, just be a nudger, a nurturer, an ally, a friend, a facilitator. There are glimpses here of what's possible. There are dreams that grow out of the stories we've been hearing and that Miles has been singing about. Miles is the song miner. I'd like to be the dream-catcher-in-residence I guess, but I don't know what that looks like yet. We're all just feeling our way here as we go along. Does that make sense?"

"Yes," I said, looking around to signify that everything was making more sense.

"Well, good then, I fooled you too!", she snorted. "Thanks for biting on that hook though, ya big walleye!" Then she got up quickly and pushed me in the water.

On the way back to the Canteen, I was thinking that there were a lot of sides to that complex and compelling woman; and also thinking on that walk that I was a little too focused on one particular side. Her backside. I know, I know, I've been lost in the sexist reporter culture too long, but I certainly detected that in Drummer's road tales too. Us boys, we have some work to do.

Of course MG had to stop in at all the campfire talking circles, where she looked at me proudly when it appeared that things were happening and decisions were being made without her. She mostly acted as cheerleader at these. Nodding encouragement and whooping at good suggestions, like when one group wondered if they needed a long term 'winterizing' team if some wanted to stick it out after the summer. Solomon's Circle was diving into the question 'What is possible here?' The group seemed equally divided between the 'let's create the conditions for a utopian society' gang and those who thought things would just organically start to happen if we let the seeds we'd planted germinate. They lost me in all the garden imagery. Hey. I live in a concrete jungle created by urban planners. MG said she was looking forward to the summary, and the wintery, later. We stopped in at the 'sanitation' group. Things were getting desperate with the outhouse situation, and Maxine was there expressing concern about the impact on her land.

"Don't worry! The cavalry is coming!" MG shouted, to some skepticism.

Lunch ran smoothly and was probably the best example I'd seen of the collaborative process. Everyone got fed, and everyone chipped in. Speaking of chips, 'Ty Dye The Fry Guy' had moved his truck into the canteen compound and was taking some of the load off the circus setup, already stretched to the limit. The menu seemed about evenly divided between 'whole food' and those who subscribed to the Northern Ontario meat-based diet, where their motto was 'if it ain't fried, it ain't food'. Refrigeration was becoming an issue for this, but as usual there was optimism that something would turn up, and in Ty's case, turnip.

Chapter Thirty

Just as we were all finishing up lunch, a loud ruckus erupted over towards the Ark entrance. Lots of horns honking, drums beating, and a dusty line of cars and trucks on Maxine's laneway.

Leading the pack was a large truck piled up with about a dozen bright blue portable toilets. A treasure for sure. The cavalry was coming to save the day! Perched on top of the load was none other than Drummer, looking for all the world like General Patton on a tank arriving to liberate a village.

I didn't really know much about Drummer 'til I listened to his audio journal of the tour, and even that didn't tell me much, but you could tell he was one shy guy. Here though, he looked like he was reveling in the attention. He leapt off the truck just as MG arrived to wrestle him to the ground where she proceeded to inflict him with an extended nuggie-fest. Once she'd finished tackling him and he'd brushed himself off, a smile broke across his face as he let MG lead him to the lounge area in front of the canteen. That's where the sanitation crew, all wearing 'Shit Disturber' T-shirts from the back of Nelly-Belle, started unloading Drummer's precious cargo.

The parade behind him was a contingent from the Pow Wow, it turned out, and more volunteers led them to the 'Arking Lot'.

I felt for Drummer then, because it seemed obvious that the flock of admirers from our Ark crew were expecting Miles, not Drummer. I could overhear some of them commenting a little too loudly. "Hey guys, it's just Drummer." In my years of covering bands for the paper, I learned that drummers are always invisible. Stuck in the back they were heard but not seen, and I'll spare you the countless drummer jokes around that. I guess countless is appropriate there because half of those jokes are about their inability to count. The crowd dispersed quickly, but there were still enough well-wishers to give Drummer a decent welcome back.

MG grabbed him by the hand, which was a clear embarrassment to Mr. Shy, and led him and his Pow Wow pals on a tour of the new festival/village/whatever it was. I tagged along, listening to the two of them catching up before reintroducing myself.

"Hey Drummer. It's Vic Penn. Folks call me Bic. That's my pen name."

He didn't recognize me at first since I was certainly more 'kempt' last time we interacted.

"Bic!", he said with an elaborate handshake. "You got the tapes!"

"I sure did, Drummer. So grateful."

"Got what you need for your story?"

"That and so much more. It was amazing. That's why I'm here. There's a new story to tell, right? And it's way bigger than a magazine article.

"No shit", said Drummer. "Though I guess enough shit that we had to come to the rescue from the Pow Wow, eh?"

He was turning in circles, trying to take everything in, and with a look of wonder said, "So this is kind of a white guy's Pow Wow, eh?"

I hadn't thought about it in that light. Cool. I asked him about something that I'd been trying to figure out from the tapes. "Those awesome tapes, Drummer. Just one question. The Nelly-Belle parts." (I tried to choose my words carefully). "What section in a book store would I look for that in?"

Drummer looked to the sky for a minute, then said, "My friend, fiction is just the truth with a groovier drumbeat." He gave a deep lusty laugh, looked around at Mittville, gave me a wink, and said, "Look at all this! Makes you believe in magic, donut? With sprinkles on top." That was my cue to leave that matter alone.

We made the rounds, with MG kind of acting as Drummer's hyperactive publicist along the way. Drummer had a permanent expression of awe and delight on his wind-burned face. That must have been one brisk ride up on that biffy-bearing truck. Since I had seen him when I handed over the tape recorder, he looked older and younger at the same time.

I'm guessing he was about forty but there were kid-like elements in his open face and his awkward gait, yet he had a kind of elder's wisdom in his deep brown eyes.

Maxine met the 'tour' as they got close to Lake Inferior, looking justifiably concerned about the growing population of her farm. She was glad to see the Pow Wow contingent, welcoming the idea of bringing some of the Wiikwemikong vibe to the place. Together they picked a good spot for a sacred fire circle, between the pond and a spruce grove. A team of Ark Angels cleared the area and a smudge ceremony got them started as the big drum was being set up.

We found a campfire to gather around, and Drummer started to talk to the circle about his experience at the Pow Wow. You could tell that taking the spotlight was new to him, and he spoke quietly and hesitantly. He reiterated some of what he'd mused about on the tapes: his sense of limbo between worlds since he didn't really identify readily with either; how he had been following Miles' quest but hadn't really determined what his own was. This weekend had helped him to understand the 'red path' more, and that felt like home to him, though he said he couldn't quite explain it yet but he wanted to find new ways to find a path for 'settlers' to follow that didn't feel like an opposing path. Sounds like Drummer had a new gig, and that he'd identify with Miles' new "Same Side" song.

. A steady parade of cars seemed to be streaming up the farm laneway carrying a growing throng of folks brandishing banners and flags. This looked like the official Miles Welcoming Committee. Quite a few false alarms as vans resembling the one they had left in with Lewis would enter. The Ark Angels were now collecting a twenty dollar 'Infrastructure tax levy' on the 'Late Bloomers', and they were starting to initiate 'Valet Arking', where Clutch's crew would find suitable spots for the growing vehicular burden on the farm. This was all great and not great at the same time. The Ark was bursting at the seams, which might mean she could sink. (I think Arks are female, but I'm not sure.)

The joint was vibrating with excitement, and soon the drum

circle was providing the rhythm for that. I was sitting beside Drummer when I was nudged by someone in a cowboy hat who squeezed in between us. He tipped his hat low to hide his face, placed his fingers to his lips and took off the hat. It was Miles. He urged the campfire circle to keep it secret. That wasn't going to last. He then engaged Drummer in one of those Canadian intimate male conversations that us guys are so skilled at.

"Yo Drummer."

"Hey."

"What's Up?"

"Nothing much". Two good laughs there. "You?"

"Holding my own, which is illegal in Alabama I think."

"Cool. Where's Dougie"?

"You didn't hear?"

"I don't hear that good, I'm a drummer."

"Dougie's buggered off. I'll tell you more about it later. Hey, don't tell anyone but I put on my Cloak of Invisibility and I've been roaming around this joint for about an hour. Holy Shit, Drummer Boy!"

Just then there was a commotion that sounded like the Beatles had come on to the field at Shea Stadium. Miles had snuck in because he had anticipated something like this. But the word was out.

"Where's Nelly-Belle and MG?" shouted a nervous Miles. MG must have been tending to her flock near the entrance, so I motioned everyone to stay put. "Follow Me!" I whispered to Drummer and Miles as we started to make a run for the Big Top just ahead of the mob. Those two jumped into Nelly-Belle while I guarded the tent's entrance. Two clowns with foam baseball bats helped with fending. I thought I'd give a little space for the band mates to catch up which meant I probably missed out on a good conversation. Maybe Nelly-Belle will report on it.

Next thing we heard was the public address system, which always started with a nice blast of feedback to get everyone's attention. It was MG, starting off with one of her signature 'yee hahs'.

"Buckaroos and Buckerettes. Yes indeedy-do, Monsieur Gerber is among us, so we've got ourselves a real shindig now! He musta snuck in, that rascal, thus missing the elaborate welcoming ceremony. You can put your twenty-one guns away. I have a warning though. That dude, after the response last night and seeing what's happening now, has a monstrous ego. Holy Moly, it's as big as Prince Edward Island. Give him a bit of space, OK? That enlarged head of his is likely to explode any minute, and our clean up crew is busy enough. Get it? Let me hear you! OK. If you haven't seen him yet, Drummer is in the house, and he's brought friends from the POW WOW who are drumming right now on the far side of Lake Inferior. They are welcoming all you Mitters to join them back there. Miles and Drummer are there now. So say hi but be as respectful as you bunch of grifters can be. Dinner is at the regular time, and we'll start the Big Top session with our special guests at 7:30 cuz I'm guessing there will be lots to talk about! Jam ya later! Over."

MG was a genius. Or a genie anyway in granting Miles' wish. She had found a way to lead the fans off the trail for a bit and let them check out the drum circle at the same time. Within minutes she had dashed past me with a wink then raced to Nelly- Belle, where a grand re-union ensued. It was hard to remember, but they actually hadn't been separated that long in time, though there was a whole new world to catch up on.

Chapter Thirty-One

Standing watch over Nelly Belle, I had a moment to pause and look out at the bustling community that the Ark of the Oven Mitt had become. I spied with my little eye:

- a flag football game going on with the latrine kings and queens, celebrating the installation of Drummer's newly delivered bounty. They had divided into 'The Real Shit Disturbers' and 'The Bog Dogs' for the big match.
- in the distance, a round dance happening around the drum circle
- a Tai Chi class happening in front of the barn
- stilt walking lessons
- a young couple demonstrating the literal definition of 'a roll in the hay'
- Solomon's visioning circle deep in animated conversation
- many hands making light work of getting dinner organized
- a large oven mitt made from straw bales and field flotsam under construction by the main entrance
- lots of hither and yawning, backing and forthing, to-ing and fro-ing, picking and grinning, chewing the low-fat, and basking with robins. Everyone looking chilled but thrilled. Everyone looking like this had always been there.

The three amigos emerged from Nelly-Belle, and joining me, we headed towards the canteen. I had to remind Miles who I was. We shook hands and he looked at me sideways and said, "Let me guess. A 'whatever-happened -to-Miles-and-Myles' story? Wow, no one has ever thought of that before."

"Yes that was my original assignment. Not anymore. I think The Rag is going to be surprised about what is emerging, and I think people will want to hear about it. I'll make sure you get to see what I've got before it goes to print."

"All righty then, Mr. Penn, sir."

As we made our way, MG's tactic seems to have worked. Miles was greeted as a friend more than an idol, which he really needed. Lots of 'hey Miles' shout-outs as we made our way. No Drummer shout-outs though, 'til we found a place to sit at the edge of the canteen lounge, which now had two sections: one regular and one that was morphing into a beer tent. Dippity came over with the bull horn and conferred briefly with Drummer, who nodded. They made their way to the centre of the action.

Dippity announced, "Friends! Hope you're all getting some chow. The fish tacos look amazing. Not sure about the squirrel stew though. We're so blessed to have Miles and Drummer back in our midst since they played such a major role in this grand creation." Lots of cheering of course, and Drummer looked proud to have been included in the creation story. "Take it away Drummer!"

Drummer took the megaphone and gave the land acknowledgement, a little meandering but straight from the heart, and then said, "I'd like to say Grace, since Grace isn't here to say it herself. Heh heh. I've got it written out here since I just heard it for the first time yesterday at the Pow Wow.

"We thank Great Spirit for the resources that made this food possible. We thank the Earth Mother for producing it, and we thank all those who laboured to bring it to us. May the wholesomeness of the food before us bring out the wholeness of the Spirit within us. Now let's eat!"

As we dug in, a pretty young woman with a large black wingspan of feathers and the head of a raven over her own head swooped in on Drummer with some good raspy raven calls and wrapped him in her arms, er, wings. Drummer and the raven had an extended cawing conversation all in pure raven, then they dissolved into giggles and hugs. MG and Miles had seriously dropped jaws.

"Hey guys," Drummer said with a huge blush, "This is Raven."

MG said, "I see that but what's your name?"

"Raven," said Raven.

"Oh," said MG. "I'm MG".

"Ya but what's your actual name?" said Raven.

"That's the million dollar question, Raven," said Miles, who then introduced himself more formally. "I'm Miles. That's my actual name."

I did my usual "I'm Vic but folks call me Bic" line. Raven looked confused, and looked at me with one eye the way ravens do.

"Why do they call you Bic?"

"Well, because I'm a reporter and I chew Bic pens. It wasn't my idea, or my parents' "

"Wow, you're a real Sharpie, ain't ya? Doesn't anyone have just a plain ol' name around here?" said Raven with an exasperated wing flap.

"You're one to talk," said Drummer.

"No, I'm one to K-Kaw!" which she did for a bit, all the while looking dreamily at Drummer.

Drummer added, "We met at the Pow Wow, and well..." He looked down at the ground but I caught the shy smile that lit up his face and could feel the sentiment behind it. I remember feeling like that. Ahh, love!

"Well fucking Pow and fucking Wow!", said MG, scooching over to make room for Raven and stroking her feathers. Judging by the still-dropped jaw of Miles, I could tell that this kind of connection with birds and other humans was a very rare thing for Drummer. Cool! The lovebirds focused on each other then, as they do, as well-wishers came around to our table to say hello.

Cher joined Dippity. They introduced themselves to the newbies, and briefly discussed how the evening would go. As I had imagined, Miles didn't feel like anything too formal.

"Remember that night outside Portage, MG? Can we do something like that to get back in the swing of things?"

I remember Drummer, or maybe it was Nelly-Belle, talking about that on the tapes. MG pointed out just how many people there were now, more coming in all the time who had seen the broadcast. Apparently Roxy had done a CTN location report from the road on her way back that day too. I bet she was bummed out that she missed Miles. It was decided that they'd make a bigger song/story circle with the addition of the new flatbed that had delivered the outhouses. (The driver was too intrigued to drive away yet). That would give some depth for a circle, or at least a horseshoe, on stage, but still let folks see what was going on.

In the brief break after dinner, MG realized she was homeless now that Roxy was gone, and so were Drummer and Miles. She led Miles up to Maxine's farmhouse, where their celebrity status probably earned them rooms.

I decided to do my job and interview some folks, realizing that the Ark residents were becoming more of a story than Miles was. He was the kindling for the fire they were burning now. Most of them told me they were there because something had felt missing in their lives. Miles came along and somehow gave them permission to actually look for that certain something. It made me think of that "Dreamin' Of A Dream" song. That woman who told a simple story seemed to just find value in articulating what was happening for her, and in hearing it back as a song? Well, she must have felt she had been validated somehow; that it was OK for a small town nobody to be a somebody in her dreams.

After grabbing some choice sound bites, I ambled back to Nelly-Belle. My dream was to catch a nap, but I found Drummer and his raven-haired Raven standing by the van. I could see they had a plan. And Raven had a small tent under her arm/wing.

"For you," she offered.

Drummer added, "If it's all right, I'd like to let Raven get to know Nelly-Belle, being that they are both such fine ladies and all." More blushing and giggling, which revealed why I had been banished from my spot in the back seat. As a reporter, I'm better with tense than with tents, but it was something. The two of them helped guide the Pow Wow flatbed in behind the other circus one, and folks started to arrive for the evening.

The always-growing house band jockeyed for position, obviously excited about Miles joining them, which he did pretty soon after. The jamming started right away, with Dylan and company catching Miles up on the songs that had been happening just in the last couple of days. Miles looked genuinely impressed, and happily got to play sideman for a change. From what I'd heard, Dougie would have been in heaven at this gathering, despite the fact that two of the younger ones with fiddles were living proof that owning a violin did not necessarily mean you could actually scrape out a tune. No one cared though.

I think MG was itchy to have some sort of structure to the evening, so she jumped in after a toe-tapper from the bluegrass faction and called everyone to attention.

"Do Burning Rubber!" yelled that same heckler guy that had been at it since I got there. I looked back at him and apparently the clowns had made him legit by giving him a big dunce cap to wear that said 'Official Heckler Guy' on it. I guess he was just doing his job.

MG deflected him with, "Well, sport, you don't have to worry about finding a rubber tonight. You ain't getting lucky with that get-up!"

It looked like she had a speech ready in her hand, but Miles clearly wasn't up for that and he stepped up to the mic to a grand reception of course.

"Thanks everyone. It's great to see you, though you know what? Last night at the Horseshoe I could FEEL you all the way down in the big city, and it felt good to know you were there for me."

"We're here for you now Miles!" shouted Heckler guy again, this time reading from a cue card, which wasn't really as much fun.

Dippity interjected: "Excuse me, recently designated Official Heckler Guy, that's not a heckle!"

Heckler Guy: "Was so!"

Dippity: "That's not a heckle either. That's a retort."

HG: "Oh, who died and made you the heckle judge?"

Dippity: "It was more of an insight. Now THAT was a heckle. We don't have an Insightful Guy. Would you like to switch jobs?"

HG: "Eat my Shorts. Oh sorry. I didn't mean that."

Dippity: "Now you see, that was a heckle, followed by a compassionate, personal, revealing moment, which kind of defeats the point."

HG whispered to the next person over- "I don't know what to say to that."

Dippity, on the megaphone: "Job Opening. Heckler Guy loses his edge! Actually becoming agreeable! Is there a shrink in the house?"

HG: "As if."

Dippity: "Now that was sarcasm, not a heckle."

Cher called the heckler-in-chief over to where she stood with Dippity. They bowed, and with a stage manager gesture, said, "And scene!"

Miles had a confused, bemused, and not that amused look on his face, and he continued, "It's pretty amazing what you folks have done here. Ark of the Oven Mitt. Who knew? I like what I've seen so far, and I'm very honoured to have played some part in the creation of this watcha-ma-callit thinga-ma-jiggy you've got going on here. It's especially cool to see that I'm not really essential to what happens here. You know me: I have a serious case of Restless Boot Syndrome and was worried I'd be locked into one spot."

"We need you Miles!" and variants thereof came from all over, not just Heckler Guy, who seemed to feel upstaged.

"Don't worry folks, I'm sticking around a while. I DO have an announcement to make though. Some guys in suits came to the Horseshoe last night. They've been following this whole shebang in the news and they've offered me a weekly radio show on the CBC starting in September, called 'Miles2Go' of course, thanks to MG here, who I'm hoping will join me on the production/research side."

The Throng didn't seem too sure if this was good or bad news. It took them a while to show their appreciation, but then there were nods of approval and you could see some were thinking 'hey, we could be on the air!' This definitely was news to MG who looked more baffled than flattered.

"Friends, it's all about the stories and the way they get shared and passed around like the gemstones they are," said Miles. "I've already heard some good ones since I got here, and it's awesome that some of you have taken up the challenge with the songwriting. Special thanks to Dougie here."

MG kicked him and corrected him on that. "Oops, my Freudian slip was showing. Dylan! But speaking of Dougie, I just figured he'd be in his regular spot over there I guess. We all miss him. It was time though I suppose. We had about 10 good years together."

"I thought it was more like 25!" shouted Drummer from his drum stool.

Miles answered, "Ya, but only about 10 of them were certifiably good, right buddy? We had some pretty lean years. Hey, why don't you say something? I bet you have some real tales to tell from your big weekend, eh?"

Drummer started to climb around but MG handed him the mic, knowing he had those protective drums to keep him in his comfort zone.

"Miigwetch everyone. Great to be here, and yes sir, the Pow Wow was a huge thing for me, and it was kind of all about sharing stories too. I'm keen to see what common threads those stories have between there and you all. Thanks to my friends who have joined the party here from Wikwemikong". He got corrected on the pronunciation by Raven. "I've got some time to get that right. And oh, this is my friend Raven. Something else to stick around for! Hey, and a shout-out to Bic Penn down there. Have you guys met him? He got me started on telling stories about this tour, and even filled in for me while I was down the road a piece. Hey Bic. Maybe I could get that job back again tomorrow, eh?"

News to me, but it made sense. That was probably more public speaking than Drummer had ever done, so he tossed the mic back with a bit of a bow, just as re-instated Heckler Guy called out, on cue, "Come on Miles, give us a song!"

After a brief discussion around key and instrumentation Miles launched into "You Know Where To Find Me",' which seemed to flow from his "Madaleina" song from the night before. It must have been an older one because MG sang backup on it, sounding for all the world like Maddie would have back in the day.

Song 33
You Know Where To Find Me

You know where to find me I'll be in between the cracks
Whistling up a westerly to whisper at my back
Following old paths and walking down the railway tracks
Counting up the ties that always bind me

You know where to find me- dilly dallying at the docks
Listening to the waves wailing their love song to the rocks
Singing with them till their rhythm resets my clock
I let the sea rewind me

You know where to find me, fighting for some hopeless cause
Performing puddle operas with the rain as my applause
Or creeping through back alleys on my little tom cat paws
Sniffing 'round for memories to remind me

Of when our future rang just like a Gibson banjo
Bright as a big yellow sun by Vincent Van Gogh
Now that the skies are gray I have lost my way
But you know where to find me

You know where to find me, I'll be digging way down deep
For what it was we had before we seemed to fall asleep
And woke to find we'd let the big bad wolf in with the sheep
I'm stuck in time and stymied

You know where to find me I'll be questioning the moon
Asking if it knew that things would fall to earth so soon
Wondering if I could recreate that Brigadoon
Or have I really left all that behind me?

You know where to find me, where we used to chant for peace
Where our legendary heroes set out for the golden fleece
Fishing streams for dreams - now it's just catch and release
Looking for the stories that define me.

OK I was there because it was my job, not because I was a fan, but I was getting converted quickly. The raggedy band turned the infectious groove into a bit of a jam-out, which ended suddenly when the lights went out onstage and a spotlight pointed to the rear entrance of the Big Top.

Chapter Thirty-Two

All eyes, and a follow spot, were on a slowly approaching procession from just outside the Big Top.

Leading the way were the stilt walkers, who were scattering rose petals ahead of a bagpiper, (where did she come from?), followed by Maxine's horse Buttermilk covered in a rich burgundy tapestry. With the same material, dressed in a long cape, with a hood mostly covering her face, I gathered by the whispers around me that it was the enigmatic Claire Voyant, riding Buttermilk bareback, looking very regal. Beside her, to some gasps from the crowd, was what appeared to be a coyote walking step for step with the horse. Above, the dancers I'd seen before swung from long white silk ropes, moving to the stately march of the piper. It was as grand an entrance as I've ever seen, choreographed perfectly and filling the tent with a sense of wonder.

It took about as long to get to the stage as it took Omar Sharif to get to Peter O'Toole in his entrance scene in Lawrence of Arabia. We stayed transfixed, just like in the movie.

As the queen and her retinue finally approached the stage, witnesses still swear that the coyote took a few steps forward as the piper stopped playing, turned, and said "Now," before darting out the other door. Claire moved forward and said in a soft voice to Miles, as a warm wash of light rose on the stage, "Found you."

There was a pregnant pause that had a spacious gestation period.

I hear that Miles liked to keep a 'poker' face when he could. His feelings came out in his songs not in his facial expressions. Here though, his face seemed to be scanning through his interior Roledex of emotions, finally settling on a combination of a 'what the fuck?' and a 'look , a double rainbow!' expression. He squinted at her like she was a blinding sun and said "Hey Maddie."

There was a collective gasp and a group inhale from the

crowd. With the two of them seemingly frozen in place, and their audience still holding their collective breath, Claire/Maddie said "Hey Miles. Fancy meeting you here. How's it going?"

"Not too shabby. You?"

"I knew you would say that."

"Oh, because you're clairvoyant?"

"No 'cuz you haven't change a bit."

"Working on that, actually."

Then MG gave a little girl's wave and said, "Hi Mom."

This time it was more of a big group EXHALE.

"Hey Molly," said Maddie.

Heckler Guy blurt out a huge "Molly?" and the crowd tossed that name around for a while like they were playing 'hot potato'.

Maddie: "So did you tell him Molly?"

Miles: "Tell me what?"

MG: "After you, Ma."

Maddie: "All righty. Miles. I believe you are acquainted with my daughter Molly Gerber?

Crowd: "Woah!"

Miles, after hearing MG's real name finally, plucked the question out of the air that was on everyone's lips.

"MG- Molly Gerber. Jesus. Who, who, who's your father?"

Molly: "What are you an owl? Ask Mom. I have no idea."

Maddie: "She's adopted. I don't know either."

Miles, looking around and seemingly noticing for the first time the crowd gathered there:

"OK, MG, I mean Molly. Did you know about all this? Were you in on this plan?

MG: "Hey, can we maybe not talk about this in front of hundreds of people?"

Maddie: "Well, our whole relationship happened on stage really. Why change that now?"

Sam, who was at that moment holding Buttermilk's reins as if she was Maddie's squire, interjected, "We'll hold space for you. I can facilitate. You can feel safe here."

MG, Miles and Maddie in their first act of unity, all said "Shut up Sam."

Miles looked around as if wondering if there were more surprises, then said, "Hey Maddie, why don't you get down off your high horse and come up here?"

That let everyone laugh nervously and breathe a bit. Maddie was just a little below stage level so she nudged Buttermilk forward and Miles, somehow embracing the scene Maddie and the circus folk had set, extended his hand in a theatrical gesture. Maddie took it with more gasping from the crowd, and gracefully planted herself onstage with Molly standing awkwardly between the erstwhile couple.

Then Maddie turned away, dropped her cape, threw it to Sam, and turned around to more gasps. This crowd was going to gasp themselves out soon. I'll be damned if she wasn't wearing her most iconic outfit from her MTV heyday: the famous 'little black dress' from the Miles and Myles "Love Flirts" video and hit single that really broke them through to the mainstream. Except for her long white hair, she was the same Maddie Myles who, with that same dress, had adorned the walls of many a pubescent boy's bedroom wall.

Heckler Guy, overcome, and back in form, yelled out, "Show us your tits!"

Miles obliged, lifting up his cowboy shirt.

More laughter, and when it subsided, Maddie took the mic and said, revealing that the Heckle dude's line had been in the script, "And that, ladies, gentlemen, and clowns, is one of the main reasons I got out of the biz." Sam handed Maddie a ringmaster's jacket to put on, with some disappointed groans from the men, though admittedly the little black dress looked a bit out character with the gang still frozen in place on the stage.

All was quiet again, when Drummer uncharacteristically made his way to the mic and said, "Hi Claire, I mean Maddie. I'm Drummer. I joined the band after you and Buck left. What we've been doing here is sharing stories with each other, and it seems to help to bring folks together. I bet if we heard your story, and yours, MG or Molly, we could..."

MG cut him off and stated, "Here? Now? What?"

Maddie jumped in, "Well as a matter of fact..." Just then there was a drum roll, and from a trampoline just off the stage, Dippity, in full Shakespearian garb with a scroll in his hands, bounced onto centre stage and in an English accent, started to read from the scroll.

"Kind villagers, allow me, with the help of the Arkitect Players here, to relate the stirring tale of Maddie Myles, aka, Claire Voyant, and ..."

"Wait!" interrupted Miles. "You're getting a theatre company to speak for you?"

Actually I thought it was weird, but I was intrigued, and the Elizabethan costume seemed appropriate since all these sudden plot twists could have been written by the Bard himself.

Maddie shot back, "Well, Mr. Gerber, you always seemed to want to speak for me, so I wanted to make sure you didn't do that this time. Just a precaution, hon. So shut up and listen."

It was clear that Maddie was well-loved too by the throng, but their loyalty was with Miles. This remark resulted in the first chorus of 'boo' that I'd heard under the Big Top, led by the Heckler-in-chief. Drummer was still by the mic, still brave, and he said, "Calm down folks. I see where that big time theatre idea came from Ms. Myles or Gerber or Voyant. I'd just like to say that what I've been seeing on this tour with these fine folks here is that the stories are first-hand, in-the-moment. Real. From the heart, not from a page, or a scroll like I see here."

"All right. All right," said Maddie.

Miles chimed in, "And while we're at it, everyone, including me, thought that grand entrance was pretty cool. But seriously, why?"

"Too Much?" Maddie waggled her LBD a bit and got a laugh, which broke the ice, which you could have skated on by then. I recognized that same 'waggle' from MG. "Ya, I guess you were right. But Miles honey, you were always in control in the band but you have to admit that I was the main draw for fans. And judging by the success of your solo career, it looked like I was right."

"ZING!", shouted Heckler Guy.

"So tonight I guess I wanted to be in control. Sorry. Really, my apologies to all. This was hard to do, and I didn't know how to do it. You probably saw me as Claire over the last few days here. I was ready to be outed but I was scared. And I guess I learned through my role with the Sycamore Sisters that, as Sam here says, 'moving from the coercive to the collaborative' is what we need to do if we are going to create the new world we all need. I wasn't observing my own rule, was I? I DO want to feel safe here, as Sam said. So you know, if it's OK with you Drummer, let's share these stories in a more intimate setting after, OK? The stage puts me in performer mode. The stage creates a wall. I built that wall; let's tear it down maybe around a campfire later."

There were nods of agreement all round. It was interesting that she talked about power, since we were all looking at one powerful, compelling woman who was now showing her own vulnerability. I guess one reason for joining the circus was that she was clearly a show person, a natural, judging by what happened next.

Maddie took the mic off its stand, and said, "You know, I write songs too. Miles here just never took them seriously. AND seriously, it was intimidating to be living with one of Canada's greatest songwriters!"

That put the crowd all back on her side. Sucking up can work wonders. She looked up, and from the top of the tent Cher, without Dippity, descended in a giant swing holding an electric keyboard, pulling off a rock-chick look that you wouldn't have guessed she had in her. Beside her, three Tina-Turner-esque backup singers landed as if from the heavens. The lighting got a little moodier, Maddie conferred with the band, and they started into a sultry R and B kind of groove. She was a belter, and man, she still had that voice!

Song 34
Miles and Miles

It took
Miles and Miles, of time and space
Miles and Miles to get to this place
Miles and Miles, and years and years
Miles and Miles to get to here
So much rain to get a sky this clear

It wasn't happiness, it wasn't wealth
It wasn't fame that I was looking for
I was searching for a sense of self
You know I couldn't find it with you anymore

I had to get so far apart
To look back and see
What was causing this pain down deep in my heart
It wasn't you it wasn't me

It wasn't the road I was travelling
It took me too long to see that was true
I found myself unravelling
And I put it all on you

It was a good thing those big tent poles were solid, or the roof would have come down. The ovation grew even louder when Miles stood beside Maddie and they stood arm in arm together. Molly, who clearly didn't inherit her mother's sentimentality that tempered her toughness, took the mic, shushed the crowd, and said, "Awww, you guys pretty well wrote the same song to each other. That's so cute it makes me want to barf!"

Miles: "Well, which one was better? I'm kidding."

Maddie: "See what I mean?"

Heckle Guy, caught up in the hoopla, called out, "So you guys getting back together, or what?"

Maddie laughed, and said, "Well Miles old man, and by the way, your song about us was really good, almost as good as mine." She dug into his ribs at that. "One thing I think we can agree on, listening to the songs, and listening to your stories about the road, is that we have a cultural assumption that if something ends it has to go on record as being a failure. Well, we made some good records together in the band; they didn't become bad records once we stopped making them. We had a good thing going between us. We loved each other." Here she looked at Miles and said, "We still do I think." A chorus of sighs from the crowd. "We affected people's lives. We done good, and we've spent twenty years beating ourselves up about who did what and what went wrong. We're both a couple of knuckleheads really. Just like the music we made together resonated in the '80s and '90s, maybe it was right for just a certain time. Our relationship had an expiry date on it too. That doesn't mean that it wasn't good before that. You moped pretty publicly about our breakup for, like, ever, and I just let it simmer on low heat all this time. Did either of those strategies work? I doubt it. What helps is that we're here now."

Heckler Guy yelled, "So cut to the chase, are you guys getting back together or not?"

MG nudged them together in the spotlight as if she was arranging them on top of a wedding cake. They looked at each other, smiled, and getting close into the mic together, said in unison, "No Fucking Way."

This got one of those delayed applauses, but it grew, until MG became MC again and said, "Well, what a beautifully poignant note to end on. Let's call it a night, shall we? One helluva' night. Class dismissed 'til tomorrow. Go do your thing. Thanks everyone."

The Arkestra started into a waltz as the crowd dispersed. Maxine approached and called Maddie, Miles, MG and Drummer over to the side of the stage. "Bedtime stories and nightcaps at my place anyone?"

Miles turned to me and said, "You might as well come too, Bic. Everyone is going to pester us for the 'amazing true story of Miles and Myles' so you might as well get it out there, and get it right, so we could let that part go, OK?"

I followed them up the hill into the night.

Chapter Thirty-Three

On our way up the path to Maxine's we were greeted by enthusiastic well-wishers. Drummer came up beside me and asked again if he could have his old job back with the tape recorder.

"I kind of miss it," he said. "But not 'til tomorrow 'cuz I'm a little distracted right now. But you could use more stuff, right?"

Drummer seemed to realize that Raven wouldn't fit in to the upcoming conversation, and after asking me to confirm that he really should be there, he pecked her beak then kissed her lips and she flew off towards the drumming circle, which had already started up again. As we got to Maxine's the little group was discussing the logistics of what might come next, as if it were some kind of summit meeting instead of a visit. I guess the agenda was to catch up on twenty years in one sitting, which seemed daunting but there seemed to be a sense that this kind of get-together might not be ongoing. Maybe it was now or never. They talked about whether I really should be there but Miles gave it a good sales pitch.

"Do we have anything to hide now? Bic here and other media like MG's pal Roxy have been forming a narrative that is already in the public realm. They'll just make shit up, like songwriters do, if they don't have the basics."

Maddie thought about it for a minute and then agreed, saying that a chat just with the three main characters in the drama might not go well if left alone. "I think we both have some anger and resentment in us, despite how well we did tonight, and we did pretty good, didn't we? Maxine is an impartial ally for sure, and you've got Drummer there, so could I have Sam along too for backup? She's got a mean left hook."

It was decided, and Maxine invited us into her slightly chaotic but welcoming farm house. Sam got a text message and showed up minutes later as Maxine tried to ease us in around her wood stove with snacks and small talk. None of these folks talked small. They lived too large.

Maddie started, "So I'm not sure you NEED to know how I got here or where I've been, but Miles, even though you don't even seem to own a phone and you haven't given an interview in a long time, even to Bic here, your whereabouts is on the record. Mine are not, so maybe we should square up on that. So should I start?"

Everyone liked that idea. She continued, though she got up from the rocking chair she was in, ('A rocker for a rocker,' Maxine had offered,) and paced the room with a whiskey in her hand. Despite her apparent nervousness she had a real grace to her movements, like a dancer, or I guess like a circus performer. Known for her imposing presence, she was smaller than I thought, and out of the spotlight she looked all of her 50-something years but she wore those years as well as that vintage dress.

"One thing I did hear about you, Miles,", she said, "is that you and Dougie were starting your shows with some lame joke about searching for the end of the music business because it's clearly in its death throes. I get that."

"It wasn't that lame really," said Miles, who was pretty well lying down on a couch.

"Hey, no interruptions. I have the talking whiskey now. Well if you ask me, the music business deserves to die. It's too sick to be resuscitated. It sounds like it's even worse than twenty years ago because at least then people appreciated their favourite acts enough to buy their merch, right Molly? When I hit the wall with it, it was so cut-throat, so soul-destroying. It wasn't about music anymore. Like we all do though, I got sucked into the allure. I have to take some of the responsibility myself, since I was a party to the creation of the image that the public came to know me by. I sold myself and they bought it gladly. That was the point I was making with this stupid dress tonight. That backfired, eh Sam? I was trying to show how ridiculous it was for women on stage back then, but all the men in the audience were drooling, same as ever. There weren't too many women in the game in our heyday, Miles, so we were making it up as we went along. A girl wants to look nice and I know that's part of the deal. Women thought I was cool 'cuz I went for this kind of 'dangerous' look. But for the men, or teenaged boys, as many of them were then, that was shaky ground we were breaking. I know I played to what would draw them in. Don't get me wrong. It's a tool of the trade. But the young people I see now who are basically whoring themselves out, well, I digress, but I don't undress. I said that the music biz deserved to die, but I couldn't kill it. I had to sever my connection to it to save myself, though I had lost track of who 'myself' was. You must know now, Miles, that we let that business kill our relationship. We forgot about caring for each other. We were just part of the machinery."

She sat down across from Miles now to speak more directly to him. She had what seemed like real compassion in her striking greenish eyes.

"I'm not saying there was nothing left that was good. It was exhilarating. We were riding a wave which had its thrills, but you can drown in a big wave too. I was drowning, Miles. I didn't know how to change things up so I could come up for air now and then, and god dammit you seemed to think everything was fine and didn't really want to recognize the call for help, the hands-up of a drowning woman."

To her credit, Sam, who had boasted about her facilitating skills, interrupted and said, "Claire, I think we're here to share stories just like what was happening on Miles's tour and here at the Ark. Can I assume, everybody, that accusations are not constructive in this safe space that Maxine has offered us?"

"Sorry," said Maddie. "Mostly sorry. I'll rephrase that; Miles and I disagreed about whether we had to shift up what we were doing. That OK, Samantha?" Both Sam and Miles nodded."So I didn't see a way that I could change the biz OR fix what was going on with us. I thought my only option was to disappear. All those years of high visibility, becoming invisible seemed very inviting. I know that was a coward's way of doing it. I know it must have messed you up a lot. I'm sorry." She put down her glass and said "Any questions?" She was looking at me.

"I'm an observer here," I said. There are some details that might be helpful in clarifying the 'Miles and Myles' story, but I am a music writer, not a tabloid writer.

Miles said "So where did you go?"

Maddie looked at the ceiling for a bit. There were flies buzzing on it, and the wallpaper was peeling off. Who wallpapers ceilings anyway? She said, "Well, does it matter?"

MG said, "Yes it does, Mommy Dearest."

Oops. A new tension in the room around that tone.

"OK kiddo. For you. I tried a 'normal' life in the U.S. where we weren't as well-known. Lucky for me, but I guess not so lucky for you, Miles. Once the hits stop coming, fans are fickle enough that they'll move on to the next flavour-of-the-month. I thought I could put everything behind. I settled for a while in Savannah, Georgia. That sweet accent is hard to lose, right 'honey chile' Molly? Remember when we toured through there the first time, Miles? We both thought if we ever settled down that might be the place. Well, one COULD live there, if you could actually settle down. I had a theory for a while that our marriage didn't work because the societal definition of a relationship was flawed. I'd never been on my own, so the urge to be looked after was huge. I guess I got that from my mother, and it resulted in three other relationships with guys after you that were such losers that they made *our* connection look pretty darn good, really. That got that 'wanting to be looked-after' crap out of me for good. At least you and I loved each other. I thought I'd try raising a kid on my own, since we had always argued about doing that together. 'Bad for business,' you always said. I thought I could at least demonstrate control over that part of my life. Great reason to raise up a kid, eh kid?"

MG butted in, "I wouldn't call what you did for me 'raising' exactly."

Sam stopped her, but Maddie waved that off, urged MG to continue, and got a nod from Miles who had only known they were mother and daughter for about an hour so he still looked dazed.

"You knew you weren't cut out for being a parent, so you cut out, after sacrificing yourself by watching me almost grow up enough that I could be on my own. I say 'almost' because

I was twelve when you ran away and joined the circus. What the fuck? Kids run away and join the circus, or they did a million years ago. What moms do that?"

"True enough," said Maddie. "I found out the hard way that the road was in my DNA as much as it was in yours, Miles, but I was too proud to come crawling back to the music biz, and don't think I didn't have lots of offers through my lawyer. There were a lot of promoters who thought I would be bigger than ever once I ditched that guy who would rather write songs with meaning than crank out the pop fluff you always hated. The Sycamore Sisters were a family that welcomed me in. They were trying to re-invent something. We were a good match, I thought, though the circus business, believe it or not, was in more trouble than the music business. When they couldn't make a go of it anymore, I was foolish enough to buy them out with that royalty money I had put away. After all, I had a new family to nurture. Wonderful caring people like Sam here."

MG made a snide aside, "Remember when you used to call that royalty money my 'college fund'? That was..." and this time Sam did cut her off.

Maddie went on, "They were a family though, just like the band was in a way, and I tried bringing Molly along with me for a while. That's where my mom came into the picture."

"Oh god," interjected Miles.

"Seriously," said MG.

"I know, I know," continued Maddie. "I had a real family in Molly, but reality wasn't exactly my specialty after years of artifice in the show business, right? And the circus was all fantasy. I could handle that. I got a new secret identity which I thought was so intriguing, a new name and a new schtick. Miles, when I was in Georgia I still used my married name, Maddie Gerber, so you didn't really try that hard to track me down."

Sam steered her back on track.

"So it was no life for a kid, and I know leaving her with Attila the Mom wasn't a life either. Remember I was just a kid too when you took me on the road, Miles. Eighteen, for Christ's sake."

MG, who had actually whispered to me that she likes being called MG better than Molly, which she thought was too 'whitebread', as well as her last name that sounded like mushy baby food, put up her hand and said, "Mother may I?"

Sam gave her blessing, with a look of affection that made me realize that when MG was tagging along with her mom in the circus, Sam must have acted as a kind of auntie. She clearly had more motherly instincts than Maddie.

Now MG paced the room as she talked. Drummer's mind was clearly elsewhere, and he was struggling to stay awake.

"Growing up, I didn't even know about Miles and Myles. Mom didn't want to talk about her past. I found an old album in a record store and started asking questions. I actually became a secret fan and learned all the songs, even though they were so old-school and white for this southern only-half-white girl. Oh ya, and speaking of that, I'm guessing my birth parents were mixed-race, but try living in Georgia as a person-of-not-quite-the-right-colour with a white mom? Ammaright? Mom wasn't really the best at answering the questions I was asking, were ya? My running away to join the circus wasn't as literal as mom's. Mom, you adopted me, but you never really adopted the mom lifestyle, did you? I needed to feel firsthand what it was that she, and I guess you, Miles, had been through. You weren't my dad, but I never had one, and I kept thinking that if I found you I'd have the missing pieces to a puzzle that I needed to solve. That's where Merch Girl came in.

Roadie, groupie, druggie, homeless, whatever. I did it all, and just like mom here, I played both sides. I hated being objectified but learned what I could get if I 'put myself out there.' Know what I'm saying? Miles, you saw me selling a lot of your albums knowing how to play the game. All the excesses, all the stupid mistakes I made, I justified as kind of a perverse research into the story I never really knew about you two. Maybe I needed to figure out why I never had a real family. Mom left you and the business. I had to leave her to maybe learn a bit about why she did that, 'cuz she never learned how to really talk about it. That's why this is pretty awesome to hear you opening up a bit here, mom. Maybe the vibe we're providing here at the Ark is helping with that."

Miles put up his hand, "So it wasn't an accident that we found you, literally, on the road?" That got one of Drummer's eyes open.

"Well, it wasn't supposed to happen quite that way. It wasn't hard to find out where you were touring, though not as easy as a band that actually had a WEBSITE! I joined up with PS, that's the Prideful Scoffers for you non-hipsters, knowing they'd get me to the same part of the world that you were meandering through. The plan was that when we hit Saskatoon, too big a place for the Disturbers to play apparently, and you were playing in some shit hole not far from there, I'd connect with you, find a way to ride along, learn about you and by extension, me. I didn't think I'd get what I wanted if you knew who I was."

Miles asked, "So what happened on that tour bus, then?"

"That's a good story. Maybe one I can't talk about in front of my mom just yet. I have to admit that because you were a legend and all Miles, I had never imagined that your career could be that much down the crapper by the time I found you. Jesus H. Christ. Travelling in a beat-up van named after Roy Rogers' Jeep. Double U Tee Eff! So when that 'turning-stories-into-songs' thing started happening, two things happened for me. I saw immediately that it was something I had always missed. Mom didn't want to tell the stories I wanted to hear. She held them inside, and no offence, Mom, but how did that turn out for ya? I was onto that whole 'Miles2Go' thing before you were, right Miles? I was dragging you into it. I needed it. You needed it, and judging by what's happening here, you can see that lots of other people needed something that was so simple- so direct, but so important to folks who found that it filled a void in their lives. I had a big void in my life too- walking on the wild side and thinking that's what I wanted. Listening to all your storytellers made me realize I wanted the same things they wanted.

Look what we made Miles! We made it together! The second thing was that I could see that this whole thing was a way for you to make a new beginning. Not the end of the music business; the start of something that had real possibilities. I needed that for you because it didn't fit my narrative that you'd be a failure. And buddy, we did it! Everyone involved from the tellers, to you guys, to the folks that decided to follow along. Not for money, not for attention, but just out of caring and love for one another. Mining for songs. Jesus, I had never really seen that before. Never shared that kind of experience.

Mom, it sounds like you found that with the Sycamore Sisters, right? That kind of connection?

Miles, we didn't know what we were doing, but we did it anyway. We followed our intuition and our imagination, tools I didn't even know I had. On one level what did we actually do? A guy listened to some stories and wrote some songs about it. Big Whoop. Why did it become more than that? Because it turns out so many people were waiting for a chance to feel that they mattered. And we made it fun, right? It helped me feel like I was a part of a family. Kind of a kinky/creepy family, since these dudes and Dougie, stuck together in that van too long, would get boners whenever I'd wear one of their lame T-shirts. I wanted that with you, mom. I don't mean the boner part, Napoleon."

She said that to me making sure I got the reportage straight.

"What do you think, Mom? Is it too late for us to be a mother and daughter?"

Wow. That little speech took an interesting turn. Obviously this 'thing' that was happening meant a lot to her, and I'm grateful that she shared why. The mother and daughter gave each other a long teary hug. Still holding MG, Maddie turned to Miles and said, "Don't take this the wrong way, Miles. I steered the circus your way because I was looking to reconnect with Molly, not you. Once she finally got a phone after she hooked up with you luddites, she let me know your whereabouts. Thanks for that kiddo. Then I realized that I had a chance to get the combo plate here, with the side of fries and the rice pudding. MG was up for it too, right hon? It was time. It was MG who figured out that we could intersect at

Espanola. God that's a long highway. And Maxine was in on it all along. Buttermilk actually used to be my horse in the circus 'til I banned animals from the act, right Maxine?"

Maxine was so involved in this conversation that it took a minute to notice that her name had come up. She nodded and passed the whiskey around again. Everyone said no except me. It was getting late, and after all, Miles had driven from Toronto early that morning.

Maddie and MG sat down, this time snuggled together, and Maddie said, "Your turn big guy," to Miles.

"Holy Shit," he said. "That's a lot. Thanks to both of you. Wow. And I guess you were right, whichever one of you said it: I've lost track. Here I thought I was the most private guy you'd ever meet. I never really thought that all along I was packing serious baggage into songs and putting them out there. My story is available on iTunes, Bic, and in delete bins at the last record stores left, so just have a listen! But I guess that story got stuck somewhere along the way. I lost the band and you at the same time, Maddie-May. I was grieving about that, and I got the dumbass idea that my only way forward was to go backwards and take back what I'd lost. Drummer, it must have been hell for you traipsing around with me all those years listening to all those maudlin songs I was writing just for my own therapy. I wasn't looking for something new, just following the old road to its end. Then this character MG drops from the sky, almost literally, and starts looking ahead and not behind. And here we are. So I guess what's left is 'What's next?' I'm losing the little bit of coherency I had to begin with cuz I'm bushed. I do my best thinking in Nelly-Belle, that much-maligned member of the band. Right Drummer? Can we meet there at the crack of 11 maybe?"

Drummer was already out the door by the time Miles finished talking. He had a date. The others agreed to the plan, though I was a bit suspicious of Miles since on one level it looked like he was just trying to weasel out of 'taking his turn'. Remembering that I had a tent to set up, I thanked all for letting me join in on the conversation, reiterated that it was off the record until I cleared things with them, let them know that I thought I had what I needed, and that I might not get a chance to say good-bye in the morning. (Actually I really suck at good-byes, so I was just looking for a way out of that. Too mushy for reporters, right?) I was going to find a way back home the next day. MG and Miles were shown to their rooms, and Maddie headed off to her caravan with Sam in tow. Outside we could still hear songs and laughter being shared around the campfires, and the stars were putting on a boffo late show. I ran into Mohan, still there and having the time of his life, and he said he had to get back in the morning too, so we agreed to meet at the canteen at 10 to take off.

Chapter Thirty-Four

Drummer Tells

Checking one two! Heh heh, it feels good to be using this recorder thingy again. I guess you got your story, Mr. Penn? More than we all bargained for, that's fer sure, eh? Glad I was some help. It helped me too, so I owe you. I was learning to be a storyteller by telling you about the adventures with Miles and his band of bumpkins, and when I got to the Pow Wow, that turned out to be a handy skill to have. I was hearing stories that were maybe thousands of years old, and that were, frankly, more exciting than your white people tales. Don't get me wrong, the stories we collected on the tour were important, but looking back now they seemed mostly to be complaints pretending to be stories. The stories I heard at the Pow Wow, part of the background I never knew, were magical, mystical, filled with laughter and tears combined. Different and often fun ways to tell the story of a people, a people that I am even more committed to connecting with now.

I have to say that doing this little job for you let me think about my own life more, even though you weren't asking for any of that personal stuff from me. I think for us travelling folk, life gets reduced to where the next meal is, where the turnoff is on the highway towards the next gig, that kind of thing. We don't pause to look at the big picture, especially when that picture can get discouraging. So thanks to you I'm going to keep talking into a tape recorder, even it's just for myself. It actually felt weird to miss a few days of recording when I went to the Pow Wow.

It also felt weird to not be here as the Ark thing got going, but Bic, I wouldn't have missed that Pow Wow for the world. That story is just for me for now, OK? Those legends and tales are not mine to tell. Maybe someday, so don't you be asking ok? You all saw one thing that I took away from that weekend, though, Raven!

All those years following Miles around feeling the pain around his lost love didn't exactly make me want to go looking for it. And son-of-a-drum if it didn't come looking for me! Holy. Miles was looking for something he couldn't have, instead of being open to what came along, and look what opened up for me!

I also wanted to confess to you that when I was recording about the tour for you, I think I was trying to impress you with big words. Words I didn't even know the meaning of! No colossal words now, (but that's a good one, eh?). Time for colossal deeds instead! Drummers are supposed to set the beat, right? We're not followers. I've done enough of that. With Raven's love and encouragement, I'm going to find a new rhythm to move forward with, one that echoes everything that has happened on this trip, and hints at the good things that can come for us if we listen like good drummers should! A rhythm that gets us all dancing together. A round dance not a square dance. Heh heh.

So happy trails to you, Bic, and next time I see you, I wanna hear your story ok? If you ask for one you've got to tell one back, right?

Chapter Thirty-Five

Nelly-Belle Tells

Hi Bic, this one's for you. It was nice sleeping with you, (blush), though I hear that you left 'the morning after.' Men. I'm not the kind of girl who would just let anyone in my passenger door. I'm hoping it meant something to you. I don't like being just a two-night van.

I couldn't seem to think straight while Drummer was away. Everything was blurry. That all changed the night he got back, though modesty prevents me from saying what he was up to in my back seat. That's a first! I guess you've got lots of material now so I'll just give you a summery summary.

The night after Miles and Drummer came back, (and I still can't figure out what happened to Dougie. I'm worried. I'm a 6-cylinder worrier), and after that wild night that left me with feathers in my wheel well, I found myself filled with passengers again, just like we were heading to the next gig. But my rad nearly boiled over when I saw that one of my riders was, could it be? Maddie Myles?

Miles, MG, Drummer, and Maddie were deep in discussion, but it was excited chatter. The dramatic tension I sensed from the stage the previous night was gone. And I should say I had a ringside seat for that, and it would have blown my engine if it wasn't blown already.

That discussion was pretty epic, so here's my Reader's Digest version:

There was general agreement that the Ark should keep going. It already had a great reputation and it had an exciting future if planned properly. They figured they could keep things rolling till September, with a growing list of activities, workshops, classes, and just plain hanging out in the cool atmosphere that had been created. MG and Maddie agreed that they would stay on. MG said to Miles at this point, "Though honoured by your invitation to help produce your new show in Toronto, no offence, but I think this opportunity to connect with Mom is top priority right now."

The mother and daughter, (gotta get used to saying that), would be getting input from everyone over the summer about the vision moving forward, and finding ways to realize that dream over the winter. And dream they did in that meeting: dreams like an 'Ark of the Oven Mitt' non-profit foundation. Maddie thought they had the skill set for that since there was surely no profit to be made in the music business or the circus these days. A retreat centre. Summer school for the circus arts, and another for sustainable agricultural practices. An 'artisan's village'. An innovation centre for building towards a new sustainable economy, with models for net-zero construction techniques starting with a straw-bale theatre that would eventually hold concerts and circus events, replacing the decrepit and unsafe Big Top. Oh dear. Was I safe under the main pole? Those gals were zooming along at hyper speed mostly with stuff I didn't understand. Spitballing. An 'earthship' as the 'interpretive centre'. Didn't know what those were. A more permanent Indigenous component, which Drummer was excited to take on after he spent the winter learning with Raven. Learning, is that what they call that now?

Outside, people were starting to disperse a bit. It was hard to tell here but I gather it was the beginning of the week. Some folks had lives and families and jobs to get back to. It was decided that there would be a lunchtime recap instead of the evening one, which could be more of a 'closing circle' and debrief.

Miles indicated that he'd stay on another month or so, continuing the 'Miles2Go' series, with the expectation that people would still be arriving to share stories and the experience. MG would ramp up the online download thing, though that would require boosting the bandwidth at the farm. Such fancy talk in a van! The CBC would actually pay Miles for that month's work gathering material for the fall. He'd spend the winter in Toronto, now that he had that paid gig and he knew the gals were going to do their own thing. That pay word led to the next part.

They needed money! They were charging admission to get in now, and folks were contributing for the food collection, but this long-term vision required sustainable funding. I can't believe that this happened so easily. That must have been quite a get-together up at Maxine's the night before. Somehow they all agreed that they could raise big sacks of cash if they put on a Miles and Myles reunion concert.

"While our fans are still alive," Miles had quipped. "They've been asking for years."

How Maddie said yes to that I'll never know. It was a good symbolic gesture to show that fences had been mended, a great way to promote the Ark, and to raise serious dough for it. They also agreed that it couldn't be held at the farm. It wouldn't have the capacity for the thousands of people they might get. MG took that task on. They'd probably do it at a festival site in Southern Ontario before the end of August. Exciting! I was hoping I'd be fixed by then. Was that even in the works? I was getting itchy tires.

Maddie mentioned that the circus usually wintered outside of Austin, Texas, the last progressive town in the southern states. They weren't sure if they even had gas money to make it down there, but if they scrounged that, Sam would run their winter activities there which made some revenue. Then they could put that property on the market and use the funds to buy into Maxine's place, which Maxine was up for. The circus folks knew their travelling days were coming to an end. As it turned out, some of them didn't migrate for the season and elected to stay on to work on Ark projects.

It was all coming together. After a text from MG, Dippity announced the lunch time gathering, for the Big Top not the Yes-U-Canteen. It was sprinkling rain outside, and inside through the many holes in the tent! Sam came over to lure them out of me to set up for the session as the crowd gathered. She ran through some of the discussion points from the meeting and it looked like everyone was shifting into the same gear.

Miles grabbed his guitar, invited the Arkestra and Drummer

up, and said, "Are you like me friends? Lots to take in, eh? Who would have imagined what's happened since I listened to a shy sheep farmer share his tale back in Needham, Sasquatchingham. I know we keep talking about how this is all about the stories, but I've been thinking. The stories are the tools we use to build connection and community. It's really all about that. And when times are tough, and they're getting tougher, it's that sense of connection that will see us through. The stories are the medium and community is the message. I think it was Marshall Dillon who said that."

He counted in the band and he debuted "Fall And Rise" for them, kind of an anthem. Everyone sang along, even me.

Song 35: Fall And Rise

All of our tears
They could fill a stream
That would flow to a sea
Of sorrow
All of our fears
All of our dashed dreams
It's hard to see
through to tomorrow

We fall and rise, we fall and rise
With all our hearts and all our minds
We call in hope into our lives
We fall and we rise

But we have the power
Of community
And you can see
It all around
In our darkest hour
It can lead
You and me
To higher ground

We fall and rise, we fall and rise
With all our hearts and all our minds
We call in hope into our lives
We fall and we rise

At such a cost
We've been driven by greed
we have built a machine
that destroys
Our spirits been lost
But we can find our way
if we all can make
a joyful noise

We fall and rise, we fall and rise
With all our hearts and all our minds
We call in hope into our lives
We fall and we rise

And so it went on for the rest of the summer. A big Summer of Love for sure. Lots of arrivals, lots of departures, but the spirit remained the same.

One day a UPS truck arrived and delivered a package addressed to Ms. Molly Gerber, Ark of The Oven Mitt, Manitoulin Island, Canada. It made it there, so we knew we were on the map. MG opened it and discovered her battered suitcase and wallet, with a note attached that said "F.U. from all of us in the P.S." Wow.

The "Arkivists" continued to revel in what should be a normal state: caring for each other, listening to each other, and I guess looking at why that wasn't normal anymore. That's what a lot of those afternoon fireside sessions were about.

The place was running like a well-oiled machine, which I wish I was at the moment. You couldn't really see the machinery though. It all looked as natural as can be.

Miles hosted song circles and storytelling sessions every night. He kept up his incredible pace, so that every time, there was at least one new song based on the previous night's stories. I won't share those here because they'll be on the radio show right?

And by the time you get this, Bic, the amazing success of the reunion concert will be already in the history books, though the production company that MG hired to put it all together sucked up a lot of the profit. The event confirmed for all the lasting popularity of Miles and Myles, raised awareness of the Ark's mission and the Miles2Go project, and it confirmed to Maddie especially that taking the 'biz' part out of 'the music biz' was wise until the revolution comes. At least that was the buzz around the Ark.

The time came for Miles to head down to Toronto. I could see that he had said personal goodbyes to Maddie already. At his last song circle, this time on the Flatbed Stage because it offered a more proper farewell platform, he talked about how grateful he was, and that while he'd been talking the talk about the value of community, all these good folks were walking the walk. Demonstrating it every darn day.

Then he said he had one more surprise for us, and he made

sure MG was sitting close by.

"Everyone. I want to give a special thanks to MG here, 'cuz I have to leave her behind when I head south. I don't really know what lies ahead for me, other than I have this radio gig to check out. I'm pleased that everyone seems to have found a path forward. I'll get there. At least I don't feel like I'm going backwards. MG has done an amazing job, and I'm still working through all that I've learned. I knew when we met that there was some sort of connection between us, but as she'll tell you, I was confused about what that was. When I learned who she was, I realized that she was almost family. Almost a daughter. So MG I'd like to make sure that I'm growing into the feeling that we can feel like part of a family, which is something I never thought that I even wanted. I learned that there are different kinds of love, and what I feel is special here and new to me. And really, we yammer on about stories and community and shit, but when it comes down to it, it's all about love, right? Let's build on that, OK? So this is embarrassing to say, but when we met we all used to play a game of trying to guess what MG stood for, since you wouldn't tell us. I somehow landed on 'Morning Glory' because it's kind of a beautiful weed, and of course there's the expression 'What's the story, Morning Glory' that Dougie used to say a lot.

So I'm going to say goodbye to you all with this song, "Miss Morning Glory", and for all of you who have given me hope and light, a purpose and a future. Love is in abundance here, and maybe you guys will have 'a bun dance tonight!' That's one last dumb pun for you Drummer. Love you too."

He sang with an emotion that felt new and brave, just like what we were building here. Bic, I think his song kind of sums everything up, so I'll leave it at that. See you in the spring I hope. And it feels good to end on the word hope!

Song 36
Morning Glory

You can feel it, can't you, that it won't be too long
Till this sweet old summer is over and gone
There'll be frost on the fields when the geese call at dawn,
They'll be heading down south just like me

I thought I had grown far too jaded and old
And I figured my still-broken heart was too cold
In this cynical age, who'd believe what's unfolded
It must have been just meant to be

Hey Morning Glory
Before we must part
Won't you tell me a story
That's straight from your heart
Something that I
Can remember you by
Until I return in the spring.

Stories are precious, like diamonds in the rough
They become smooth and warm if you tell them enough
You and I both like to think we're so tough,
But hey look our soft sides are showin'

Love, when you share it, more comes back to you
It's the same with stories, when they're honest and true,
We are richer for the knowing, they are what'll get us through
When the wild winter winds are blowin'.

Hey Morning Glory
Before we must part
Won't you tell me a story
That's straight from your heart
Something that I
Can remember you by
Until I return in the spring.

THE END